LITTLE DORRIT

Published by Priory Books,
© Peter Haddock Publishing,
United Kingdom, YO16 6BT.

LITTLE DORRIT

BOOK THE FIRST

POVERTY

CHAPTER 1

Sun and Shadow

One day, thirty years ago, Marseilles lay burning in the sun.

In Marseilles that day there was a villainous prison. In one of its chambers were two men. Besides the two men there was a notched and disfigured bench, immovable from the wall, with a draught-board rudely hacked upon it with a knife, a set of draughts, made of old buttons and soup bones, a set of dominoes, two mats, and two or three wine bottles. That was all the chamber held, exclusive of rats and other unseen vermin, in addition to the seen vermin – the two men.

It received such light as it got, through a grating of iron bars fashioned like a pretty large window. There was a broad strong ledge of stone to this grating where the bottom of it was let into the masonry, three or four feet above the ground. Upon it, one of the two men lolled, half sitting and half lying, with his knees drawn up, and his feet and shoulders planted against the opposite sides of the aperture. As the captive men were faded and haggard, so the iron was rusty, the stone was slimy, the wood was rotten, the air was faint, the light was dim.

The man who lay on the ledge of the grating was even chilled. He jerked his great cloak more heavily upon him by an impatient movement of one shoulder, and growled, "To the devil with this Brigand of a Sun that never shines in here!"

He was waiting to be fed, looking sideways through the bars that he might see the further down the stairs, with much of the expression of a wild beast in similar expectation. But his eyes were sharp rather than bright – pointed weapons with little surface to betray them. He had a hook nose, handsome after its kind, and for the rest, he was large and tall in frame, had thin lips, where his thick moustache showed them at all, and a quantity of dry hair, of no definable colour, in its shaggy state, but shot with red. The hand with which he held the grating (seamed all over the back with ugly scratches newly healed), was unusually small and plump; would have been unusually white but for the prison grime.

The other man was lying on the stone floor, covered with a coarse brown coat.

"Get up, pig!" growled the first. "Don't sleep when I am hungry."

"It's all one, master," said the pig, in a submissive manner, and not without cheerfulness; "I can wake when I will, I can sleep when I will. It's all the same."

As he said it, he rose, shook himself, scratched himself, tied his brown coat loosely round his neck by the sleeves (he had previously used it as a coverlet), and sat down upon the pavement yawning, with his back against the wall opposite to the grating.

"Say what the hour is," grumbled the first man.

"The mid-day bells will ring – in forty minutes."

"You are a clock. How is it that you always know?"

"I always know what the hour is, and where I am. I was brought in here at night, and out of a boat, but I know where I am. See here! Marseilles harbour."

He remained on his knees, looking up at his fellow-prisoner with a lively look for a prison. A sunburnt, quick, lithe, little man, though rather thick-set. Earrings in his brown ears, white teeth lighting up his grotesque brown face, intensely black hair clustering about his brown throat, a ragged red shirt open at his brown breast. Loose, seaman-like trousers, decent shoes, a long red cap, a red sash round his waist, and a knife in it.

Some lock below gurgled in its throat immediately afterwards, and then a door crashed. Slow steps began ascending the stairs; the prattle of a sweet little voice mingled with the noise they made; and the prison-keeper appeared carrying his daughter, three or four years old, and a basket.

"How goes the world this forenoon, Signor John Baptist?" said he.

"Poor birds!" said the child.

The fair little face, touched with divine compassion, as it peeped shrinkingly through the grate, was like an angel's in the prison.

John Baptist rose and moved towards it, as if it had a good attraction for him. The other bird remained as before, except for an impatient glance at the basket.

"Stay!" said the jailer, putting his little daughter on the outer ledge of the grate. "This big loaf is for Signor John Baptist. We must break it to get it through into the cage. So, there's a tame bird to kiss the little hand! This sausage in a vine leaf is for Monsieur Blandois. Again – this veal in savoury jelly is for Monsieur Blandois. Again – these three white little loaves are for Monsieur Blandois. Again, this cheese – again, this wine – again, this tobacco – all for Monsieur Blandois. Lucky bird!"

The child put all these things between the bars into the soft, smooth, well-shaped hand, with evident dread – whereas she had put the lump of coarse bread into the swart, scaled, knotted hands of John Baptist with ready confidence; and, when he kissed her hand, had herself passed it caressingly over his face.

Monsieur Blandois propitiated the father by laughing and nodding at the daughter. When he laughed, his moustache went up under his nose, and his nose came down over his moustache, in a very sinister and cruel manner.

"There!" said the jailer, turning his basket upside down to beat the crumbs out, "I have expended all the money I received; here is the note of it, and that's a thing accomplished. Monsieur Blandois, as I expected yesterday, the President will look for the pleasure of your society at an hour after mid-day, today."

"To try me, eh?" said Blandois, pausing, morsel in mouth.

"You have said it. To try you."

"There is no news for me?" asked John Baptist, who had begun, contentedly, to munch his bread.

The jailer shrugged his shoulders.

"Adieu, my birds!" he said, taking his pretty child in his arms, and dictating the words with a kiss.

"Adieu, my birds!" the pretty child repeated.

The door clashed.

"What an infernal hole this is!" said Monsieur Blandois. "Look at the light of day. So slack and dead! John Baptist," said Monsieur Blandois, "you know me for a gentleman?"

"Surely, surely!"

"How long have we been here?"

5

"I, eleven weeks, tomorrow night at midnight. You, nine weeks and three days, at five this afternoon."

"You knew from the first moment when you saw me here, that I was a gentleman?"

"I believe you!"

"Haha! You are right! A gentleman I am! And a gentleman I'll live, and a gentleman I'll die! It's my intent to be a gentleman. It's my game. Death of my soul, I play it out wherever I go!"

He changed his posture to a sitting one, crying with a triumphant air:

"Here I am! See me! Shaken out of destiny's dice-box into the company of a mere smuggler; – shut up with a poor little contraband trader, whose papers are wrong, and whom the police lay hold of besides, for placing his boat (as a means of getting beyond the frontier) at the disposition of other little people whose papers are wrong; and he instinctively recognises my position, even by this light and in this place. It's well done! By Heaven! I win, however the game goes. The President will have a gentleman before him soon. Come! Shall I tell you on what accusation? It must be now, or never, for I shall not return here. Either I shall go free, or I shall go to be made ready for shaving. You know where they keep the razor."

"I am a" – Monsieur Blandois stood up to say it – "I am a cosmopolitan gentleman. I own no particular country. My father was Swiss – Canton de Vaud. My mother was French by blood, English by birth. I myself was born in Belgium. I am a citizen of the world. Call me five-and-thirty years of age. I have seen the world. I have lived here, and lived there, and lived like a gentleman everywhere. I have been treated and respected as a gentleman universally. Two years ago I came to Marseilles. I put up at the Cross of Gold – I had lived in the house some four months when Monsieur Henri Barronneau had the misfortune to die. He left a widow. She was two-and-twenty. She had gained a reputation for beauty, and (which is often another thing) *was* beautiful. I continued to live at the Cross of Gold. I married Madame Barronneau. It is not for me to say whether there was any great disparity in such a match. Be it as it may, Madame Barronneau approved of me. That is not to prejudice me, I hope?"

His eye happening to light upon John Baptist with this inquiry, that little man briskly shook his head in the negative.

"Now came the difficulties of our position. Unfortunately, the property of Madame Blandois was settled upon herself. Such was the insane act of her late husband. More unfortunately still, she had relations. Quarrels began to arise between us; and, propagated and exaggerated by the slanders of the relations of Madame Blandois, to become notorious to the neighbours. Alas, we were brought into frequent and unfortunate collision. Even when I wanted any little sum of money for my personal expenses, I could not obtain it without collision – and I, too, a man whose character it is to govern! One night, Madame Blandois and myself were walking amicably – I may say like lovers – on a height overhanging the sea. An evil star occasioned Madame Blandois to talk about her relations. We began to argue. At length, Madame Blandois, in an access of fury that I must ever deplore, threw herself upon me with screams of passion; trampled and trod the dust; and finally leaped over, dashing herself to death upon the rocks below. Such is the train of incidents which malice has perverted into my assassinating her!"

He stepped aside to the ledge where the vine leaves yet lay strewn about, collected two or three, and stood wiping his hands upon them, with his back to the light.

"Well," he demanded after a silence, "have you nothing to say to all that?"

"It's ugly," returned the little man, who had risen, and was brightening his knife upon his shoe, as he leaned an arm against the wall. Nothing more was said on either side, though they both began walking to and fro, and necessarily crossed at every turn.

By-and-by the noise of the key in the lock arrested them both. The sound of voices succeeded, and the tread of feet. The door clashed, the voices and the feet came on, and the prison-keeper slowly ascended the stairs, followed by a guard of soldiers.

"Now, Monsieur Blandois," said he, pausing for a moment at the grate, with his keys in his hands, "have the goodness to come out."

"I am to depart in state, I see?"

He lighted another of his paper cigars, put it tightly between his teeth; covered his head with a soft slouched hat; threw the end of his cloak over his shoulder again; and walked out into the side gallery on which the door opened, without taking any further notice of Signor John Baptist.

CHAPTER 2

Fellow Travellers

"Ah! but these people are always howling. Never happy otherwise."

"Do you mean the Marseilles people?"

"I mean the French people. They're always at it. As to Marseilles, we know what Marseilles is. It sent the most insurrectionary tune into the world that was ever composed. And it would be more creditable to you, I think, to let people about their lawful business instead of shutting 'em up in quarantine for fear of the plague caught in the East."

"Tiresome enough," said the other, "but we shall be out today."

"Out! What have we ever been in for?"

The speaker, with a whimsical good humour upon him all the time, looked over the parapet-wall with the greatest disparagement of Marseilles; and taking up a determined position by putting his hands in his pockets and rattling his money at it, apostrophised it with a short laugh.

"You bear it very well, Mr Meagles," said the second speaker, smiling.

"No. If you knew the real state of the case, that's the last observation you would think of making. I have been waking up night after night, and saying, *now* I have got the plague, *now* it has developed itself."

"Well, Mr Meagles, say no more about it now it's over," urged a cheerful feminine voice.

It was Mrs Meagles who had spoken to Mr Meagles; and Mrs Meagles was, like Mr Meagles, comely and healthy, with a pleasant English face which had been looking at homely things for five-and-fifty years or more, and shone with a bright reflection of them.

"There! Never mind, Father, never mind!" said Mrs Meagles. "For goodness sake content yourself with Pet."

"With Pet?" repeated Mr Meagles in his injured vein. Pet, however, being close behind him, touched him on the shoulder, and Mr Meagles immediately forgave Marseilles from the bottom of his heart.

Pet was about twenty. A fair girl with rich brown hair hanging free in natural ringlets. A lovely girl, with a frank face, and wonderful eyes; so large, so soft, so bright, set to such perfection in her kind good head. She was round and fresh and dimpled and spoilt, and there was in Pet an air of timidity and dependence which was the best weakness in the world, and gave her the only crowning charm a girl so pretty and pleasant could have been without.

"Now, Pet, my darling," said Mr Meagles, "you had better go along with Mother and get ready for the boat. Tattycoram, stick you close to your young mistress."

He spoke to a handsome girl with lustrous dark hair and eyes, and very neatly dressed, who replied with a half curtsey as she passed off in the train of Mrs Meagles and Pet. They crossed the bare scorched terrace all three together, and disappeared through a staring white archway. Mr Meagles's companion, a grave dark man of forty, still stood looking towards this archway after they were gone; until Mr Meagles tapped him on the arm.

"I beg your pardon," said he, starting.

"Not at all," said Mr Meagles.

They took one silent turn backward and forward in the shade of the wall, getting, at the height on which the quarantine barracks are placed, what cool refreshment of sea breeze there was at seven in the morning. Mr Meagles's companion resumed the conversation.

"May I ask you," he said, "what is the name of – "

"Tattycoram?" Mr Meagles struck in. "One day, five or six years ago now, when we took Pet to church at the Foundling – you have heard of the Foundling Hospital in London? Similar to the Institution for the Found Children in Paris?"

"I have seen it."

"Well! One day we took Pet to church there to hear the music – and we were so moved by the plight of the children that the next day I said to Mrs Meagles 'Now, Mother, I have a proposition to make that I think you'll approve of. Let us take one of those same little children to be a little maid to Pet.' And that's the way we came by Tattycoram."

"And the name itself – "

"By George!" said Mr Meagles, "I was forgetting the name itself. Why, she was called in the Institution, Harriet Beadle – an arbitrary name, of course. Now, Harriet we changed into Hattey, and then into Tatty, because, as practical people, we thought even a playful name might be a new thing to her, and might have a softening and affectionate kind of effect, don't you see? At one time she was Tatty, and at one time she was

9

Coram, until we got into a way of mixing the two names together, and now she is always Tattycoram."

"Your daughter," said the other, when they had taken another silent turn to and fro, and, after standing for a moment at the wall glancing down at the sea, had resumed their walk, "is she your only child, Mr Meagles?"

"No. No," said Mr Meagles. "We have, er, one other child."

"I am afraid I have inadvertently touched upon a tender theme."

"Never mind," said Mr Meagles. "If I am grave about it, I am not at all sorrowful. It quiets me for a moment, but does not make me unhappy. Pet had a twin sister who died when we could just see her eyes – exactly like Pet's – above the table, as she stood on tiptoe holding by it."

"Ah! indeed, indeed!"

"Yes, and being practical people, a result has gradually sprung up in the minds of Mrs Meagles and myself which perhaps you may – or perhaps you may not – understand. Pet and her baby sister were so exactly alike, and so completely one, that in our thoughts we have never been able to separate them since. As Pet has grown, that child has grown."

"I understand you," said the other, gently.

"Her mother and I were not young when we married, and Pet has always had a sort of grown-up life with us, though we have tried to adapt ourselves to her. We have been advised more than once when she has been a little ailing, to change climate and air for her as often as we could – especially at about this time of her life – and to keep her amused. So, as I have no need to stick at a bank-desk now (though I have been poor enough in my time I assure you, or I should have married Mrs Meagles long before), we go trotting about the world. This is how Tattycoram will be a greater traveller in course of time than Captain Cook."

"I thank you," said the other, "very heartily for your confidence."

"Don't mention it," returned Mr Meagles, "I am sure you are quite welcome. And now, Mr Clennam, perhaps I may ask you whether you have yet come to a decision where to go next?"

"Indeed, no. I am such a waif and stray everywhere, that I am liable to be drifted where any current may set."

"It's extraordinary to me – if you'll excuse my freedom in saying so – that you don't go straight to London," said Mr Meagles, in the tone of a confidential adviser.

"Perhaps I shall."

"Ay! But I mean with a will."

"I have no will. That is to say," he coloured a little, "next to none that I can put in action now. Trained by main force; broken, not bent; heavily ironed with an object on which I was never consulted and which was never mine; shipped away to the other end of the world before I was of age, and exiled there until my father's death there, a year ago; always grinding in a mill I always hated; what is to be expected from me in middle life? Will, purpose, hope? All those lights were extinguished before I could sound the words."

"Light 'em up again!" said Mr Meagles.

"Ah! Easily said. I am the son, Mr Meagles, of a hard father and mother. I am the only child of parents who weighed, measured, and priced everything; for whom what could not be weighed, measured, and priced, had no existence. But enough of me. Here is the boat, bringing more company."

Everybody reassembled at a great hotel, where a great table in a great room was soon profusely covered with a superb repast.

They were about thirty together, and all talking; but necessarily in groups. Father and Mother Meagles sat with their daughter between them, the last three on one side of the table: on the opposite side sat Mr Clennam; a tall French gentleman with raven hair and beard, of a swart and terrible, not to say genteelly diabolical aspect, but who had shown himself the mildest of men; and a handsome young Englishwoman, travelling quite alone, who had a proud observant face, and had either withdrawn herself from the rest or been avoided by the rest – nobody, herself excepted perhaps, could have quite decided which. She rose with the rest, and silently withdrew to a remote corner of the great room, where she sat herself on a couch in a window, seeming to watch the reflection of the water as it made a silver quivering on the bars of the lattice. She sat, turned away from the whole length of the apartment, as if she were lonely of her own haughty choice.

Now Pet and Mr Clennam moved up to her.

"Are you – " Pet faltered – "expecting any one to meet you here, Miss Wade?"

"I? No."

"We are afraid," said Pet, sitting down beside her, shyly and half tenderly, "that you will feel quite deserted when we are all gone."

"Indeed!"

"In short," said Pet, timidly touching her hand as it lay impassive on the sofa between them, "will you not allow Father to tender you any slight assistance or service? He will be very glad."

"Very glad," said Mr Meagles, coming forward with his wife. "Anything short of speaking the language, I shall be delighted to undertake, I am sure."

"I am obliged to you," she returned, "but my arrangements are made, and I prefer to go my own way in my own manner."

"A pleasant journey to you then," said Mr Meagles. "Good-bye!"

With the coldest of farewells, and with a certain worn expression on her beauty that gave it, though scarcely yet in its prime, a wasted look, she left the room.

Now, there were many stairs and passages that she had to traverse in passing from that part of the spacious house to the chamber she had secured for her own occupation. When she had almost completed the journey, and was passing along the gallery in which her room was, she heard an angry sound of muttering and sobbing. A door stood open, and within she saw the attendant upon the girl she had just left; the maid with the curious name. She stood still, to look at this maid. A sullen, passionate girl! Her rich black hair was all about her face, her face was flushed and hot, and as she sobbed and raged, she plucked at her lips with an unsparing hand.

"Selfish brutes!" said the girl, sobbing and heaving between whiles. "Not caring what becomes of me! Leaving me here hungry and thirsty and tired, to starve, for anything they care! Beasts! Devils! Wretches!"

"My poor girl, what is the matter?"

She looked up with reddened eyes, and with her hands suspended, in the act of pinching her neck, freshly disfigured with great scarlet blots. "It's nothing to you what's the matter. It don't signify to any one."

"Oh yes it does; I am sorry to see you so."

"You are not sorry," said the girl. "You are glad. You know you are glad. I never was like this but twice over in the quarantine yonder; and both times you found me. I am afraid of you."

"Afraid of me?"

"Yes. You seem to come like my own anger, my own malice, my own – whatever it is – I don't know what it is. But I am ill-used, I am ill-used!"

Here the sobs and the tears, and the tearing hand, which had all been suspended together since the first surprise, went on together anew.

The girl raged and battled with all the force of youth and fullness of life. The day passed on and the hot night was on Marseilles; and through it the caravan of the morning, all dispersed, went their appointed ways.

CHAPTER 3

Home

It was a Sunday evening in London, gloomy, close, and stale.

Mr Arthur Clennam, newly arrived from Marseilles by way of Dover, and by Dover coach the Blue-eyed Maid, sat in the window of a coffee-house on Ludgate Hill.

"Beg pardon, sir," said a brisk waiter, rubbing the table. "Wish see bedroom?"

"No!" said Clennam, rousing himself. "I am not going to sleep here. I am going home."

Mr Arthur Clennam took up his hat and buttoned his coat, and walked out. He came at last to the house he sought. An old brick house, so dingy as to be all but black, standing by itself within a gateway. Before it, a square courtyard where a shrub or two and a patch of grass were as rank (which is saying much) as the iron railings enclosing them were rusty; behind it, a jumble of roots. It was a double house, with long, narrow, heavily-framed windows. Many years ago, it had had it in its mind to slide down sideways; it had been propped up, however, and was leaning on some half-dozen gigantic crutches.

"Nothing changed," said the traveller, stopping to look round. "Dark and miserable as ever. A light in my mother's window, which seems never to have been extinguished since I came home twice a year from school, and dragged my box over this pavement. Well, well, well!"

He went up to the door and knocked. A shuffling step was soon heard on the stone floor of the hall, and the door was opened by an old man, bent and dried, but with keen eyes.

He had a candle in his hand, and he held it up for a moment to assist

13

his keen eyes. "Ah, Mr Arthur?" he said, without any emotion, "you are come at last? Step in."

Mr Arthur stepped in and shut the door.

"Your figure is filled out, and set," said the old man, turning to look at him with the light raised again, and shaking his head; "but you don't come up to your father in my opinion. Nor yet your mother."

"How is my mother?"

"She is as she always is now. Keeps her room when not actually bedridden, and hasn't been out of it fifteen times in as many years, Arthur." They had walked into a spare, meagre dining-room.

The old man had put the candlestick upon the table, and, supporting his right elbow with his left hand, was smoothing his leathern jaws while he looked at the visitor. The visitor offered his hand.

"Will you tell Mother that I have come home?"

"Yes, Arthur, yes. Oh, to be sure! I'll tell her that you have come home. Please to wait here. You won't find the room changed."

"How weak am I," said Arthur Clennam, when he was gone, "that I could shed tears at this reception! I, who have never experienced anything else; who have never expected anything else." But here was the old man come back, saying, "Arthur, I'll go before and light you."

Arthur followed him up the staircase, which was panelled off into spaces like so many mourning tablets, into a dim bed-chamber, the floor of which had gradually so sunk and settled, that the fire-place was in a dell. On a black bier-like sofa in this hollow, propped up behind with one great angular black bolster like the block at a state execution in the good old times, sat his mother in a widow's dress.

She and his father had been at variance from his earliest remembrance. She gave him one glassy kiss, and four stiff fingers muffled in worsted.

This embrace concluded, he sat down on the opposite side of her table. There was a fire in the grate, as there had been night and day for fifteen years. There was a kettle on the hob, as there had been night and day for fifteen years, and there was a smell of black dye in the airless room, which the fire had been drawing out of the crape and stuff of the widow's dress for fifteen months, and out of the bier-like sofa for fifteen years.

The old influence of his mother's presence and her stern strong voice, so gathered about her son, that he felt conscious of a renewal of the timid chill and reserve of his childhood.

"Do you never leave your room, mother?"

"What with my rheumatic affection I never leave my room. I have not been outside this door for – tell him for how long," she said, speaking over her shoulder.

"A dozen year next Christmas," returned a cracked voice out of the dimness behind.

"Is that Affery?" said Arthur, looking towards it.

The cracked voice replied that it was Affery: and an old woman came forward into what doubtful light there was, and kissed her hand once; then subsided again into the dimness.

"I am able," said Mrs Clennam, with a slight motion of her worsted-muffled right hand toward a chair on wheels, standing before a tall writing cabinet close shut up, "I am able to attend to my business duties, and I am thankful for the privilege. It is a great privilege. But no more of business on this day. It is a bad night, is it not?"

"Yes, mother."

"Does it snow?"

"Snow, mother? And we only yet in September?"

On her little table lay two or three books, her handkerchief, a pair of steel spectacles newly taken off, and an old-fashioned gold watch in a heavy double case. Upon this last object her son's eyes and her own now rested together.

"I see that you received the packet I sent you on my father's death, safely, mother. I never knew my father to show so much anxiety on any subject, as that his watch should be sent straight to you."

"I keep it here as a remembrance of your father."

"It was not until the last, that he expressed the wish; when he could only put his hand upon it, and very indistinctly say to me 'your mother.' A moment before, I thought him wandering in his mind, as he had been for many hours – I think he had no consciousness of pain in his short illness – when I saw him turn himself in his bed and try to open it."

"Was your father, then, not wandering in his mind when he tried to open it?"

"No. He was quite sensible at that time."

Mrs Clennam signified assent; then added, "No more of business on this day. Affery, it is nine o'clock."

Upon this, the old woman cleared the little table, went out of the room,

15

and quickly returned with a tray on which was a dish of little rusks and a small precise pat of butter, cool, symmetrical, white, and plump. The old man who had been standing by the door in one attitude during the whole interview, looking at the mother upstairs as he had looked at the son downstairs, went out at the same time, and, after a longer absence, returned with another tray on which was the greater part of a bottle of port wine (which, to judge by his panting, he had brought from the cellar), a lemon, a sugar-basin, and a spice box. She then put on the spectacles and read certain passages aloud from a book – sternly, fiercely, wrathfully – praying that her enemies (she made them by her tone and manner expressly hers) might be put to the edge of the sword, consumed by fire, smitten by plagues and leprosy, that their bones might be ground to dust, and that they might be utterly exterminated. As she read on, years seemed to fall away from her son like the imaginings of a dream, and all the old dark horrors of his usual preparation for the sleep of an innocent child to overshadow him. Then the sick woman was ready for bed.

"Good-night, Arthur. Affery will see to your accommodation. Only touch me, for my hand is tender." He touched the worsted muffling of her hand – that was nothing; if his mother had been sheathed in brass there would have been no new barrier between them—and followed the old man and woman downstairs.

"Have something to drink, then," said Affery; "you shall have some of her bottle of port, if you like."

No; nor would he have that, either.

"It's no reason, Arthur," said the old woman, bending over him to whisper, "that because I am afeared of my life of 'em, you should be. You've got half the property, haven't you?"

"Yes, yes."

"Well then, don't you be cowed. You're clever, Arthur, an't you?"

He nodded, as she seemed to expect an answer in the affirmative.

"Then stand up against them! She's awful clever, and none but a clever one durst say a word to her. *He's* a clever one – oh, he's a clever one! – and he gives it her when he has a mind to't, he does!"

"Your husband does?"

"Does? It makes me shake from head to foot, to hear him give it her. My husband, Jeremiah Flintwinch, can conquer even your mother. What can he be but a clever one to do that!"

16

His shuffling footstep coming towards them caused her to retreat to the other end of the room and she collapsed before the little keen-eyed crab-like old man.

"Now, Affery," said he; "make his bed. Stir yourself." His neck was so twisted that the knotted ends of his white cravat usually dangled under one ear. He addressed Arthur.

"You'll have bitter words together tomorrow, Arthur; you and your Mother. Your having given up the business on your father's death – which she suspects, though we have left it to you to tell her – won't go off smoothly."

"I have given up everything in life for the business, and the time came for me to give up that."

"Good!" cried Jeremiah, evidently meaning Bad. "Very good! Only don't expect me to stand between your mother and you, Arthur. I stood between your mother and your father, fending off this, and fending off that, and getting crushed and pounded betwixt 'em; and I've done with such work."

"You will never be asked to do it again for me, Jeremiah."

Arthur Clennam wished the old man good-night, and went upstairs with Affery to the top of the house.

They mounted up and up, through the musty smell of an old close house, little used, to a large garret bedroom. Meagre and spare, like all the other rooms, it was even uglier and grimmer than the rest, by being the place of banishment for the worn-out furniture. Arthur opened the long low window, and looked out upon the old blasted and blackened forest of chimneys, and the old red glare in the sky. He drew in his head again, sat down at the bedside, and looked on at Affery Flintwinch making the bed.

"Affery, you were not married when I went away. How did it happen? Was it my mother's project, then?"

"The Lord bless you, Arthur, and forgive me the wish!" cried Affery, speaking always in a low tone. "If they hadn't been both of a mind in it, how could it ever have been? Jeremiah said to me one day, he said, 'Affery,' he said, 'now I am going to tell you something. What do you think of the name of Flintwinch?'

'What do I think of it?' I says. 'Yes,' he said, 'because you're going to take it,' he said. 'Take it?' I says. 'Jere-*mi*-ah?' Oh! he's a clever one!"

Mrs Flintwinch went on to spread the upper sheet over the bed, and the blanket over that, and the counterpane over that, as if she had quite concluded her story.

"Affery, what girl was that in my mother's room just now?"

"Girl?" said Mrs Flintwinch in a rather sharp key.

"It was a girl, surely – almost hidden in the dark corner?"

"Oh! She? Little Dorrit? She's nothing; she's a whim of – hers."

It was a peculiarity of Affery Flintwinch that she never spoke of Mrs Clennam by name. "But there's another sort of girl than that about. Have you forgot your old sweetheart? Long and long ago, I'll be bound."

"I suffered enough from my mother's separating us, to remember her."

"Have you got another?"

"No."

"Here's news for you, then. She's well to do now, and a widow. And if you like to have her, why you can."

"And how do you know that, Affery?"

"Them two clever ones have been speaking about it. – There's Jeremiah on the stairs!" She was gone in a moment.

Little more than a week ago at Marseilles, the face of the pretty girl from whom he had parted with regret, had had an unusual interest for him, and a tender hold upon him, because of some resemblance, real or imagined, to this first face that had soared out of his gloomy life into the bright glories of fancy. He leaned upon the sill of the long low window, and looking out upon the blackened forest of chimneys again, began to dream; for it had been the uniform tendency of this man's life – so much was wanting in it to think about, so much that might have been better directed and happier to speculate upon – to make him a dreamer, after all.

CHAPTER 4

Family Affairs

As the city clocks struck nine on Monday morning, Mrs Clennam was wheeled by Jeremiah Flintwinch to her tall cabinet. When she had unlocked and opened it, and had settled herself at its desk, Jeremiah withdrew and her son appeared.

18

"Are you any better this morning, mother? Shall I speak of our affairs, mother? Are you inclined to enter upon business?"

"Am I inclined, Arthur? Rather, are you? Your father has been dead a year and more. I have been at your disposal, and waiting your pleasure, ever since."

"There was much to arrange before I could leave; and when I did leave, I travelled a little for rest and relief. Besides, mother, you being sole executrix, and having the direction and management of the estate, there remained little business, or I might say none, that I could transact, until you had had time to arrange matters to your satisfaction."

"The accounts are made out," she returned. "I have them here. The vouchers have all been examined and passed. You can inspect them when you like, Arthur; now, if you please."

"It is quite enough, mother, to know that the business is completed. Shall I proceed then?"

"Why not?" she said, in her frozen way.

"Mother, our House has done less and less for some years past, and our dealings have been progressively on the decline. We have never shown much confidence, or invited much; we have attached no people to us; the track we have kept is not the track of the time; and we have been left far behind. I need not dwell on this to you, mother. You know it necessarily."

"I know what you mean," she answered, in a qualified tone.

"You have anticipated, mother, that I decide for my part, to abandon the business. I have done with it. I will not take upon myself to advise you; you will continue it, I see. If I had any influence with you, I would simply use it to soften your judgement of me in causing you this disappointment: to represent to you that I have lived the half of a long term of life, and have never before set my own will against yours."

"Have you finished, Arthur, or have you anything more to say to me?"

"Mother, I have yet something more to say. It has been upon my mind, night and day, this long time. It is far more difficult to say than what I have said. That concerned myself; this concerns us all."

"Us all! Who are us all?"

"Yourself, myself, my dead father."

She took her hands from the desk; folded them in her lap; and sat looking towards the fire, with the impenetrability of an old Egyptian sculpture.

19

"You knew my father infinitely better than I ever knew him; and his reserve with me yielded to you. You were much the stronger, mother, and directed him. As a child, I knew it as well as I know it now. I knew that your ascendancy over him was the cause of his going to China to take care of the business there, while you took care of it here (though I do not even now know whether these were really terms of separation that you agreed upon); and that it was your will that I should remain with you until I was twenty, and then go to him as I did. You will not be offended by my recalling this, after twenty years?"

"I am waiting to hear why you recall it."

He lowered his voice, and said, with manifest reluctance, and against his will:

"I want to ask you, whether it ever occurred to you to suspect – "

At the word suspect, she turned her eyes momentarily upon her son, with a dark frown.

" – that he had any secret remembrance which caused him trouble of mind – remorse? Whether you ever observed anything in his conduct suggesting that. Is it possible, mother," her son leaned forward to be the nearer to her while he whispered it, and laid his hand nervously upon her desk, "is it possible, mother, that he had unhappily wronged any one, and made no reparation?"

Looking at him wrathfully, she bent herself back in her chair to keep him further off, but gave him no reply.

"I am deeply sensible, mother, that if this thought has never at any time flashed upon you, it must seem cruel and unnatural in me, even in this confidence, to breathe it. But I cannot shake it off. Time and change (I have tried both before breaking silence) do nothing to wear it out. Remember, I was with my father. Remember I saw his face when he gave the watch into my keeping, and struggled to express that he sent it as a token you would understand, to you. Remember, I saw him at the last with the pencil in his failing hand, trying to write some word for you to read, but to which he could give no shape.

"For Heaven's sake, let us examine sacredly whether there is any wrong entrusted to us to set right. No one can help towards it, mother, but you."

She looked at him in a fixed silence.

"In grasping at money and in driving hard bargains – I have begun, and

I must speak of such things now, mother – some one may have been grievously deceived, injured, ruined. You were the moving power of all this machinery before my birth; your stronger spirit has been infused into all my father's dealings for more than two score years. You can set these doubts at rest, I think, if you will really help me to discover the truth. Will you, mother?"

He stopped in the hope that she would speak.

There was a bell-rope hanging on the panelled wall, some two or three yards from the cabinet. By a swift and sudden action of her foot, she drove her wheeled chair rapidly back to it and pulled it violently – holding her arm up in a shield-like posture, as if he were striking at her, and she warding off the blow.

A girl came hurrying in, frightened.

"Send Flintwinch here!"

In a moment the girl had withdrawn, and the old man stood within the door. "What! You're hammer and tongs, already, you two?" he said, coolly stroking his face. "I thought you would be. I was pretty sure of it."

"Flintwinch!" said the mother, "look at my son. Look at him!"

"Well, I *am* looking at him," said Flintwinch.

She stretched out the arm with which she had shielded herself, and as she went on, pointed at the object of her anger.

"In the very hour of his return almost – before the shoe upon his foot is dry – he asperses his father's memory to his mother! Asks his mother to become, with him, a spy upon his father's transactions through a lifetime Reparation! It is easy for him to talk of reparation, fresh from journeying and junketing in foreign lands, and living a life of vanity and pleasure. But let him look at me, in prison, and in bonds here. I endure without murmuring, because it is appointed that I shall so make reparation for my sins. Reparation! Is there none in this room? Has there been none here this fifteen years? Flintwinch, give me that book!"

The old man handed it to her from the table. She put two fingers between the leaves, closed the book upon them, and held it up to her son in a threatening way.

"If you ever renew that theme with me, I will renounce you."

"Mrs Clennam," said Flintwinch. "Let us see how we stand. Have you told Mr Arthur that he mustn't lay offences at his father's door? That he has no right to do it? That he has no ground to go upon?"

"I tell him so now."

He put his hands to the back of the wheeled chair. "Has Arthur told you what he means to do about the business?"

"He has relinquished it."

"In favour of nobody, I suppose?"

Mrs Clennam glanced at her son, leaning against one of the windows. He observed the look and said, "To my mother, of course. She does what she pleases."

She spoke bitterly. "Jeremiah, the captain deserts the ship, but you and I will sink or float with it."

Jeremiah, whose eyes glistened as if they saw money, told the mother that he thanked her, and that Affery thanked her, and that he would never desert her, and that Affery would never desert her.

Finally, he hauled up his watch from its depths, and said, "Eleven. Time for your oysters!" and with that change of subject, which involved no change of expression or manner, rang the bell.

This refection of oysters was not presided over by Affery, but by the girl who had appeared when the bell was rung; the same who had been in the dimly-lighted room last night. Now that he had an opportunity of observing her, Arthur found that her diminutive figure, small features, and slight spare dress, gave her the appearance of being much younger than she was. A woman, probably of not less than two-and-twenty, she might have been passed in the street for little more than half that age. Not that her face was very youthful, for in truth there was more consideration and care in it than naturally belonged to her utmost years; but she was so little and light, so noiseless and shy, and appeared so conscious of being out of place among the three hard elders, that she had all the manner and much of the appearance of a subdued child. This was Amy, or Little Dorrit as she was called. She let herself out to do needlework. At so much a day – or at so little – from eight to eight, Little Dorrit was to be hired. Punctual to the moment, Little Dorrit appeared; punctual to the moment, Little Dorrit vanished. What became of Little Dorrit between the two eights was a mystery.

Another of the moral phenomena of Little Dorrit: besides her consideration money, her daily contract included meals. She had an extraordinary repugnance to dining in company; would never do so, if it were possible to escape.

It was not easy to make out Little Dorrit's face but it seemed to be a pale transparent face, quick in expression, though not beautiful in feature, its soft hazel eyes excepted. A delicately bent head, a tiny form, a quick little pair of busy hands, and a shabby dress – it must needs have been very shabby to look at all so, being so neat – were Little Dorrit as she sat at work.

At two o'clock, when Arthur dined with Mr Flintwinch, the new partner, Mr Flintwinch informed him that his mother had recovered her equanimity now, and that he need not fear her again.

"And don't you lay offences at your father's door, Mr Arthur," added Jeremiah, "once for all, don't do it! Now, we have done with the subject."

It was then Mr Arthur announced his intention of lodging at the coffee-house where he had left his luggage.

Daily business hours were agreed upon, which his mother, Mr Flintwinch, and he, were to devote together to a necessary checking of books and papers; and he left the home he had so lately found, with depressed heart.

But Little Dorrit? His original curiosity augmented every day, as he watched for her, saw or did not see her, and speculated about her. Influenced by his predominant idea, he even fell into a habit of discussing with himself the possibility of her being in some way associated with it. At last he resolved to watch Little Dorrit and know more of her story.

CHAPTER 5

The Father of the Marshalsea

Thirty years ago there stood, a few doors short of the church of Saint George, in the borough of Southwark, on the left-hand side of the way going southward, the Marshalsea Prison. It is gone now, and the world is none the worse without it.

Itself a close and confined prison for debtors, it contained within it a much closer and more confined jail for smugglers. Offenders against the revenue laws, and defaulters to excise or customs who had incurred fines which they were unable to pay, were supposed to be incarcerated behind an iron-plated door closing up a second prison. However, in reality smugglers habitually consorted with the debtors (who received them with open arms), except at certain constitutional moments when somebody came from some Office, to go through some form of overlooking something which neither he nor anybody else knew anything about.

There had been taken to the Marshalsea Prison, long before the day when the sun shone on Marseilles and on the opening of this narrative, a debtor with whom this narrative has some concern.

He was, at that time, a very amiable and very helpless middle-aged gentleman, who was going out again directly. Necessarily, he was going out again directly, because the Marshalsea lock never turned upon a debtor who was not. He brought in a portmanteau with him, which he doubted its being worthwhile to unpack; he was so perfectly clear – like all the rest of them, the turnkey on the lock said – that he was going out again directly.

He was a shy, retiring man; well-looking, though in an effeminate style; with a mild voice, curling hair, and irresolute hands – rings upon the fingers in those days – which nervously wandered to his trembling lip a hundred times in the first half-hour of his acquaintance with the jail. His principal anxiety was about his wife.

"Do you think, sir," he asked the turnkey, "that she will be very much shocked, if she should come to the gate tomorrow morning?"

The turnkey gave it as the result of his experience that some of 'em was and some of 'em wasn't. In general, more no than yes. "What like is she, you see?" he philosophically asked: "that's what it hinges on."

"She is very delicate and inexperienced indeed."

"That," said the turnkey, "is agen her."

"She is so little used to go out alone," said the debtor, "I fear – I hope it is not against the rules – that she will bring the children."

"The children?" said the turnkey. "And the rules? Why, lord set you up like a corner pin, we've a reg'lar playground o' children here."

He was right in all his particulars. She came next day with a little boy of three years old, and a little girl of two, and he stood entirely corroborated.

"Got a room now; haven't you?" the turnkey asked the debtor after a week or two.

"Yes, I have got a very good room."

24

"Any little sticks a coming to furnish it?" said the turnkey.

"I expect a few necessary articles of furniture to be delivered by the carrier, this afternoon."

"Missis and little 'uns a coming to keep you company?" asked the turnkey.

"Why, yes, we think it better that we should not be scattered, even for a few weeks."

"Even for a few weeks, *of* course," replied the turnkey. And he followed him again with his eyes, and nodded his head seven times when he was gone.

The affairs of this debtor were perplexed by a partnership, of which he knew no more than that he had invested money in it. And as nobody on the face of the earth could be more incapable of explaining any single item in the heap of confusion than the debtor himself, nothing comprehensible could be made of his case.

He had been in the Marshalsea for some time, when his wife had a baby.

"A very nice little girl indeed," said the doctor; "little, but well-formed."

By this time, the rings had begun to fall from the debtor's irresolute hands, like leaves from a wintry tree. Not one was left upon them that night, when he put them with something else that chinked into the doctor's greasy palm. "I am very happy and very thankful to have had your help," said the debtor, "though I little thought once, that – "

"That a child would be born to you in a place like this?" said the doctor. "Bah, bah, sir, what does it signify? Elsewhere, people are restless, worried, hurried about, anxious respecting one thing, anxious respecting another. Nothing of the kind here, sir. We have done all that – we know the worst of it; we have got to the bottom, we can't fall, and what have we found? Peace. That's the word for it. Peace."

Now, the debtor was a very different man from the doctor, but he had already begun to travel, by his opposite segment of the circle, to the same point. Crushed at first by his imprisonment, he had soon found a dull relief in it. He was under lock and key; but the lock and key that kept him in, kept numbers of his troubles out.

If he had been a man with strength of purpose to face those troubles and fight them, he might have broken the net that held him, or broken his heart; but being what he was, he languidly slipped into this smooth descent, and never more took one step upward.

Time passed. He had unpacked the portmanteau long ago; and his elder children now played regularly about the yard, and everybody knew the baby, and claimed a kind of proprietorship in her.

"Why, I'm getting proud of you," said his friend the turnkey, one day. "You'll be the oldest inhabitant soon. The Marshalsea wouldn't be like the Marshalsea now, without you and your family. You'll find some characters behind other locks, I don't say you won't; but if you want the top sawyer in such respects as I've mentioned, you must come to the Marshalsea."

When his youngest child was eight years old, his wife went upon a visit to a poor friend and old nurse in the country, and died there. He remained shut up in his room for a fortnight afterwards and when he appeared again he was greyer and his hands went often to his trembling lips again, as they had used to do when he first came in.

Time went on, and the turnkey began to fail. His chest swelled, his legs got weak, and he was short of breath. The well-worn wooden stool was "beyond him," he complained. He sat in an armchair, and sometimes wheezed so, for minutes together, that he couldn't turn the key. When he was overpowered by these fits, the debtor often turned it for him.

"You and me," said the turnkey, one snowy winter's night when the lodge, with a bright fire in it, was pretty full of company, "is the oldest inhabitants. I wasn't here myself above seven year before you. I shan't last long. When I'm off the lock for good and all, you'll be the Father of the Marshalsea."

The turnkey went off the lock of this world next day. His words were remembered and repeated; and tradition afterwards handed down from generation to generation – a Marshalsea generation might be calculated as about three months – that the shabby old debtor with the soft manner and the white hair, was the Father of the Marshalsea. Yes, he was the Father of the place. So the world was kind enough to call him; and so he was, if more than twenty years of residence gave him a claim to the title.

It became a not unusual circumstance for letters to be put under his door at night, enclosing half-a-crown, two half-crowns, now and then at long intervals even half-a-sovereign, for the Father of the Marshalsea. "With the compliments of a collegian taking leave."

26

CHAPTER 6

The Child of the Marshalsea

The baby whose first draught of air had been taken in the Marshalsea, was handed down among the generations of collegians, like the tradition of their common parent. In the earlier stages of her existence, she was handed down in a literal and prosaic sense; it being almost a part of the entrance footing of every new collegian to nurse the child who had been born in the college.

"By rights," remarked the turnkey when she was first shown to him, "I ought to be her godfather."

The debtor irresolutely thought of it for a minute, and said,

"Perhaps you wouldn't object to really being her godfather?"

"Oh! – I – don't object," replied the turnkey, "if you don't."

Thus it came to pass that she was christened one Sunday afternoon; and that the turnkey went up to the font of Saint George's Church, and promised and vowed and renounced on her behalf, as he himself related when he came back, "like a good 'un."

This invested the turnkey with a new proprietary share in the child, over and above his former official one. The child, for her part, soon grew so fond of the turnkey that she would come climbing up the lodge-steps of her own accord at all hours of the day.

At what period of her early life the little creature began to perceive that it was not the habit of all the world to live locked up in narrow yards surrounded by high walls with spikes at the top, would be a difficult question to settle.

With a pitiful and plaintive look for everything, this Child of the Marshalsea and the child of the Father of the Marshalsea, sat by her friend the turnkey in the lodge, kept the family room, or wandered about the prison-yard, for the first eight years of her life. With a pitiful and plaintive look for her wayward sister; for her idle brother; for the high blank walls; for the faded crowd they shut in; for the games of the prison children as they whooped and ran, and played at hide-and-seek, and made the iron bars of the inner gateway "Home."

Wistful and wondering, the Child of the Marshalsea took upon herself a new relation towards the Father.

At first, such a baby could do little more than sit with him, deserting her livelier place by the high fender, and quietly watching him. But this made her so far necessary to him that he became accustomed to her, and began to be sensible of missing her when she was not there. Through this little gate, she passed out of childhood into the care-laden world.

What her pitiful look saw, at that early time, in her father, in her sister, in her brother, in the jail; how much of the wretched truth it pleased God to make visible to her; lies hidden with many mysteries. It is enough that she was inspired to be something which was not what the rest were, and to be that something, different and laborious, for the sake of the rest.

At thirteen, she could read and keep accounts, that is, could put down in words and figures how much the bare necessaries that they wanted would cost, and how much less they had to buy them with.

She had been, by snatches of a few weeks at a time, to an evening school outside, and got her sister and brother sent to day-schools by desultory starts, during three or four years. There was no instruction for any of them at home; but she knew well – no one better – that a man so broken as to be the Father of the Marshalsea, could be no father to his own children.

To these scanty means of improvement, she added another of her own contriving. Once, among the heterogeneous crowd of inmates, there appeared a dancing-master. Her sister had a great desire to learn the dancing-master's art, and seemed to have a taste that way. At thirteen years old, the Child of the Marshalsea presented herself to the dancing-master, with a little bag in her hand, and preferred her humble petition.

"And what can I do for you?" said the dancing-master.

"Nothing for me, sir, thank you," anxiously undrawing the strings of the little bag; "but if, while you stay here, you could be so kind as to teach my sister cheap – "

"My child, I'll teach her for nothing," said the dancing-master.

The success of this beginning, which led to the dancing-master's continuing his instruction after his release, emboldened the poor child to try again. She watched and waited months for a seamstress. In the fullness of time a milliner came in, and to her she repaired on her own behalf.

"I beg your pardon, ma'am," she said, looking timidly round the door of the milliner, whom she found in tears and in bed: "but I was born here."

Everybody seemed to hear of her as soon as they arrived; for the milliner sat up in bed, drying her eyes, and said:

"Oh! You are the child, are you?"

"Yes, ma'am. If you please I want to learn needlework."

The milliner, who was not morose or hard-hearted, only newly insolvent – was touched, took her in hand with goodwill, found her the most patient and earnest of pupils, and made her a cunning work-woman in course of time.

In course of time, and in the very self-same course of time, the Father of the Marshalsea gradually developed a new flower of character. The more Fatherly he grew as to the Marshalsea, and the more dependent he became on the contributions of his changing family, the greater stand he made by his forlorn gentility.

The sister became a dancer. There was a ruined uncle in the family group – Frederick, ruined by his brother, the Father of the Marshalsea, and knowing no more how than his ruiner did, but accepting the fact as an inevitable certainty – on whom her protection devolved.

Naturally a retired and simple man, he had shown no particular sense of being ruined at the time when that calamity fell upon him, further than that he left off washing himself when the shock was announced, and never took to that luxury any more. He had been a very indifferent musical amateur in his better days; and when he fell with his brother, resorted for support to playing a clarionet as dirty as himself in a small Theatre Orchestra. It was the theatre in which his niece became a dancer. To enable this girl to earn her few weekly shillings, it was necessary for the Child of the Marshalsea to go through an elaborate form with the Father.

"Fanny is not going to live with us just now, father. She will be here a good deal in the day, but she is going to live outside with uncle."

"You surprise me. Why?"

"I think uncle wants a companion, father. He should be attended to, and looked after."

"A companion? He passes much of his time here. And you attend to him and look after him, Amy, a great deal more than ever your sister will. You all go out so much; you all go out so much. But you and Fanny and your uncle, my dear, shall have your own way. Good, good. I'll not meddle; don't mind me."

To get her brother Tip out of the prison she found him a position in the office of an attorney. Tip languished in Clifford's Inn for six months, and at the expiration of that term sauntered back one evening with his hands in his pockets, and incidentally observed to his sister that he was not going back again.

"I am so tired of it," said Tip, "that I have cut it."

Tip tired of everything. Wherever he went, he appeared to take the prison walls with him, then the Marshalsea walls asserted their fascination over him, and brought him back.

At length he found a pursuit for himself, and announced it.

"Amy, I have got a situation."

"Have you really and truly, Tip?"

"All right. I shall do now. You needn't look anxious about me any more, old girl."

"What is it, Tip?"

"Why, you know Slingo by sight?"

"Not the man they call the dealer?"

"That's the chap. He'll be out on Monday, and he's going to give me a berth."

"What is he a dealer in, Tip?"

"Horses. All right! I shall do now, Amy."

She lost sight of him for months afterwards, and only heard from him once. Then one evening she was alone at work – standing up at the window, to save the twilight lingering above the wall – when he opened the door and walked in.

"I am afraid, Amy, you'll be vexed this time. Upon my life I am!"

"Oh! Don't say you are a prisoner, Tip! Don't, don't!"

"Well, I don't want to say it," he returned in a reluctant tone; "but if you can't understand me without my saying it, what am I to do? I am in for forty pound odd."

This was the life, and this the history, of Little Dorrit; now going home upon a dull September evening, observed at a distance by Arthur Clennam; turning at the end of London Bridge, recrossing it, going back again, passing on to Saint George's Church, turning back suddenly once more, and flitting in at the open outer gate and little courtyard of the Marshalsea.

CHAPTER 7

The Lock

Arthur Clennam stood in the street, waiting to ask some passer-by what place that was.

"This is the Marshalsea, sir," said an old man who was passing by.

"The debtors' prison?"

"Yes."

"Can any one go in here?"

"Any one can go *in*," replied the old man; plainly adding by the significance of his emphasis, "but it is not every one who can go out."

"Pardon me once more. Are you familiar with the place?"

"Sir," returned the old man, squeezing his little packet of snuff in his hand, and turning upon his interrogator as if such questions hurt him. "I am."

"I beg you to excuse me. I am not impertinently curious, but have a good object. Do you know the name of Dorrit here?"

"My name, sir," replied the old man most unexpectedly, "is Dorrit."

Arthur pulled off his hat to him. "I have recently come home to England after a long absence. I have seen at my mother's – Mrs Clennam in the city – a young woman working at her needle, whom I have only heard spoken of as Little Dorrit. I have felt sincerely interested in her, and have had a great desire to know something more about her. I saw her, not a minute before you came up, pass in at that door."

The old man looked at him attentively. "The young woman whom you saw go in here is my brother's child. My brother is William Dorrit; I am Frederick. Come and see."

The night was dark; and the prison lamps in the yard, and the candles in the prison windows faintly shining behind many sorts of wry old curtain and blind, had not the air of making it lighter.

A few people loitered about, but the greater part of the population was within doors. The old man, taking the right-hand side of the yard, turned in at the third or fourth doorway, began to ascend the stairs and paused for a moment before opening a door on the second storey.

He had no sooner turned the handle than the visitor saw Little Dorrit, and saw the reason of her setting so much store by dining alone.

31

She had brought the meat home that she should have eaten herself, and was already warming it on a gridiron over the fire for her father, clad in an old grey gown and a black cap, awaiting his supper at the table. A clean cloth was spread before him, with knife, fork, and spoon, salt-cellar, pepper-box, glass, and pewter ale-pot. Such zests as his particular little phial of cayenne pepper and his pennyworth of pickles in a saucer, were not wanting.

"This is my brother William, sir," said Frederick.

"I hope," said Arthur, very doubtful what to say, "that my respect for your daughter may explain and justify my desire to be presented to you, sir. She works for my mother, Mrs Clennam."

"You are welcome to the Marshalsea, sir," said the prisoner with a deep bow. "I have welcomed many gentlemen to these walls. Perhaps you are aware – my daughter Amy may have mentioned, that I am the Father of this place."

"I – so I have understood," said Arthur, dashing at the assertion.

"You know, I dare say, that my daughter Amy was born here. A good girl, sir, a dear girl, and long a comfort and support to me."

Arthur was to speak, when a bell began to ring, and footsteps approached the door. A pretty girl of a far better figure and much more developed than Little Dorrit, though looking much younger in the face when the two were observed together, stopped in the doorway on seeing a stranger; and a young man who was with her, stopped too.

"Mr Clennam, Fanny. My eldest daughter and my son, Mr Clennam. The bell is a signal for visitors to retire, and so they have come to say good-night; but there is plenty of time, plenty of time."

Mr Clennam had two things to do before he went; one, to offer his testimonial to the Father of the Marshalsea, without giving pain to his child; the other to say something to that child, though it were but a word, in explanation of his having come there.

She had slipped out after the rest, and they were alone.

"Pray forgive me," he said, "for speaking to you here; pray forgive me for coming here at all! I followed you tonight. I did so, that I might endeavour to render you and your family some service. What I have seen here, in this short time, has greatly increased my heartfelt wish to be a friend to you. It would recompense me for much disappointment if I could hope to gain your confidence."

She was scared at first, but seemed to take courage while he spoke to her.

"You are very good, sir. You speak very earnestly to me. But I – but I wish you had not watched me."

He understood the emotion with which she said it, to arise in her father's behalf; and he respected it, and was silent.

"Mrs Clennam has been of great service to me; I don't know what we should have done without the employment she has given me; I am afraid it may not be a good return to become secret with her; I can say no more tonight, sir. I am sure you mean to be kind to us. Thank you, thank you."

"Let me ask you one question before I leave. Have you known my mother long?"

"I think two years, sir, – The bell has stopped."

"How did you know her first? Did she send here for you?"

"No. She does not even know that I live here. We have a friend, father and I – a poor labouring man, but the best of friends – and I wrote out that I wished to do needlework, and gave his address. And he got what I wrote out displayed at a few places where it cost nothing, and Mrs Clennam found me that way, and sent for me. The gate will be locked, sir!"

He remained too late. The inner gate was locked, and the lodge closed. After a little fruitless knocking with his hand, a voice accosted him from behind.

"Caught, eh?" said the voice. "You won't go home till morning. Oh! It's you, is it, Mr Clennam?"

The voice was Tip's; and they stood looking at one another in the prison-yard, as it began to rain.

"You've done it," observed Tip; "you must be sharper than that next time."

"But you are locked in too," said Arthur.

"I believe I am!" said Tip, sarcastically. "About! But not in your way. I belong to the shop, only my sister has a theory that our governor must never know it. I don't see why, myself."

"Can I get any shelter?" asked Arthur. "What had I better do?"

"We had better get hold of Amy first of all," said Tip, referring any difficulty to her as a matter of course.

"I would rather walk about all night – it's not much to do – than give that trouble."

33

"You needn't do that, if you don't mind paying for a bed. They'll make you up one on the Snuggery table, under the circumstances. If you'll come along, I'll introduce you there."

As they passed down the yard, Arthur looked up at the window of the room he had lately left, where the light was still burning. "Yes, sir," said Tip, following his glance. "The governor sleeps up in the room, and she has a lodging at the turnkey's. First house there," said Tip, pointing out the doorway into which she had retired. "She pays twice as much for it as she would for one twice as good outside. But she stands by the governor, poor dear girl, day and night."

The Snuggery turned out to be a cooped-up apartment, and while he tried to repose on two Windsor chairs Arthur's mind was in turmoil.

What if his mother had an old reason she well knew for softening to this poor girl! What if the prisoner now sleeping quietly – Heaven grant it! – by the light of the great Day of judgement should trace back his fall to her. What if any act of hers and of his father's, should have even remotely brought the grey heads of those two brothers so low!

CHAPTER 8

Little Mother

Though little rested by the night, Arthur Clennam turned out as soon as he could distinguish objects about him, and paced the yard for two heavy hours before the gate was opened.

At last the lodge-gate turned, and the turnkey, standing on the step, taking an early comb at his hair, was ready to let him out.

There was a string of people already straggling in. These insolvent waiters upon insolvency, was a sight to see.

As these people passed him standing still in the courtyard, and one of them turned back to inquire if he could assist him with his services, it came into Arthur Clennam's mind that he would speak to Little Dorrit again before he went away. She would have recovered her first surprise, and might feel easier with him. He asked this member of the fraternity (who had two red herrings in his hand, and a loaf and a blacking brush under his arm), where was the nearest place to get a cup of coffee at. The nondescript replied in encouraging terms, and brought him to a coffee-shop in the street within a stone's throw.

"Do you know Miss Dorrit?" asked the new client.

The nondescript knew two Miss Dorrits; one who was born inside – that was the one! Arthur entrusted the nondescript with a confidential message to her, importing that the visitor who had waited on her father last night, begged the favour of a few words with her at her uncle's lodging; he obtained from the same source full directions to the house, which was very near.

The door was opened by the poor old man himself.

"Ha!" said he, very slowly remembering Arthur, "you were shut in last night?"

"Yes, Mr Dorrit. I hope to meet your niece here presently."

"Oh!" said he, pondering. "Out of my brother's way? True. Would you come upstairs and wait for her? Her sister is getting dressed."

"Thank you."

Turning himself as slowly as he turned in his mind whatever he heard or said, he led the way up the narrow stairs and into the back garret then sat down in his chair, and began warming his hands at the fire.

"My brother would have been quite lost without Amy," he said. "We should all have been lost without Amy. She is a very good girl, Amy. She does her duty."

At length, a bell rang. That was Amy, he said, and went down to let her in; Amy came up in the usual plain dress, and with the usual timid manner. Her lips were a little parted, as if her heart beat faster than usual.

"Mr Clennam, Amy," said her uncle, "has been expecting you some time."

"I took the liberty of sending you a message."

"I received the message, sir."

"Are you going to my mother's this morning? I think not, for it is past your usual hour."

"Not today, sir. I am not wanted today."

"Will you allow me to walk a little way in whatever direction you may be going? I can then speak to you as we walk, both without detaining you here, and without intruding longer here myself."

She looked embarrassed, but said, if he pleased. Mr Arthur Clennam

35

offered his arm to Little Dorrit, and Little Dorrit took it. "Will you go by the Iron Bridge," said he, "where there is an escape from the noise of the street?" Little Dorrit answered, if he pleased, and presently ventured to hope that he would "not mind" Mr Cripples's boys, for she had herself received her education, such as it was, in Mr Cripples's evening academy.

The morning remained squally, and the streets were miserably muddy, but no rain fell as they walked towards the Iron Bridge.

Little Dorrit spoke gently. "I am sorry to hear you were so inconvenienced last night, sir, as to be locked in. It was very unfortunate."

It was nothing, he returned. He had had a very good bed.

"I asked you last night," said Clennam, after a pause, "how you had become acquainted with my mother. Did you ever hear her name before she sent for you?"

"No, sir."

"Do you think your father ever did?"

"No, sir."

"I have a reason for asking, which I cannot very well explain; but you must, on no account, suppose it to be of a nature to cause you the least alarm or anxiety. Quite the reverse. And you think that at no time of your father's life was my name of Clennam ever familiar to him?"

"No, sir."

Thus they emerged upon the Iron Bridge, which was as quiet after the roaring streets as though it had been open country.

"Let me put you in a coach," said Clennam, very nearly adding "my poor child."

She hurriedly declined, saying that wet or dry made little difference to her; she was used to go about in all weathers.

"I wished very much to say to you – " she hesitated and trembled, and tears rose in her eyes, but did not fall.

"To say to me – ?"

"That I hope you will not misunderstand my father. Don't judge him, sir, as you would judge others outside the gates. He has been there so long. He is not to be blamed for being in need, poor love. Who could be in prison a quarter of a century, and be prosperous!"

What affection in her words, what compassion in her repressed tears, what a great soul of fidelity within her, how true the light that shed false brightness round him!

"I feel permitted now," he said, "to ask you a little more concerning your father. Has he many creditors?"

"Oh! a great number."

"I mean detaining creditors, who keep him where he is?"

"Oh yes! a great number."

"Can you tell me – I can get the information, no doubt, elsewhere, if you cannot – who is the most influential of them?"

Little Dorrit said, after considering a little, that she used to hear long ago of Mr Tite Barnacle as a man of great power. He was a commissioner, or a board, or a trustee, "or something." He lived in Grosvenor Square, she thought, or very near it, high in the Circumlocution Office.

"It can do no harm," thought Arthur, "if I see this Mr Tite Barnacle."

The thought did not present itself so quietly but that her quickness intercepted it. "Ah!" said Little Dorrit, shaking her head with the mild despair of a lifetime. "Many people used to think once of getting my poor father out, but you don't know how hopeless it is."

"You would be glad to have your brother set at liberty?"

"Oh very, very glad, sir!"

"Well, we will hope for him at least. You told me last night of a friend you had?"

His name was Plornish, Little Dorrit said.

And where did Plornish live? Plornish lived in Bleeding Heart Yard. He was "only a plasterer," Little Dorrit said, as a caution to him not to form high social expectations of Plornish. He lived at the last house in Bleeding Heart Yard, and his name was over a little gateway.

Arthur took down the address and gave her his.

They came into the High Street, where the prison stood, when a voice cried, "Little mother, little mother!" Little Dorrit stopping and looking back, an excited figure of a strange kind bounced against them (still crying "little mother"), fell down, and scattered the contents of a large basket, filled with potatoes, in the mud.

"Oh, Maggy," said Little Dorrit, "what a clumsy child you are!"

Maggy was not hurt, but picked herself up immediately, and then began to pick up the potatoes, in which both Little Dorrit and Arthur Clennam helped. She was about eight-and-twenty, with large bones, large features, large feet and hands, large eyes and no hair. Her large eyes were limpid and almost colourless; they seemed to be very little affected by light, and to stand unnaturally still. There was also that attentive listening expression in her face, which is seen in the faces of the blind; but she was not blind, having one tolerably serviceable eye.

Arthur Clennam looked at Little Dorrit with the expression of one saying, "May I ask who this is?"

"This is Maggy, sir."

"Maggy, sir," echoed the personage presented. "Little mother!"

"She is the grand-daughter – " said Little Dorrit.

"Grand-daughter," echoed Maggy.

"Of my old nurse, who has been dead a long time. Maggy, how old are you?"

"Ten, mother," said Maggy.

"You can't think how good she is, sir," said Little Dorrit, with infinite tenderness.

"Good *she* is," echoed Maggy, transferring the pronoun in a most expressive way from herself to her little mother.

"Or how clever," said Little Dorrit. "she goes on errands as well as any one." Maggy laughed. "And is as trustworthy as the Bank of England." Maggy laughed. "She earns her own living entirely. Entirely, sir!" said Little Dorrit, in a lower and triumphant tone. "Really does!"

"What is her history?" asked Clennam.

"Think of that, Maggy?" said Little Dorrit, taking her two large hands and clapping them together. "A gentleman from thousands of miles away, wanting to know your history!"

"My history?" cried Maggy. "Little mother."

"She means me," said Little Dorrit, rather confused; "she is very much attached to me. Her old grandmother was not so kind to her as she should have been; was she, Maggy?"

Maggy shook her head, made a drinking vessel of her clenched left hand, drank out of it, and said, "Gin." Then beat an imaginary child, and said, "Broom-handles and pokers."

"When Maggy was ten years old," said Little Dorrit, watching her face while she spoke, "she had a bad fever, sir, and she has never grown any older ever since. Her grandmother did not know what to do with her, and for some years was very unkind to her indeed. At length, in course of time, Maggy began to take pains to improve herself, and to be very attentive and very industrious; and by degrees was allowed to come in

38

and out as often as she liked, and got enough to do to support herself, and does support herself. And that," said Little Dorrit, clapping the two great hands together again, "is Maggy's history, as Maggy knows!"

The courtyard received them at last, the little mother attended by her big child.

CHAPTER 9

Containing the Whole Science of Government

Arthur went to the Circumlocution Office to learn that Tite Barnacle, who ran it in a lordly manner, was at home at 24 Mews Street, Grosvenor Square, nursing an attack of gout. On his arrival the footman pondered over the card a little; then said, "Walk in."

Mr Barnacle would see him. Would he walk upstairs? He would, and he did; and in the drawing-room, with his leg on a rest, Mr Barnacle greeted Arthur.

"Mr Clennam?" said Mr Barnacle. "Be seated."

Mr Clennam became seated.

"You have called on me, I believe," said Mr Barnacle, "at the Circumlocution – " giving it the air of a word of about five-and-twenty syllables – "Office."

"I have taken that liberty. Mr Barnacle, allow me to observe that I have been for some years in China, am quite a stranger at home, and have no personal motive or interest in the inquiry I am about to make."

Mr Barnacle tapped his fingers on the table and nodded.

"I have found a debtor in the Marshalsea Prison of the name of Dorrit, who has been there many years. I wish to investigate his confused affairs so far as to ascertain whether it may not be possible, after this lapse of time, to ameliorate his unhappy condition. The name of Mr Tite Barnacle has been mentioned to me as representing some highly influential interest among his creditors. Am I correctly informed?"

"I must refer you," returned Mr Barnacle, ringing the bell, "to the Department itself for a formal answer to that inquiry."

"I want to know," said Arthur, and repeated his case.

"Well, I tell you what. Look here. You had better try the Secretarial Department," Mr Barnacle said at last, sidling to the bell and ringing it. "Jenkinson," to the messenger, "take this man back to the Circumlocution office to Mr Wobbler!"

Arthur Clennam accompanied the messenger to another floor of the building from where he had come, and in the appointed apartment, found two gentlemen sitting face to face at a large and easy desk, one of whom was polishing a gun-barrel on his pocket-handkerchief, while the other was spreading marmalade on bread with a paper-knife.

"Mr Wobbler?" inquired the suitor.

Both gentlemen glanced at him, and seemed surprised at his assurance.

"What's the matter?" then said Mr Wobbler, with his mouth full.

"I want to know – " and Arthur Clennam again mechanically set forth what he wanted to know.

"Can't inform you," observed Mr Wobbler, apparently to his lunch. "Never heard of it. Nothing at all to do with it. Better try Mr Clive, second door on the left in the next passage."

A few steps brought him to the second door on the left in the next passage. In that room he found three gentlemen doing nothing in particular and a fourth, a vivacious, well-looking, well-dressed, agreeable young fellow – he was a Barnacle, but on the more sprightly side of the family – and he said in an easy way, "Oh! you had better not bother yourself about it, I think. I don't say it would be hopeless, but I don't think you'd go on with it. However, of course, you can do as you like. I suppose there was a failure in the performance of a contract, or something of that kind, was there?"

"I really don't know."

"Well! That you can find out. Then you'll find out what department the contract was in, and then you'll find out all about it there."

"But surely this is not the way to do the business," Arthur Clennam could not help saying to which the engaging young Barnacle replied, "You had better take a lot of forms away with you."

Arthur Clennam put his forms in his pocket gloomily enough, and went his way down the long stone passage and the long stone staircase. He had come to the swing doors leading into the street, and was waiting, not over patiently, for two people who were between him and them to pass out and let him follow, when the voice of one of them struck familiarly on his ear.

He looked at the speaker and recognised Mr Meagles, who was collaring a short man and shouting, "Come out, you rascal, come out!"

Clennam stood still for the moment exchanging looks of surprise with the porter. He followed, however, quickly; and saw Mr Meagles going down the street with his enemy at his side. He soon came up with his old travelling companion, and touched him on the back. The choleric face which Mr Meagles turned upon him smoothed when he saw who it was, and he put out his friendly hand.

"How are you?" said Mr Meagles. "How d'ye do? I have only just come over from abroad. I am glad to see you."

"And I am rejoiced to see you."

"Thank'ee. Thank'ee!"

"Mrs Meagles and your daughter – ?"

"Are as well as possible," said Mr Meagles. "I only wish you had come upon me in a more prepossessing condition as to coolness."

"You have been ruffled, Mr Meagles. What is the matter?"

"Wait a bit, and I'll tell you. Have you leisure for a turn in the park?"

"As much as you please."

"Come along then! You keep with us," said Mr Meagles, in a threatening kind of way to the short man, "and I'll introduce you presently. Now then!"

Clennam wondered within himself, as they took the nearest way to the park, what this unknown (who complied in the gentlest manner) could have been doing.

At length, they being among the trees, Mr Meagles stopped short, and said: "Mr Clennam, will you do me the favour to look at this man? His name is Doyce, Daniel Doyce. You wouldn't suppose this man to be a notorious rascal; would you? You wouldn't suppose him to be a public offender; would you?"

"I certainly should not." It was really a disconcerting question, with the man there.

"No. But he is. He is a public offender. What has he been guilty of? Murder, manslaughter, arson, forgery, swindling, house-breaking, highway robbery, larceny, conspiracy, fraud? Which should you say, now?"

"I should say," returned Arthur Clennam, observing a faint smile in Daniel Doyce's face, "not one of them."

"You are right," said Mr Meagles. "But he has been ingenious, and he has been trying to turn his ingenuity to his country's service. That makes him a public offender directly, sir."

Arthur looked at the man himself, who only shook his head.

"This Doyce," said Mr Meagles, "is a smith and engineer. He is not in a large way, but he is well known as a very ingenious man. A dozen years ago, he perfects an invention of great importance to his country and his fellow-creatures. I won't say how much money it cost him, or how many years of his life he had been about it, but he brought it to perfection a dozen years ago. He is the most exasperating man in the world; he never complains! Mr Clennam, he addresses himself to the Government. The moment he addresses himself to the Government, he becomes a public offender! He is treated from that instant as a man who has done some infernal action, a man with no rights in his own time, or his own property. Don't stand there, Doyce, turning your spectacle-case over and over," cried Mr Meagles, "but tell Mr Clennam what you confessed to me."

"I undoubtedly was made to feel," said the inventor, "as if I had committed an offence. In dancing attendance at the various offices, I was always treated, more or less, as if it was a very bad offence yet I only wanted to effect a great saving and a great improvement."

"There!" said Mr Meagles. "Judge whether I exaggerate. Now you'll be able to believe me when I tell you the rest of the case."

With this prelude, Mr Meagles went through the narrative of how, after interminable attendance and correspondence, the Circumlocution Office shelved the business.

"Upon which," concluded Mr Meagles, "as a practical man, I then and there, in that presence, took Doyce by the collar and took him away. I brought him out of the office door by the collar, that the very porter might know I was a practical man who appreciated the official estimate of such characters; and here we are! Now you know all about Doyce."

Daniel Doyce looked rueful. "I ought to have let the Circumlocution Office alone. I shall go back to the factory."

"Why then, we'll all go back to the factory, or walk in that direction," returned Mr Meagles cheerfully. "Mr Clennam won't be deterred by its being in Bleeding Heart Yard."

"Bleeding Heart Yard?" said Clennam. "I want to go there."

"So much the better," cried Mr Meagles. "Come along!"

CHAPTER 10

Let Loose

A late, dull autumn night was closing in upon the river Saone. The stream, like a sullied looking-glass in a gloomy place, reflected the clouds heavily.

One man slowly moving on towards Chalons was the only visible figure in the landscape. He glanced here, and he glanced there, sullenly but shrinkingly.

At long last there was the hotel with its gateway, and its savoury smell of cooking; and there in a dark back street, he found suitable accommodation. The curtained windows clouded the "Break of Day" but it seemed light and warm, and he went in and made his way to an empty little table in a corner of the room behind the stove. He put down his knapsack and his cloak upon the ground. As he raised his head from stooping to do so, he found the landlady beside him.

"One can lodge here tonight, madame?"

"Perfectly!" said the landlady in a high, sing-song, cheery voice.

"Good. One can dine – sup – what you please to call it?"

"Ah, perfectly!" cried the landlady as before.

"Dispatch then, madame, if you please. Something to eat, as quickly as you can; and some wine at once. I am exhausted."

His hoarse voice failed him, and he rested his head upon his hands until a bottle of wine was brought from the counter. Having filled and emptied his little tumbler twice, and having broken off an end from the great loaf that was set before him he rested his back against the corner of the wall and began to chew crust, until such time as his repast should be ready.

The other customers had done glancing at him, and were talking again.

"That's the true reason," said one of them, bringing a story he had been telling, to a close, "that's the true reason why they said that the devil was let loose."

The landlady, having given her directions for the new guest's entertainment to her husband, who acted as cook to the Break of Day, had resumed her needlework behind her counter. She struck into the conversation with several laughing nods of her head, but without looking up from her work.

"Ah Heaven, then," said she. "When the boat came up from Lyons, and brought the news that the devil was actually let loose at Marseilles, some fly-catchers swallowed it. But I? No, not I."

"Madame, you are always right," returned a tall Swiss man.

"He was a wicked wretch," said the landlady, "and well merited what he had the good fortune to escape. So much the worse."

The tall Swiss nodded. "It was because the man was acquitted on his trial that people said at Marseilles that the devil was let loose. That was how the phrase began to circulate, and what it meant; nothing more."

"How do they call him?" said the landlady. "Biraud, is it not?"

"Blandois, madame," returned the tall Swiss.

"Blandois! To be sure."

The traveller's soup was succeeded by a dish of meat, and that by a dish of vegetables. As he became refreshed, he became overbearing; and patronised the company at the Daybreak in certain small talk at which he assisted, as if his condition were far above his appearance.

"Pardon me, madame – that Biraud."

"Blandois, monsieur."

"Blandois. Pardon me again – has contracted your displeasure, how?"

The landlady, who had been at one moment thinking within herself that this was a handsome man, at another moment that this was an ill-looking man, observed the nose coming down and the moustache going up, and strongly inclined to the latter decision. Blandois was a criminal, she said, who had killed his wife.

"Ay, ay? Death of my life, that's a criminal indeed. But how do you know it?"

"All the world knows it."

"Hah! And yet he escaped justice?"

"Monsieur, the law could not prove it against him to its satisfaction. Nevertheless, all the world knows he did it. The people knew it so well, that they tried to tear him to pieces."

"Did you mention, madame – or was it mentioned among the gentlemen – what became of him?"

The landlady shook her head.

Now the traveller yawned. "May one ask to be shown to bed, madame?"

"Very willingly, monsieur. Hola, my husband!"

My husband would conduct him upstairs. There was another traveller there, asleep, who had gone to bed very early indeed, being overpowered by fatigue; but it was a large chamber with two beds in it, and space enough for twenty. This the landlady chirpingly explained, calling between whiles, "Hola, my husband!" out at the side door.

Presenting himself in his cook's cap, "my husband" lighted the traveller up a steep and narrow staircase to a large room, with a rough splintery floor, unplastered rafters overhead, and two bedsteads on opposite sides.

"The bed to the right!" he said and left him to his repose.

The guest looked contemptuously at the clean coarse bedding prepared for him, and, sitting down on the rush chair at the bedside, drew his money out of his pocket, and told it over in his hand. "One must eat," he muttered to himself, "but by Heaven I must eat at the cost of some other man tomorrow!"

As he sat pondering, the deep breathing of the traveller in the other bed fell so regularly upon his hearing that it attracted his eyes in that direction and became at length a strong incentive to get a glimpse of the sleeper's face.

"Death of my soul!" he whispered, falling back, "here's John Baptist!"

The little Italian opened his eyes and with a cry of surprise and alarm, sprang out of bed.

"Hush! What's the matter? Keep quiet! It's I. You know me?" cried the other, in a suppressed voice.

But John Baptist, seeing his old prison comrade, fell back upon the door, and set his shoulders against it.

"John Baptist! Give me your hand. Do not use the name you used to call me – don't use that – Lagnier, say Lagnier. You know Lagnier, the gentleman. Touch the hand of a gentleman!"

Submitting himself to the old tone of condescending authority, John Baptist, not at all steady on his legs as yet, advanced and put his hand in his patron's. Monsieur Lagnier laughed; and having given it a squeeze, tossed it up and let it go.

"Then you were – " faltered John Baptist.

"Not shaved? No. See here!" cried Lagnier, giving his head a twirl; "as tight on as your own. How long have you been out?"

"Two days after you, my master."

"How do you come here?"

"I was cautioned not to stay there, and so I left the town at once, and

45

since then I have changed about." As he spoke, he rapidly mapped the places out with his sunburnt hand upon the floor.

"And where are you going?"

"Going, my master?"

"Ay!"

John Baptist seemed to desire to evade the question without knowing how. "By Bacchus!" he said at last, as if he were forced to the admission, "I have sometimes thought of going to Paris, and perhaps to England."

"John Baptist. This is in confidence. I also am going to Paris and perhaps to England. We'll go together."

The little man nodded his head, and showed his teeth; and yet seemed not quite convinced that it was a surpassingly desirable arrangement.

"I am a man," said Monsieur Lagnier, "whom society has deeply wronged since you last saw me. You know that I am sensitive and brave, and that it is my character to govern. How has society respected those qualities in me? I have been shrieked at through the streets. I have lain in prison for security, with the place of my confinement kept a secret, lest I should be torn out of it and felled by a hundred blows. But society shall pay for it." All this he said in his companion's ear, and with his hand before his lips.

As he stretched out his length upon his bed, with a ragged handkerchief bound round his wicked head, only his wicked head showed above the bedclothes.

When John Baptist started up at daybreak, he rose, took his shoes in his hand, turned the key in the door with great caution, and crept downstairs. He was running away from his patron.

CHAPTER 11

Bleeding Heart Yard

Bleeding Heart Yard was a place much changed in feature and in fortune, yet with some relish of ancient greatness about it.

Down in to the yard, by way of the steps, came Daniel Doyce, Mr Meagles, and Clennam. Passing along the yard, and between the open doors on either hand, all abundantly garnished with light children nursing heavy ones, they arrived at its opposite boundary, the gateway. Here Arthur Clennam stopped to look about him for the domicile of Plornish, plasterer, whose name, according to the custom of Londoners, Daniel Doyce had never seen or heard of to that hour.

It was plain enough, nevertheless, as Little Dorrit had said; over a lime-splashed gateway in the corner, within which Plornish kept a ladder and a barrel or two. The last house in Bleeding Heart Yard which she had described as his place of habitation, was a large house, let off to various tenants; but Plornish ingeniously hinted that he lived in the parlour, by means of a painted hand under his name that referred all inquirers to that apartment.

Parting from his companions, after arranging another meeting with Mr Meagles, Clennam went alone into the entry, and knocked with his knuckles at the parlour door. It was opened presently by a woman with a child in her arms, whose unoccupied hand was hastily rearranging the upper part of her dress. This was Mrs Plornish, and this maternal action was the action of Mrs Plornish during a large part of her waking existence.

Was Mr Plornish at home? "Well, sir," said Mrs Plornish, a civil woman, "not to deceive you, he's gone to look for a job."

Even as Mrs Plornish spoke these words, Mr Plornish returned.

He was a smooth-cheeked, fresh-coloured, sandy-whiskered man of thirty. Long in the legs, yielding at the knees, foolish in the face, flannel-jacketed, lime-whitened.

"This is Plornish, sir."

"I came," said Clennam, rising, "to beg the favour of a little conversation with you on the subject of the Dorrit family."

"Mr Clennam, is it? Oh! I've heard of you, sir."

"And I of you," said Arthur.

"Please to sit down again, sir, and consider yourself welcome. – Why, yes," said Plornish, taking a chair, and lifting the elder child upon his knee, that he might have the moral support of speaking to a stranger over his head, "I have been on the wrong side of the Lock myself, and in that way we come to know Miss Dorrit. Me and my wife Sally, we are well acquainted with Miss Dorrit."

"Intimate!" cried Mrs Plornish. Indeed, she was so proud of the acquaintance, that she had awakened some bitterness of spirit in the Yard by magnifying to an enormous amount the sum for which Miss Dorrit's father had become insolvent. "It was her father that I got acquainted with first. And through getting acquainted with him, you see – why – I got acquainted with her. Miss Dorrit and her sister dursn't let him know that they work for a living. No!"

"Without admiring him for that," Clennam quietly observed, "I am very sorry for him. Pray how did you introduce her at my mother's!"

Mr Plornish, unequal to the task of lucid explanation, turned to his wife.

"Miss Dorrit," said Sally, hushing the baby from side to side, and laying her chin upon the little hand as it tried to disarrange the gown again, "came here one afternoon with a bit of writing, telling how she wished for needlework, and asked if it would be considered any ill-conwenience in case she was to give her address here. Me and Plornish says, 'No, Miss Dorrit, no ill-conwenience' and she wrote it in, according. 'Have you thought of copying it three or four times, as the way to make it known in more places than one?' we asked her. 'No,' says Miss Dorrit, 'I have not, but I will.' She copied it out according, on this table, in a sweet writing, and Plornish, he took it where he worked, having a job just then, and likewise to the landlord of the Yard; through which it was that Mrs Clennam first happened to employ Miss Dorrit."

"The landlord of the yard," said Arthur Clennam, "is – "

"He is Mr Casby, by name, he is," said Plornish, "and Pancks, he collects the rents."

"Ay?" returned Clennam, thoughtful in his turn. "Mr Casby, too! An old acquaintance of mine, long ago!"

Arthur Clennam went on to the present purport of his visit; namely, to make Plornish the instrument of effecting Tip's release, with as little detriment as possible to the self-reliance and self-helpfulness of the young man. Plornish told him Tip was but a seller of horses – and that he (Plornish) considered that ten shillings in the pound "would settle handsome."

They soon drove off together to a stable-yard in High Holborn and there found a gentleman, one Captain Maroon, who happened also to be the Plaintiff in the Tip case. He referred Mr Plornish to his solicitor and declined to treat with Mr Plornish, or even to endure his presence in the yard, unless he appeared there with a twenty-pound note. Mr Plornish retired and presently came back with the required money. Captain Maroon gave him a receipt in full and discharged the prisoner.

"Mr Plornish," said Arthur, "I trust to you, if you please, to keep my secret. If you will undertake to let the young man know that he is free, and to tell him that you were employed to compound for the debt by some one whom you are not at liberty to name, you will not only do me a service, but may do him one, and his sister also."

"Your wishes, sir, shall be attended to."

"And if you will be so good, in your better knowledge of the family, as to communicate freely with me, and to point out to me any means by which you think I may be delicately and really useful to Little Dorrit, I shall feel under an obligation to you."

They drove off in the direction of the Marshalsea Gate and on the way, Arthur elicited from his new friend a confused summary of the interior life of Bleeding Heart Yard. They was all hard up there, Mr Plornish said, uncommon hard up, to be sure!

CHAPTER 12

Patriarchal

The mention of Mr Casby again revived in Clennam's memory the smouldering embers of curiosity and interest which Mrs Flintwinch had fanned on the night of his arrival. Flora Casby had been the beloved of his boyhood; and Flora was the daughter and only child of wooden-headed old Christopher who was reputed to be rich in weekly tenants, and to get a good quantity of blood out of the stones of several unpromising courts and alleys.

After some days of inquiry, Arthur Clennam became convinced that the case of the Father of the Marshalsea was indeed a hopeless one, and sorrowfully resigned the idea of helping him to freedom again. He had no hopeful inquiry to make at present, concerning Little Dorrit either; but he argued with himself that it might – for anything he knew – it might be serviceable to the poor child, if he renewed this acquaintance.

Mr Casby lived in a street in the Gray's Inn Road.

"The house," thought Clennam, as he crossed to the door, "is as little changed as my mother's, and looks almost as gloomy. But the likeness ends outside. The smell of its jars of old rose-leaves and lavender seems to come upon me even here."

Patriarch was the name which many people delighted to give Old Christopher Casby. So grey, so slow, so quiet, so impassionate, so very bumpy in the head, Patriarch was the word for him. He now sat in his silent parlour while Arthur Clennam moved to attract his attention.

"I beg your pardon," said Clennam, "I fear you did not hear me announced?"

"No, sir, I did not. Did you wish to see me, sir?"

"I wished to pay my respects."

"I believe I am not mistaken in supposing that I am acquainted with those features? I think I address a gentleman of whose return to this country I was informed by Mr Flintwinch?"

"That is your present visitor."

"Mr Clennam, I am glad to see you. How have you been since we met? To think your respected father is no more! I was grieved to hear it, Mr Clennam, I was grieved. There was a time when your parents and myself were not on friendly terms. There was a little family misunderstanding among us. Your respected mother was rather jealous of your worthy self. Those times, however, are past and gone, past and gone. I do myself the pleasure of making a visit to your respected mother occasionally, and of admiring the fortitude and strength of mind with which she bears her trials."

"I have heard that you were kind enough on one of those occasions," said Arthur, "to mention Little Dorrit to my mother."

"Little – Dorrit? That's the seamstress who was mentioned to me by a small tenant of mine? Yes, yes. Dorrit? That's the name. Ah, yes, yes! You call her Little Dorrit?"

Mr Casby turned to a subject close to his heart. "My daughter Flora, as you may have heard, Mr Clennam, was married and established in life, several years ago. She had the misfortune to lose her husband, Mr Finching, when she had been married a few months. She resides with me again. She will be glad to see you, if you will permit me to let her know that you are here."

"By all means," returned Clennam.

Upon this Mr Casby rose up in his list shoes, and with a slow, heavy step (he was of an elephantine build), made for the door.

He had scarcely left the room, when a quick hand turned a latchkey in the house-door, opened it, and shut it. Immediately afterwards, a quick and eager short dark man came into the room so fast that he was within a foot of Clennam before he could stop.

"Halloa!" he said, "where's Mr Casby?"

"He will be here directly, if you want him."

"*I* want him?" said the short dark man. "Don't you? Oh!" said he, when Arthur told him how he came to be there. "Very well! If he should ask for Pancks, will you be so good as to say that Pancks is come in?" And so, with a snort and a puff, he walked out by another door.

Mr Casby returned with his daughter. Flora, always tall, had grown to be very broad too, and short of breath; but that was not much. Flora, whom he had left a lily, had become a peony; but that was not much. Flora, who had seemed enchanting in all she said and thought, was diffuse and silly. That was much. Flora, who had been spoiled and artless long ago, was determined to be spoiled and artless now. That was a fatal blow.

This is Flora!

All the while the Patriarch glowed with vacant serenity.

"You mustn't think of going yet," said Flora, for Arthur had looked at his hat, being in a ludicrous dismay, and not knowing what to do.

"No one could dispute, Arthur – Mr Clennam – that it's quite right you should be formally friendly to me under the altered circumstances, and indeed you couldn't be anything else, at least I suppose not. You ought to know, but I can't help recalling that there was a time when things were very different."

"My dear Mrs Finching," Arthur began, struck by the good tone again.

"Oh not that nasty ugly name, say Flora!"

"Flora. I assure you, Flora, I am happy in seeing you once more, and in finding that, like me, you have not forgotten the old foolish dreams, when we saw all before us in the light of our youth and hope."

"You don't seem so," pouted Flora.

"My dear Mrs Finching," urged Clennam – "it was all so long ago and so long concluded, is it worth while seriously to – "

51

"But here is Papa," returned Flora, "who is always tiresome and putting in his nose everywhere where he is not wanted."

The Patriarch insisted on his staying to dinner, and Flora signalled "Yes!" Clennam so wished he could have done more than stay to dinner – so heartily wished he could have found the Flora that had been, or that never had been – that he thought the least atonement he could make for the disappointment he almost felt ashamed of, was to give himself up to the family desire. Therefore, he stayed to dinner.

Pancks dined with them and there was a fourth and most original figure who also appeared before dinner. This was an amazing little old woman, with a face like a staring wooden doll too cheap for expression, and a stiff yellow wig perched unevenly on the top of her head. This little old woman had no name but Mr F's Aunt. Flora said, perhaps Mr Clennam might not have heard that Mr F had left her Mr F's Aunt as a legacy.

All through dinner, Flora combined her present appetite for eating and drinking with her past appetite for romantic love, in a way that made Clennam afraid to lift his eyes from his plate; since he could not look towards her without receiving some glance of mysterious meaning or warning, as if they were engaged in a plot.

Mr F's Aunt sat silently defying him with an aspect of the greatest bitterness. Foreseeing then that Mr Pancks would shortly leave, and that the Patriarch would go to sleep, Arthur pleaded the necessity of visiting his mother, and asked Mr Pancks in which direction he was going?

"Citywards, sir," said Pancks.

"Shall we walk together?" said Arthur.

"Quite agreeable," said Pancks.

Meanwhile Flora was murmuring that she should be at home tomorrow at half-past one, while he tried, at parting, to give his hand in frankness to the existing Flora. But Flora wouldn't have it and he left the house miserably enough.

"You lead such a busy life?" he asked Pancks.

"Yes, I have always some of 'em to look up, or something to look after. But I like business," said Pancks, getting on a little faster. "What's a man made for?"

"For nothing else?" said Clennam.

When they had walked a little further in silence, Clennam said:

"Have you no taste for anything, Mr Pancks?"

"What's taste?" drily retorted Pancks.

"Let us say inclination."

"I have an inclination to get money, sir," said Pancks, "You're not of the Clennams of Cornwall, Mr Clennam?"

"Not that I ever heard of."

"I know you're not. I asked your mother, sir. She has too much character to let a chance escape her."

"Supposing I had been of the Clennams of Cornwall?"

"You'd have heard of something to your advantage."

"Indeed! I have heard of little enough to my advantage for some time."

"There's a Cornish property going a begging, sir, and not a Cornish Clennam to have it for the asking," said Pancks, taking his note-book from his breast pocket and putting it in again. "I turn off here. I wish you good-night."

"Good-night!" said Clennam.

He turned slowly down Aldersgate Street, and was pondering his way along towards Saint Paul's, when a crowd of people flocked towards him on the same pavement, and he stood aside against a shop to let them pass. As they came up, he made out that they were gathered around a something that was carried on men's shoulders. A muddy bundle carried by one man, and a muddy hat carried by another, informed him that an accident had occurred. The litter stopped under a lamp and he found himself in the midst of the array.

"An accident going to the Hospital?" he asked an old man beside him, who stood shaking his head, inviting conversation.

"Yes," said the man, "along of them Mails. They come a racing out of Lad Lane and Wood Street at twelve or fourteen mile a hour, them Mails do."

"This person is not killed, I hope?"

"I don't know!" said the man. "What can you expect from a poor foreigner who don't know nothing about them!"

He now heard a feeble voice asking, both in Italian and in French, for water. Clennam begged to be allowed to pass, as he understood the poor creature. He was immediately handed to the front, to speak to him.

"First, he wants some water," said he, looking round. (A dozen good fellows dispersed to get it.) "Are you badly hurt, my friend?" he asked the man on the litter, in Italian.

53

"Yes, sir; yes, yes, yes. It's my leg, it's my leg. But it pleases me to hear the old music, though I am very bad."

"You are a traveller! Stay! See, the water! Let me give you some."

They had rested the litter on a pile of paving stones. It was at a convenient height from the ground, and by stooping he could lightly raise the head with one hand and hold the glass to his lips with the other. A little, muscular, brown man, with black hair and white teeth. A lively face, apparently. Earrings in his ears.

"That's well. You are a traveller?"

"Surely, sir."

"A stranger in this city?"

"Surely, surely, altogether. I am arrived this unhappy evening."

"From what country?"

"Marseilles."

"Why, see there! I also! Almost as much a stranger here as you, though born here, I came from Marseilles a little while ago. Don't be cast down."

Arthur Clennam turned; and walking beside the litter, and saying an encouraging word now and then, accompanied it to the neighbouring hospital of Saint Bartholomew. None of the crowd but the bearers and he being admitted, the disabled man was soon laid on a table in a cool, methodical way, and carefully examined by a surgeon who was as near at hand.

"It's a serious injury, I suppose?" said Clennam.

"Ye-es," replied the surgeon.

Clennam remained until everything possible to be done had been skilfully and promptly done – the poor belated wanderer in a strange land movingly besought that favour of him – and lingered by the bed to which he was in due time removed, until he had fallen into a doze. Even then he wrote a few words for him on his card, with a promise to return tomorrow, and left it to be given to him when he should awake.

All these proceedings occupied so long that it struck eleven o'clock at night as he came out at the Hospital Gate. He had hired a lodging for the present in Covent Garden, and he took the nearest way to that quarter, by Snow Hill and Holborn.

When he got to his lodging, he sat down before the dying fire. Left to himself again, after the solicitude and compassion of his last adventure, he was naturally in a thoughtful mood. As naturally, he could not think for ten minutes without recalling Flora. She necessarily recalled to him his life, with all its misdirection and little happiness.

He was a dreamer in such wise, because he was a man who had, deep-rooted in his nature, a belief in all the gentle and good things his life had been without. Bred in meanness and hard dealing, this had rescued him to be a man of honourable mind and open hand.

He reviewed all that had happened to him. "From the unhappy suppression of my youngest days, through the rigid and unloving home that followed them, through my departure, my long exile, my return, my mother's welcome, my intercourse with her since, down to the afternoon of this day with poor Flora," said Arthur Clennam, "what have I found!"

His door was softly opened, and these spoken words startled him, and came as if they were an answer:

"Little Dorrit."

CHAPTER 13

Little Dorrit's Party

Arthur Clennam rose hastily, and saw her standing at the door.

"My poor child! Here at midnight?"

"I said Little Dorrit, sir, on purpose to prepare you. I knew you must be very much surprised."

"Are you alone?"

"No sir, I have got Maggy with me."

Considering her entrance sufficiently prepared for by this mention of her name, Maggy appeared from the landing outside.

"I have no fire," said Clennam. "And it is so cold."

Putting the chair from which he had risen nearer to the grate, he made her sit down in it; and hurriedly bringing wood and coal, heaped them together and got a blaze.

"Your foot is like marble, my child;" he had happened to touch it, while stooping on one knee at his work of kindling the fire; "put it nearer the warmth." Little Dorrit thanked him hastily.

"What I was going to tell you, sir," she said, "is, that my brother is at large."

Arthur was rejoiced to hear it, and hoped he would do well.

"And what I was going to tell you, sir," said Little Dorrit, trembling in all her little figure and in her voice, "is, that I am not to know whose generosity released him but if I knew him, and I might, I would go down on my knees to him, and take his hand and kiss it."

Little Dorrit had put his hand to her lips, and would have kneeled to him, but he gently prevented her, and replaced her in her chair.

"Why are you out at midnight, and what it is that brings you so far through the streets at this late hour, Little Dorrit!"

"Maggy and I have been tonight," she answered, subduing herself with the quiet effort that had long been natural to her, "to the theatre where my sister is engaged. We went there because I like sometimes to know, of my own knowledge, that my sister is doing well; and like to see her there, with my own eyes, when neither she nor Uncle is aware. It is very seldom indeed that I can do that, because when I am not out at work, I am with my father, and even when I am out at work, I hurry home to him. But I pretend tonight that I am at a party."

He asked where the supposititious party was? At a place where she worked, answered Little Dorrit, blushing. She had said very little about it; only a few words to make her father easy. Her father did not believe it to be a grand party – indeed he might suppose that. And she glanced for an instant at the shawl she wore.

"It is the first night," said Little Dorrit, "that I have ever been away from home. And London looks so large, so barren, and so wild. But this is not," she added, "what I have come to trouble you with, sir. My sister's having found a friend, a lady she has told me of and made me rather anxious about, was the first cause of my coming away from home. And being away and coming (on purpose) round by where you lived and seeing a light in the window – "

Not for the first time. No, not for the first time. In Little Dorrit's eyes, the outside of that window had been a distant star on other nights than this. She had toiled out of her way, tired and troubled, to look up at it, and wonder about the grave, brown gentleman from so far off, who had spoken to her as a friend and protector.

"There were three things," said Little Dorrit, "that I thought I would like to say, if you were alone and I might come upstairs. First, what I have tried to say, but never can – never shall – "

56

"Hush, hush! That is done with, and disposed of. Let us pass to the second," said Clennam, smiling her agitation away, making the blaze shine upon her, and putting wine and cake and fruit on the table.

"I think," said Little Dorrit – "this is the second thing, sir – I think Mrs Clennam must have found out my secret, and must know where I come from and where I go to. Where I live, I mean."

"Indeed!" returned Clennam quickly. He asked her, after short consideration, why she supposed so.

"I think," replied Little Dorrit, "that Mr Flintwinch must have watched me. I have met him twice. Both times near home. Both times at night, when I was going back. Both times I thought that he hardly looked as if he had met me by accident."

"Did he say anything?"

"No; he only nodded and put his head on one side."

"Little Dorrit," said Clennam, "do nothing. I will have some talk with my old friend, Mrs Affery. Do nothing, Little Dorrit – except refresh yourself with such means as there are here. I entreat you to do that."

"Thank you, I am not hungry. Nor," said Little Dorrit, as he softly put her glass towards her, "nor thirsty. – I think Maggy might like something, perhaps."

"We will fill her basket presently with all there is here," said Clennam: "but before that, there was a third thing to say."

"Yes. You will not be offended, sir?"

"I promise that, unreservedly."

Little Dorrit folded her small hands tightly in one another. "Don't encourage my father to ask for money. Don't understand him if he does ask. Don't give it to him. Save him and spare him that, and you will be able to think better of him!" Her eyes filled with tears. "You have been so good to us, so delicately and truly good, that I want him to be better in your eyes than in anybody's. And I cannot bear to think," cried Little Dorrit, covering her tears with her hands, "I cannot bear to think that you of all the world should see him in his only moments of degradation."

"Pray," said Clennam, "do not be so distressed. Pray, pray, Little Dorrit! This is quite understood now." Arthur Clennam looked at the clock. "But the gates will have been locked long ago. Where are you going?"

"I am going to Maggy's lodging," answered Little Dorrit. "I shall be quite safe, quite well taken care of. Come, Maggy, we shall do very well; we know the way by this time. Maggy?"

"Yes, yes, little mother; we know the way," chuckled Maggy. And away they went. Little Dorrit turned at the door to say, "God bless you!"

Arthur Clennam suffered them to pass the corner of the street before he followed at a distance; not with any idea of encroaching a second time on Little Dorrit's privacy, but to satisfy his mind by seeing her secure in the neighbourhood to which she was accustomed. So diminutive she looked, so fragile and defenceless against the bleak damp weather, flitting along in the shuffling shadow of her charge, that he felt, in his compassion, and in his habit of considering her a child apart from the rest of the rough world, as if he would have been glad to take her up in his arms and carry her to her journey's end.

In course of time she came into the thoroughfare where the Marshalsea was, and then he saw them slacken their pace, and soon turn down a by-street. He stopped, felt that he had no right to go further, and slowly left them. He had no suspicion that they ran any risk of being houseless until morning; had no idea of the truth until long, long afterwards.

But, said Little Dorrit, when they stopped at a poor dwelling all in darkness, and heard no sound on listening at the door, "Now, this is a good lodging for you, Maggy, and we must not give offence. Consequently, we will only knock twice, and not very loud; and if we cannot wake them so, we must walk about till day."

Once, Little Dorrit knocked with a careful hand, and listened.

Twice, Little Dorrit knocked with a careful hand, and listened.

All was close and still. "Maggy, we must do the best we can, my dear. We must be patient, and wait for day."

It was a chill dark night, with a damp wind blowing, when they came out into the street again, and heard the clocks strike half-past one.

"In only five hours and a half," said Little Dorrit, "we shall be able to go home." To speak of home, and to go and look at it, it being so near, was a natural sequence. They went to the closed gate, and peeped through into the courtyard.

The gate was so familiar, and so like a companion, that they put down Maggy's basket in a corner to serve for a seat, and keeping close together, rested there for some time. While the street was empty and silent, Little Dorrit was not afraid; but when she heard a footstep at a distance she insisted that they should wander about a little, and come back again.

58

As long as eating was a novelty and an amusement, Maggy kept up pretty well. But that period going by, she became querulous about the cold, and shivered and whimpered. "It will soon be over, dear," said Little Dorrit patiently.

"Oh it's all very fine for you, little mother," returned Maggy, "but I'm a poor thing, only ten years old." At last, in the dead of the night, when the street was very still indeed, Little Dorrit laid the heavy head upon her bosom, and soothed her to sleep. And thus she sat at the gate, as it were alone; looking up at the stars, and seeing the clouds pass over them in their wild flight – which was the dance at Little Dorrit's party. She sat looking up at the stars, quite lost, until Maggy woke and was querulous again, and wanted to get up and walk.

They were walking slowly towards the east, already looking for the first pale streak of day, then they went back again to the gate, intending to wait there now until it should be opened; but the air was so raw and cold that Little Dorrit, leading Maggy about, kept in motion. Going round by the Church, she saw lights there, and the door open; and went up the steps and looked in.

"Who's that?" cried a stout old man, who was putting on a nightcap as if he were going to bed in a vault. "Stop! Let's have a look at you! I thought so! I know *you*."

"We have often seen each other," said Little Dorrit, recognising the sexton, or the beadle, or the verger, or whatever he was, "when I have been at church here."

"More than that, we've got your birth in our Register, you know; you're one of our curiosities."

"Indeed!" said Little Dorrit.

He was a very good old fellow, in his familiar way; and having stirred the vestry fire, he looked round the shelves of registers for a particular volume. "Here you are, you see," he said, taking it down and turning the leaves. "Here you'll find yourself, as large as life. Amy, daughter of William and Fanny Dorrit. Born, Marshalsea Prison, Parish of St George. And we tell people that you have lived there, without so much as a day's or a night's absence, ever since. Is it true?"

"Quite true, till last night."

"Lord! I am sorry to see that you are faint and tired. Stay a bit. I'll get some cushions out of the church, and you and your friend shall lie down before the fire. Don't be afraid of not going in to join your father when the gate opens. I'll call you."

He soon brought in the cushions, and strewed them on the ground.

"There you are, you see. Again as large as life. Oh, never mind thanking. I've daughters of my own."

This was Little Dorrit's party.

CHAPTER 14

Nobody's Weakness

The time being come for the renewal of his acquaintance with the Meagles family, Clennam turned his face on a certain Saturday towards Twickenham, where Mr Meagles had a cottage-residence of his own.

He had crossed the heath and was leaving it behind when he gained upon a figure which had been in advance of him for some time, and which he thought he knew to be Daniel Doyce.

"How do you do, Mr Doyce?" said Clennam, overtaking him. "I am glad to see you again, and in a healthier place than the Circumlocution Office." They were soon quite intimate, and lightened the way with a variety of conversation.

Mr Doyce was the son of a north-country blacksmith, and had originally been apprenticed by his widowed mother to a lock-maker; he had "struck out a few little things" at the lock-maker's, then worked his way on, until, after a dozen years of constant suit and service, he had been enrolled in the Great British Legion of Honour, the Legion of the Rebuffed of the Circumlocution Office.

As he knew the house well, he conducted Arthur to it by the way that showed it to the best advantage. It was a charming place on the road by the river, and just what the residence of the Meagles family ought to be.

The bell at the gate had scarcely sounded when Mr Meagles came out to receive them. Mr Meagles had scarcely come out, when Mrs Meagles came out. Mrs Meagles had scarcely come out, when Pet came out. Pet scarcely had come out, when Tattycoram came out. Never had visitors a more hospitable reception.

Mr Meagles invited them in and showed them all his spoils, while Clennam's eyes strayed to a picture on the wall, of two pretty little girls with their arms entwined.

"Their names?" said Arthur.

"Ah to be sure! You have never heard any name but Pet. Pet's name is Minnie; her sister's Lillie."

Pet herself was now standing in the doorway.

"I might have thought that both of them were meant for you, both are still so like you. Indeed," said Clennam, glancing from the fair original to the picture and back, "I cannot even now say which is not your portrait."

"D'ye hear that, Mother?" cried Mr Meagles to his wife, who had followed her daughter. "It's always the same, Clennam; nobody can decide. The child to your left is Minnie, though we call her Pet."

The picture happened to be near a looking-glass. As Arthur looked at it again, he saw, by the reflection of the mirror, Tattycoram stop in passing outside the door, listen to what was going on, and pass away with an angry and contemptuous frown upon her face, that changed its beauty into ugliness.

Arthur Clennam was a retiring man, with a sense of many deficiencies; and he so exalted the merits of the beautiful Pet in his mind, and depressed his own, that when he pinned himself to this point, his hopes began to fail him. He came to the final resolution, as he made himself ready for dinner, that he would not allow himself to fall in love with Pet.

There were only five, at a round table, and it was very pleasant indeed. They had so many places and people to recall, and they were all easy and cheerful together.

"And Miss Wade," said Mr Meagles, after they had recalled a number of fellow-travellers. "Has anybody seen Miss Wade?"

"I have," said Tattycoram. "I met her near the church."

"What was she doing there, I wonder!" said Mr Meagles. "Not going to it, I should think."

"She knew, when we were travelling, where you lived," said Tattycoram, "and she had seen me not quite – not quite – "

"Not quite in a good temper, Tattycoram?" suggested Mr Meagles, shaking his head at the dark eyes with a quiet caution.

She pressed her lips together again, and took a long deep breath.

"So she wrote to me to say that if I ever felt myself hurt," she looked down at her young mistress, "or found myself worried," she looked down at her again, "I might go to her, and be considerately treated. I was to think of it, and could speak to her by the church. So I went there to thank her."

"Now there," said Mr Meagles softly, as he gave a turn to the dumb-waiter on his right hand to twirl the sugar towards himself, "there's a girl who might be lost and ruined, if she wasn't among practical people."

Time passed pleasantly among the little group and as they broke up for the night, Arthur overheard Doyce ask his host if he could give him half an hour's conversation before breakfast in the morning? The host replying willingly, Arthur lingered behind a moment, having his own word to add to that topic.

"Mr Meagles," he said, on their being left alone, "do you remember when you advised me to go straight to London?"

"Perfectly well."

"And when you gave me some other good advice which I needed at that time?"

"I won't say what it was worth," answered Mr Meagles: "but of course I remember our being very pleasant and confidential together."

"I have acted on your advice; and having disembarrassed myself of an occupation that was painful to me for many reasons, wish to devote myself and what means I have, to another pursuit."

"Right! You can't do it too soon," said Mr Meagles.

"Now, as I came down today, I found that your friend, Mr Doyce, is looking for a partner in his business – not a partner in his mechanical knowledge, but in the ways and means of turning the business arising from it to the best account. – And I shall be glad to enter into the subject, provided Mr Doyce responds, and you think well of it. If you will at present, therefore, allow me to place it in your hands, you will much oblige me."

"Clennam, I accept the trust with readiness," said Mr Meagles. "Of one thing you may be perfectly certain. Daniel is an honest man."

Clennam went back to his room, sat down again before his fire, and made up his mind again that he was glad he had resolved not to fall in love with Pet.

CHAPTER 15

Nobody's Rival

Before breakfast in the morning, Arthur walked out to look about him. As the morning was fine and he had an hour on his hands, he crossed the river by the ferry, and strolled along a footpath through some meadows. When he came back to the towing-path, he found the ferry-boat on the opposite side, and a gentleman hailing it and waiting to be taken over.

This gentleman looked barely thirty. He was throwing stones into the river, preoccupied by his thoughts, as his face showed, and he was taking no notice of a fine Newfoundland dog, who watched him attentively, and watched every stone too, in its turn, eager to spring into the river on receiving his master's sign.

Clennam followed the man and the dog into the boat, and took his seat. Man and dog both jumped lightly out as soon as they touched the other side, and went away.

The church clock struck the breakfast hour as he walked up the little lane by which the garden-gate was approached. The moment he pulled the bell, a deep loud barking assailed him from within the wall.

"I heard no dog last night," thought Clennam. The gate was opened by one of the rosy maids who had served the meal last night. On the lawn were the Newfoundland dog and the man.

"Odd enough, Mr Clennam, that we should have met just now," said the man. Upon which the dog became mute. "Allow me to introduce myself – Henry Gowan. A pretty place this, and looks wonderfully well this morning!"

The manner was easy, and the voice agreeable; but still Clennam thought, he had taken a dislike to this Henry Gowan.

Pet appeared and ah! how beaming she looked, and how glad! How she caressed the dog, and how the dog knew her! How expressive that heightened colour in her face, that fluttered manner, her downcast eyes, her irresolute happiness! When had Clennam seen her look like this?

He stood at a little distance from them. This Gowan had gone up to her and taken her hand. She had laughed and welcomed him, and made far too much of the dog – that is to say, supposing there had been any third person looking on who had resolved not to fall in love with her.

She disengaged herself now, and came to Clennam, and put her hand in his and wished him good morning, and gracefully made as if she would take his arm and be escorted into the house. To this Gowan had no objection. No, he knew he was too safe.

"Well, Gowan," said Mr Meagles, over breakfast. "How goes the world with you this morning?"

"Very well sir. I have taken the liberty of making an addition to your family dinner-party today, which I hope will not be inconvenient to you or to Mr Meagles. I couldn't very well get out of it. A young fellow wrote to propose himself to me; and as he is well connected, I thought you would not object to my transferring him here."

"Who is the young fellow?" asked Mr Meagles with peculiar complacency.

"He is one of the Barnacles."

"Aye, aye?" said Meagles. "A Barnacle is he? We know something of that family, eh, Dan?"

More than once or twice when Pet caressed the dog, it appeared to Clennam that her father was unhappy in seeing her do it; and, in one particular instance when Gowan stood on the other side of the dog, and bent his head at the same time, Arthur fancied that he saw tears rise to Mr Meagles's eyes as he hurried out of the room.

This Gowan had plenty to say for himself, and said it in an off-hand and amusing manner. He appeared to be an artist by profession, and to have been at Rome some time; yet he had a slight, careless, amateur way with him – a perceptible limp, both in his devotion to art and his attainments – which Clennam could scarcely understand.

He applied to Daniel Doyce for help, as they stood together, looking out of a window.

"You know Mr Gowan?" he said in a low voice.

"I have seen him here. Comes here every Sunday when they are at home."

Pursuing his inquiries, Clennam found that the Gowan family were a very distant ramification of the Barnacles.

About an hour or so after dinner time, Young Barnacle appeared, attended by his eye-glass; in honour of whose family connections, Mr Meagles had cashiered the pretty parlour-maids for the day, and had placed on duty in their stead two dingy men. Young Barnacle was in the

64

last degree amazed and disconcerted at sight of Arthur and had murmured involuntarily, "Look here! upon my soul, you know!" before his presence of mind returned.

Even then, he was obliged to embrace the earliest opportunity of taking his friend into a window, and saying, in a nasal way that was a part of his general debility:

"I want to speak to you, Gowan. I say. Look here. Who is that fellow?"

"A friend of our host's. None of mine."

"Ecod, sir, he was pitching into our people the other day in the most tremendous manner. He said he wanted to know, you know! Pervaded our Department – without an appointment – and said he wanted to know!"

At last the wet Sunday wore itself out in a wet night; and Young Barnacle went home in a cab, feebly smoking; and the objectionable Gowan went away on foot, accompanied by the objectionable dog.

When Arthur had gone to his own room, and had again thrown himself into the chair by the fire, Mr Doyce knocked at the door, candle in hand, to ask him how and at what hour he proposed returning on the morrow? After settling this question, Clennam said, "I thought our good friend Mr Meagles a little changed and out of spirits."

"Yes," returned Doyce.

"But not his daughter?" said Clennam.

"No," said Doyce.

"There is an engagement between them, of course?" said Clennam airily.

"No. As I am told, certainly not. All that there is between Miss Minnie and Mr Gowan, I have no doubt we see."

"Ah! We see enough!" cried Arthur.

CHAPTER 16

Little Dorrit's Lover

Little Dorrit had not attained her twenty-second birthday without finding a lover. Little Dorrit's lover, however, was not a Collegian. He was the sentimental son of a turnkey.

Young John was small of stature, with rather weak legs and very weak light hair. One of his eyes was also weak, and looked larger than the other, as if it couldn't collect itself. Young John was gentle likewise. But he was great of soul. Poetical, expansive, faithful.

The Chivery parents were not ignorant of their son's attachment – indeed it had, on some exceptional occasions, thrown him into a state of mind that had impelled him to conduct himself with irascibility towards the customers, and damage the business – but they, in their turns, had worked it out to desirable conclusions.

Mrs Chivery, a prudent woman, had desired her husband to take notice that their John's prospects of the Lock would certainly be strengthened by an alliance with Miss Dorrit, who had herself a kind of claim upon the College and was much respected there.

The Father of the Marshalsea was supposed to know nothing about the matter, of course: his poor dignity could not see so low.

One Sunday after an early dinner of baked viands, Young John issued forth on his usual Sunday errand; not empty-handed, but with his offering of cigars.

The Collegians were entertaining a considerable number of visitors that Sunday afternoon, and their Father kept his room for the purpose of receiving presentations. After making the tour of the yard, Little Dorrit's lover with a hurried heart went upstairs, and knocked with his knuckles at the Father's door.

"Come in, come in!" said a gracious voice. The Father's voice, her father's, the Marshalsea's father's. He was seated in his black velvet cap, with his newspaper, three-and-sixpence accidentally left on the table, and two chairs arranged. Everything prepared for holding his Court.

" – A few cigars, sir."

"Oh!" (For the moment, excessively surprised.) "Thank you, Young John, thank you."

"Miss Amy quite well, sir?"

"Yes, John, yes; very well. She is out, gone for an airing on the Iron Bridge. She has become quite partial to the Iron Bridge of late, and seems to like to walk there better than anywhere." He returned to conversation. "Your father is not on duty at present, I think, John?"

"No, sir, he comes on later in the afternoon," Young John said, rising. "I am afraid I must wish you good-day, sir."

Little Dorrit's lover very soon came upon the Iron Bridge looking about him for the well-known and well-beloved figure. He saw her standing still, looking at the water. She was absorbed in thought, and he wondered what she might be thinking about.

When he said "Miss Dorrit!" she started and fell back from him, with an expression in her face of fright and something like dislike that caused him unutterable dismay. That momentary look had said, "You, of all people! I would rather have seen any one on earth than you!"

To the inexpressible consternation of her lover, Little Dorrit, with her hands to her averted face, and rocking herself where she stood as if she were in pain, murmured, "Oh father, how can you! Oh dear, dear father, how can you, can you, do it! Oh, I don't know what to do, I don't know what to do!"

"Miss Amy," he then stammered, "I have had for a long time – ages they seem to me – revolving ages – a heart-cherished wish to say something to you. May I say it?"

"If you please, John Chivery," she returned, trembling, but in a quiet way, "since you are so considerate as to ask me whether you shall say any more – if you please, no."

"Never, Miss Amy?"

"No, if you please. Never. And I particularly want you to remember, that when I come outside the gate, I am unprotected and solitary." Her slight colour faded. "Good-bye, John. I hope you will have a good wife one day, and be a happy man. I am sure you will deserve to be happy, and you will be, John. Oh, don't cry," said Little Dorrit piteously as he wept openly in front of her. "Don't, don't! Good-bye, John. God bless you!"

He pulled himself up. "Good-bye, Miss Amy. Good-bye!"

CHAPTER 17

The Father of the Marshalsea in Two or Three Relations

The brothers William and Frederick Dorrit walked up and down the College-yard on the evening of Little Dorrit's Sunday interview with her lover on the Iron Bridge.

"You are a little low this evening, Frederick," said the Father of the Marshalsea. "Anything the matter?"

"The matter?" He stared for a moment, and then dropped his head and eyes again. "No, William, no. Nothing is the matter."

"If you could be persuaded to smarten yourself up a little, Frederick. Consider my case, Frederick. I am a kind of example. Necessity and time have taught me what to do, how to dress. At certain stated hours of the day, you will find me on the parade, in my room, in the Lodge, reading the paper, receiving company, eating and drinking. I have impressed upon Amy during many years, that I must have my meals punctually. Amy has grown up in a sense of the importance of these arrangements, and you know what a good girl she is."

The brother only sighed again, as he plodded dreamily along, "Hah! Yes, yes, yes, yes."

Shaking hands with his brother, and touching his greasy hat to the company in the Lodge, Frederick slowly shuffled out of the door which Mr Chivery unlocked for him. The Father of the Marshalsea showed the amiable solicitude of a superior being that he should come to no harm.

"Be so kind as to keep the door open a moment, Chivery, that I may see him go along the passage and down the steps. Take care, Frederick! (He is very infirm.) Mind the steps! (He is so very absent.) Be careful how you cross, Frederick. (I really don't like the notion of his going wandering at large, he is so extremely liable to be run over.)"

Mr Chivery did not respond to these asides and when the Father of the Marshalsea had bid his brother farewell, he turned into the sallow yard and up his own poor shabby staircase to his own poor shabby room.

There, the table was laid for his supper, and his old grey gown was ready for him on his chair-back at the fire. His daughter rose to welcome him. As she stood behind him, leaning over his chair so lovingly, he looked with downcast eyes at the fire.

"I – hem! – I can't think, Amy, what has given Chivery offence. He is generally so – so very attentive and respectful. And tonight he was quite – quite short with me. Why, good Heaven! if I was to lose the support and recognition of Chivery and his brother officers, I might starve to death here." He shrugged his bent shoulders. "What does it matter whether I eat or starve? What does it matter whether such a blighted life as mine comes to an end, now, next week, or next year? What am I worth to anyone? A poor prisoner, fed on alms and broken victuals!"

"Father, father! Dear father, loved father, darling of my heart!"

"Amy! Is your father so universally despised?"

Thus, now boasting, now despairing, in either fit a captive with the jail-rot upon him, and the impurity of his prison worn into the grain of his soul, he revealed his degenerate state to his affectionate child.

She soothed him; asked him for his forgiveness if she had been, or seemed to have been, undutiful, and soon he was free from that touch of shame, and had recovered his usual bearing. She prepared the remains of his supper afresh, and, sitting by his side, rejoiced to see him eat and drink.

While he smoked out his cigar in peace, she made his bed, and put the small room in order for his repose. All this time he had never once thought of *her* dress, her shoes, her need of anything. She said quietly, "Father, dear, I am not tired; let me come back presently, when you are in bed, and sit by you."

"Come back by all means."

She never left him all that night. Not until the morning came to protect him and encourage him, did she give him a kiss and leave the small room.

CHAPTER 18

Moving in Society

Tip had turned his liberty to hopeful account by becoming a billiard-marker and now occasionally looked in at the little skittle-ground in a green Newmarket coat (second-hand), with a shining collar and bright buttons (new), and drank the beer of the Collegians.

One solid stationary point in the looseness of this gentleman's character was, that he respected and admired his sister Amy.

Little Dorrit was late on the Monday morning, for her father slept late, and afterwards there was his breakfast to prepare and his room to arrange. She had no engagement to go out to work so she put on her bonnet to go and see her sister who was at the theatre which was on that side of the river. She reached the theatre, a dark, confusing place, and heard her sister say, "Why, good gracious, Amy, what ever brought you here?"

"I wanted to see you, Fanny dear."

"Well! And what have you got on your mind, Amy?" She spoke as if her sister, between two and three years her junior, were her prejudiced grandmother.

"I have not been quite easy on your account, and indeed want to know a little more if you will confide more to me."

There was a great empty well before them and looking down into its depths Fanny said, "Now, Uncle!"

Little Dorrit, as her eyes became used to the darkness, faintly made him out at the bottom of the well, in an obscure corner by himself, with his instrument in its ragged case under his arm.

He did not hear her until she had spoken to him three or four times; nor was he at all surprised by the presence of two nieces instead of one, but merely said in his tremulous voice, "I am coming, I am coming!" and crept forth by some underground way which emitted a cellarous smell.

"And so, Amy," said her sister, when the three together passed out through the door, "you are curious about me?"

She was pretty, and conscious, and rather flaunting; and the condescension with which she put aside the superiority of her charms, and of her worldly experience, and addressed her sister on almost equal terms, had a vast deal of the family in it.

"I am interested, Fanny, and concerned in anything that concerns you."

"So you are, so you are, and you are the best of Amys. If I am ever a little provoking, I am sure you'll consider what a thing it is to occupy my position and feel a consciousness of being superior to it. I shouldn't care," said the Daughter of the Father of the Marshalsea, "if the others were not so common. None of them have come down in the world as we have." Fanny took out her handkerchief, and rather angrily wiped her eyes. "I was not born where you were, you know, Amy, and perhaps that makes a difference. My dear child, when we get rid of Uncle, you shall know all about it. We'll drop him at the cook's shop where he is going to dine."

They walked on with him until they came to a dirty shop window in a dirty street, which was made almost opaque by the steam of hot meats, vegetables, and puddings.

"Dinner?" muttered Uncle. "Ha! Yes, yes, yes!" and he slowly vanished from them into the mist.

"Now, Amy," said her sister, "come with me, if you are not too tired to

70

walk to Harley Street, Cavendish Square." Arriving at that grand destination, Fanny singled out the handsomest house, and knocking at the door, inquired for Mrs Merdle. The footman opened the door and Fanny walked in, taking her sister with her. They went upstairs and were left in a spacious semicircular drawing-room, one of several drawing-rooms, where there was a parrot on the outside of a golden cage holding on by its beak. Through a curtained doorway came a lady, raising the curtain with a heavily ringed hand as she entered.

She had large unfeeling handsome eyes, and dark unfeeling handsome hair, and a broad unfeeling handsome bosom.

"Mrs Merdle," said Fanny. "My sister, ma'am."

"I am glad to see your sister, Miss Dorrit. I did not remember that you had a sister."

"I did not mention that I had," said Fanny.

"Ah!" Mrs Merdle curled the little finger of her left hand. "Also professional?" said Mrs Merdle, looking at Little Dorrit through an eye-glass.

Fanny answered No. "My sister has been asking me to tell her, as between sisters, how I came to have the honour of knowing you. And as I had engaged to call upon you once more, I thought I might take the liberty of bringing her with me, when perhaps you would tell her."

"I cannot object to comply with her request, I am sure," said Mrs Merdle. "I have a son (I was first married extremely young) of two or three-and-twenty."

Fanny set her lips, and her eyes looked half triumphantly at her sister.

"He is a little gay, a thing Society is accustomed to in young men, and he is very impressible. When I heard that my son was supposed to be fascinated by a dancer, I was much surprised and much distressed. But when I found that your sister, by rejecting my son's advances (I must add, in an unexpected manner), had brought him to the point of proposing marriage, my feelings were of the profoundest anguish. There is very little more to tell, but it is to your sister's credit. I pointed out to your sister the plain state of the case; the impossibility of the Society in which we moved recognising the Society in which she moved – though charming, I have no doubt – "

"Let my sister know, if you please, Mrs Merdle," Fanny pouted, with a toss of her gauzy bonnet, "that I had already had the honour of telling your son that I wished to have nothing whatever to say to him."

"Well, Miss Dorrit," assented Mrs Merdle, "perhaps I might have mentioned that before." She lifted her unfeeling, handsome chin and made a sign that the interview was ended.

The sisters rose at the same time and came downstairs, the elder sister haughty and the younger sister humbled, and were shut out into Harley Street. They spoke no more all the way back to the lodging where Fanny and her uncle lived. When they arrived there, they found the old man practising his clarionet in the dolefullest manner in a corner of the room. Fanny had a composite meal to make, of chops, and porter, and tea; and indignantly pretended to prepare it for herself, though her sister did all that in quiet reality. When at last Fanny sat down to eat and drink, she angrily threw the table implements about. "If you despise me," she said, bursting into vehement tears, "because I am a dancer, why did you put me in the way of being one? It was your doing, Amy!"

"Oh Fanny!"

"And Tip, too, poor fellow. Why, it was your doing, Amy. And your father, your poor father, Amy. Because he is not free to show himself and to speak for himself, you would let such people insult him with impunity."

Poor Little Dorrit felt the injustice of this taunt rather sharply.

Fanny was passionate with the tea-cups as long as her passion lasted, and then protested that she was the wretchedest girl in the world, and she wished she was dead. After that, her crying became remorseful, and she got up and put her arms round her sister and said "Forgive me, Amy," almost as passionately as she had said what she regretted.

Little Dorrit parted from them, and hastened back to the Marshalsea. It fell dark there sooner than elsewhere, and going into it that evening was like going into a deep trench. The shadow of the wall was on every object, not least upon the figure in the old grey gown and the black velvet cap, as it turned towards her when she opened the door of the dim room.

CHAPTER 19

Mr Merdle's Complaint

Society was aware of Mr and Mrs Merdle. Society had said "Let us license them; let us know them."

Mrs Merdle's first husband had been a colonel, whose son was Mrs Merdle's only child. He was of a chuckle-headed, high-shouldered make, with a general appearance of being, not so much a young man as a swelled boy. He had given so few signs of reason, that a by-word went among his companions that his brain had been frozen up in a mighty frost which prevailed at St John's, New Brunswick, at the period of his birth there, and had never thawed from that hour.

As for Mr Merdle, he did not want a son-in-law for himself; he wanted a son-in-law for Society. Mr Sparkler being in the habit of frequenting all the races, and all the lounges, and all the parties, and being well known, Society was satisfied with its son-in-law.

There was a dinner giving in the Harley Street establishment, while Little Dorrit was stitching at her father's new shirts by his side that night; and there were magnates from every quarter. Mrs Merdle was magnificent and the chief butler was the stateliest man in the company. Among the evening magnates was a famous physician, who knew everybody, and whom everybody knew. On entering at the door, he came upon Mr Merdle who had been feeling under the weather for some time and was now drinking his tea in a corner.

Mr Merdle started. "Oh! It's you!"

"Any better today?"

"No," said Mr Merdle, "I am no better. A pity I didn't see you this morning. Pray come to me tomorrow, or let me come to you."

"Well!" he replied. "I will come tomorrow as I drive by." He turned to Mrs Merdle. "I may as well tell you that I can find nothing the matter with Mr Merdle. As to nerves, Mr Merdle is of a cool temperament, so how he should suppose himself unwell without reason, you may think strange."

Society and Mr Merdle had so much to do with one another in all things else, that it is hard to imagine his complaint, if he had one, being solely his own affair. Had he a deep-seated complaint, and could any doctor find it out?

CHAPTER 20

A Puzzle

The Father of the Marshalsea was happy to receive Mr Clennam when he called to pay his respects; but he didn't find that he got on with him personally. There appeared to be something (he didn't know what it was) wanting in him. However, in the threefold capacity, of the gentleman from outside who had been accidentally locked in on the night of his first appearance, of the gentleman from outside who had inquired into the affairs of the Father of the Marshalsea with the stupendous idea of getting him out, and of the gentleman from outside who took an interest in the child of the Marshalsea, Clennam soon became a visitor of mark.

One day Mr Chivery, who was on the lock when Arthur came out of the Marshalsea, asked him which way he might be going.

"I am going over the Bridge."

"I ask your pardon again," said Mr Chivery, "but could you go round by Horsemonger Lane? Could you by any means find time to look in at that address?" handing him a little card on which was printed: Chivery and Co., Tobacconists, Importers of pure Havannah Cigars, fine Snuffs, &C. &C.

"It an't tobacco business, the truth is, it's my wife. She's wishful to say a word to you, sir, upon a point respecting – yes," said Mr Chivery, answering Clennam's look of apprehension with a nod, "respecting Little Dorrit."

"I will make a point of seeing your wife directly."

"Thank you, sir. Much obliged. It an't above ten minutes out of your way. Please to ask for Mrs Chivery!"

Arthur Clennam speedily arrived there. It was a very small establishment, wherein a decent woman sat behind the counter working at her needle. Little jars of tobacco, little boxes of cigars, a little assortment of pipes, a little jar or two of snuff, and a little instrument like a shoeing horn for serving it out, composed the retail stock in trade.

Arthur mentioned his name, and his having promised to call, on the solicitation of Mr Chivery. About something relating to Miss Dorrit, he believed. Mrs Chivery at once laid aside her work, rose up from her seat behind the counter, and deploringly shook her head.

74

"You may see him now," said she, "if you'll condescend to take a peep."

With these mysterious words, she preceded the visitor into a little parlour behind the shop, with a little window in it commanding a very little dull back-yard where sheets and table-cloths were drying. Among those flapping articles was sitting in a chair, a little woe-begone young man.

"Our John," said Mrs Chivery.

Not to be deficient in interest, Clennam asked what he might be doing there?

"It's the only change he takes," said Mrs Chivery, shaking her head afresh. "He won't go out, even in the back-yard, when there's no linen; but when there's linen to keep the neighbours' eyes off, he'll sit there, hours." Mrs Chivery shook her head and reconducted her visitor into the regions of the business.

"Please to take a seat, sir," said Mrs Chivery. "Miss Dorrit is the matter with Our John, sir; he's a breaking his heart for her, and I would wish to take the liberty to ask how it's to be made good to his parents when bust?" She began to shake her head and dry her eyes.

"Does she know your son?" asked Arthur.

"Brought up together, sir," said Mrs Chivery. "Played together."

"Does she know your son as her admirer?"

"Oh! bless you, sir," said Mrs Chivery, with a sort of triumphant shiver, "she never could have seen him on a Sunday without knowing he was that."

"May I ask you how he came to fall into the desponding state which causes you so much uneasiness?"

"Our John has everyone's good word and everyone's good wish. He played with her as a child and has known her ever since. He went out upon the Sunday afternoon and made his offer to her. 'No, John,' she replied, 'I cannot have you, I cannot have any husband, it is not my intentions ever to become a wife, it is my intentions to be always a sacrifice. Farewell, find another worthy of you, and forget me!'"

Clennam told the worthy Mrs Chivery, after turning these things over in his mind – he did that, indeed, while she was yet speaking – that he might be relied upon to do his utmost at all times to promote the happiness of Miss Dorrit, and to further the wishes of her heart if it were in his power to do so, and if he could discover what they were. At the

75

same time he cautioned her against assumptions and appearances; enjoined strict silence and secrecy, lest Miss Dorrit should be made unhappy; and particularly advised her to endeavour to win her son's confidence and so to make quite sure of the state of the case.

They then parted good friends, and Arthur walked away towards the Iron Bridge. He had scarcely set foot upon it, when he saw Little Dorrit walking on before him. It was a timely chance, favourable to his wish of observing her face and manner when no one else was by. He quickened his pace; but before he reached her, she turned her head.

"Have I startled you?" he asked.

"I thought I knew the step," she answered, hesitating.

"And did you know it, Little Dorrit? You could hardly have expected mine."

"I did not expect any. But when I heard a step, I thought it – sounded like yours."

"Are you going further?"

"No, sir, I am only walking here for a little change."

They walked together and he gathered from a tremor on her lip, and a passing shadow of great agitation on her face, that her mind was with her father. The Little Dorrit, trembling on his arm, was less in unison than ever with Mrs Chivery's theory, and yet was not irreconcilable with a new fancy which sprung up within him, that there might be someone else in the hopeless unattainable distance.

They turned, and Clennam said, Here was Maggy coming! Little Dorrit looked up, surprised, and they confronted Maggy, who brought herself at sight of them to a dead stop.

"Maggy, you promised me to stop near Father."

"So I would, Little Mother, only he wouldn't let me. If he takes and sends me out I must go. If he takes and says, 'Maggy, you hurry away and back with that letter', Lor, Little Mother, what's a poor thing of ten year old to do? And if Mr Tip – if he happens to be a-coming in as I come out, and if he says, 'Where are you going, Maggy?' and if I says, 'I'm a-going So and So,' and if he says, 'I'll have a Try too,' and if he goes into the George and writes a letter and if he gives it me and says, 'Take that one to the same place, and if the answer's a good 'un I'll give you a shilling,' it ain't my fault, mother!"

"Give them me here," said Clennam in a low voice.

"Well, then, come across the road," answered Maggy in a very loud whisper. "Little Mother wasn't to know nothing of it."

Clennam crossed to the other side, and hurriedly opened the letters. That from the father mentioned that most unexpectedly finding himself in the novel position of having been disappointed of a remittance from the City, he took up his pen to entreat Mr Clennam to advance him the sum of Three Pounds Ten Shillings upon his I.O.U., which he begged to enclose. That from the son set forth that Mr Clennam would, he knew, be gratified to hear that he had at length obtained permanent employment of a highly satisfactory nature, but that the temporary inability of his employer to pay him his arrears of salary to that date combined with the fraudulent conduct of a false friend had reduced him to the verge of ruin, unless he could by a quarter before six that evening raise the sum of eight pounds. This sum, Mr Clennam would be happy to learn, he had already raised, with the exception of a trifling balance of one pound seventeen and fourpence balance.

These letters Clennam answered with the aid of his pencil and pocket-book, on the spot; sending the father what he asked for, and excusing himself from compliance with the demand of the son. He then commissioned Maggy to return with his replies, and gave her a shilling.

When he rejoined Little Dorrit, and they had begun walking as before, she said all at once:

"I think I had better go. I had better go home. Good-bye. I had far better stay at home!"

"Don't call it home, my child!" he entreated. "It is always painful to me to hear you call it home."

"But it is home! What else can I call home? It is better for me to stay there; much more dutiful, much happier. Please don't go with me, let me go by myself. Good-bye, God bless you. Thank you, thank you."

That night he thought of his poor child and Little Dorrit thought of him – too faithfully, ah, too faithfully! – in the shadow of the Marshalsea wall.

CHAPTER 21

Machinery in Motion

Mr Meagles bestirred himself with such prompt activity in the matter of the negotiation with Daniel Doyce which Clennam had entrusted to him, that he soon brought it into business train, and called on Clennam at nine o'clock one morning to make his report.

"Doyce is highly gratified by your good opinion," he opened the business by saying, "and desires nothing so much as that you should examine the affairs of the Works for yourself, and entirely understand them. He has handed me the keys of all his books and papers – here they are jingling in this pocket – and the only charge he has given me is 'Let Mr Clennam have the means of putting himself on a perfect equality with me as to knowing whatever I know. If it should come to nothing after all, he will respect my confidence. Unless I was sure of that to begin with, I should have nothing to do with him.' And there, you see," said Mr Meagles, "you have Daniel Doyce all over."

"A very honourable character."

"Indeed. And now," added Mr Meagles, "you can begin to look into matters as soon as you think proper. I avow, Mr Clennam," – with a cordial shake of the hand – "that if I had looked high and low for a partner, I believe I could not have found one more to my mind."

"I say the same," said Clennam.

"And I say of both of you," added Mr Meagles, "that you are well matched. Each of you will be a right hand to the other. Here's my own right hand upon it, as a practical man, to both of you."

The purchase was completed within a month. It left Arthur in possession of private personal means not exceeding a few hundred pounds; but it opened to him an active and promising career. Soon nothing seemed new in the partnership but the paint of the inscription on the door-posts, DOYCE AND CLENNAM.

The workshop was arrived at by a step-ladder from the outer yard below, where it served as a shelter for the large grindstone where tools were sharpened.

Raising his eyes one day, Clennam was surprised to see a bonnet labouring up the step-ladder. The unusual apparition was followed by another bonnet. He then perceived that the first bonnet was on the head of Mr F's Aunt, and that the second bonnet was on the head of Flora, who seemed to have propelled her legacy up the steep ascent with considerable difficulty. Though not altogether enraptured at the sight of these visitors, Clennam lost no time in opening the counting-house door, and placing chairs for them in the counting-house.

As Flora dropped into hers, she bestowed the old look upon him.

"Dear Arthur – force of habit, Mr Clennam every way more delicate and adapted to existing circumstances – I thought I might so far presume upon old times for ever faded never more to bloom as to call with Mr F's Aunt to congratulate and offer best wishes."

"I am very happy to see you," said Clennam, "and I thank you, Flora, very much for your kind remembrance."

"My goodness, Arthur – Doyce and Clennam really easier to me with old remembrances. When Pancks told us I made up my mind that I would come and call because when Papa happened to mention her I said at the moment Good gracious!"

"When you say Her," observed Mr Clennam, by this time pretty well bewildered, "do you mean Mr F's – "

"My goodness, Arthur – who ever heard of Mr F's Aunt doing needlework and going out by the day?"

"Going out by the day! Do you speak of Little Dorrit?"

"Why yes of course," returned Flora; "and of all the strangest names I ever heard the strangest."

"Then, Flora," said Arthur, with a sudden interest in the conversation, "Mr Casby was so kind as to mention Little Dorrit to you, was he? What did he say?"

"I must admit, Papa said you had spoken of her in an earnest way and I said what I have told you and that's all."

"That's all?" said Arthur, a little disappointed.

"Except that when Pancks told us of your having embarked in this business and with difficulty persuaded us that it was really you I said to Mr F's Aunt then we would come and ask you if it would be agreeable to all parties that Little Dorrit should be engaged at our house when required for I know she often goes to your mama's and I know that your mama has a very touchy temper Arthur – Doyce and Clennam – or I never might

79

have married Mr F and might have been at this hour but I am running into nonsense."

"It was very kind of you, Flora, to think of this."

Once more he put out his hand frankly to poor Flora; once more poor Flora couldn't accept it frankly, found it worth nothing openly, must make the old intrigue and mystery of it.

The Patriarch, meanwhile, came inanely beaming towards the counting-house in the wake of Pancks. Pancks opened the door for him, towed him in, and retired to his own moorings in a corner.

"I heard from Flora," said the Patriarch with his benevolent smile, "that she was coming to call, coming to call. And being out, I thought I'd come also, thought I'd come also."

"Mrs Finching has been telling me, sir," said Arthur, "that she hopes occasionally to employ the young needlewoman you recommended to my mother. For which I have been thanking her."

The Patriarch turning his head in a lumbering way towards Pancks, that assistant put up the note-book in which he had been absorbed, and took him in tow.

"The name was mentioned to you, and you passed it on. That's what *you* did."

"Well!" said Clennam. "As she justifies any recommendation, it is much the same thing."

"You are glad she turns out well," said Pancks, "but it wouldn't have been your fault if she had turned out ill. You knew nothing about her."

"You are not acquainted, then," said Arthur, hazarding a random question, "with any of her family?"

"You can't be acquainted with people you never heard of, can you?" returned Pancks.

A momentary silence that ensued was broken by Mr F's Aunt, who had been sitting upright in a cataleptic state. With the deadliest animosity she observed, "You can't make a head and brains out of a brass knob with nothing in it."

Mr Pancks was not slow to reply, with his usual calmness, "Indeed, ma'am! Bless my soul! I'm surprised to hear it. Favour me with your arm, ma'am; we'll have a little walk together." And so he escorted Mr F's Aunt down the private staircase of the counting-house along with Mr Casby and his daughter. On return he addressed Mr Clennam.

80

"I am in want of information, sir."

"Connected with this firm?" asked Clennam.

"No," said Pancks.

"With what then, Mr Pancks? That is to say, assuming that you want it of me."

"Yes, sir; yes, I want it of you," said Pancks. "Motive good. Nothing to do with my proprietor. Not stateable at present, but good. Desiring to serve young person, name of Dorrit."

"What do you want to know?" asked Clennam.

Mr Pancks replied with a pause and a puff, "I want supplementary information of any sort."

After a little consideration, Arthur resolved to supply Mr Pancks with such leading information as it was in his power to impart him; well knowing that Mr Pancks, if he failed in his present research, was pretty sure to find other means of getting it.

He, therefore, first requested Mr Pancks to remember his voluntary declaration that his proprietor had no part in the disclosure, and that his own intentions were good. Then he openly told him that as to the Dorrit lineage or former place of habitation, he had no information to communicate, and that his knowledge of the family did not extend beyond the fact that it appeared to be now reduced to five members; namely, to two brothers, of whom one was single, and one a widower with three children. The ages of the whole family he made known to Mr Pancks, as nearly as he could guess at them; and finally he described to him the position of the Father of the Marshalsea, and the course of time and events through which he had become invested with that character.

"In conclusion, Mr Pancks," said Arthur, "I wish to make a fair bargain with you, that you shall enlighten me concerning the Dorrit family when you have it in your power, as I have enlightened you."

Mr Pancks laughed. "It's a bargain, sir," said he. "You shall find me stick to it. And now I'll wish you good day, as it's collecting day in the yard. By-the-bye, the lame foreigner with the stick wants a top room down the yard. Is he good for it?"

"I will answer for him," said Clennam.

"He has been in the hospital, I believe?"

81

"Yes. Through having met with an accident. He is only just now discharged."

"Many thanks," said Pancks, descending the workshop ladder swift as a monkey.

Throughout the remainder of the day, Bleeding Heart Yard was in consternation, as the grim Pancks cruised in it; haranguing the inhabitants on their backslidings in respect of payment, demanding his bond, sending a swell of terror on before him, and leaving it in his wake.

CHAPTER 22

Fortune-telling

Little Dorrit received a call that same evening from Mr Plornish, who, having intimated that he wished to speak to her privately, told Miss Dorrit that Mr Casby's daughter would be glad for to engage her. "'She was a old and a dear friend,' she said, 'particular of Mr Clennam, and hoped for to prove herself a useful friend to his friend.' Them was her words. Wishing to know whether Miss Dorrit could come tomorrow morning, I said I would see you, Miss."

"I can go tomorrow, thank you," said Little Dorrit. "This is very kind of you, but you are always kind."

Early in the morning, Little Dorrit, leaving Maggy in high domestic trust, set off for the Patriarchal tent. At five minutes before eight her hand was on the Patriarchal knocker, which was quite as high as she could reach.

She gave Mrs Finching's card to the young woman who opened the door, and the young woman told her that "Miss Flora" – Flora having, on her return to the parental roof, reinvested herself with the title under which she had lived there – was not yet out of her bedroom, but she was to please to walk up into Miss Flora's sitting-room. Little Dorrit was still sitting near the door with her bonnet on, when Flora came in in a hurry half an hour afterwards, so sorry to have kept her waiting, and good gracious why did she sit out there in the cold when she had expected to find her by the fire reading the paper. "Why, what a good little thing you are, my dear!" she said and pressed her face between her hands like the gentlest of women. "Really so sorry that I should happen to be late on this morning of all mornings because my intention and my wish was to be ready to meet you when you came in and to say that any one that interested Arthur Clennam half so much must interest me. You are coming here on the footing of a friend and companion you know if you will let me take that liberty and I should be ashamed of myself indeed if you could come here upon any other, besides which Arthur Clennam spoke in such terms. Have you known Arthur long?"

Little Dorrit answered that she had known Mr Clennam ever since his return. She looked timidly about.

"Shall I find my work anywhere, ma'am?" she asked; "can I get it?"

Her earnestness was so expressive of her being uneasy without her work, that Flora answered, "Well my dear, whatever you like best," and produced a basket of white handkerchiefs. Little Dorrit gladly put it by her side, took out her little pocket-housewife, threaded the needle, and began to hem.

Flora put her feet upon the fender, and settled herself for a thorough good romantic disclosure.

"For Arthur's sake I will always be a friend to you my dear girl and in Arthur's name you may always rely upon me. Now tell me about yourself."

Quietly pursuing her task, Little Dorrit condensed the narrative of her life into a few scanty words about herself and a glowing eulogy upon her father; and Flora took it all in with a natural tenderness that quite understood it, and in which there was no incoherence.

When dinner-time came, Flora drew the arm of her new charge through hers, and led her downstairs, and presented her to the Patriarch and Mr Pancks.

When she had left the table for half an hour, and was at work alone, Mr Pancks softly appeared before her, urbanely nodding.

"Find it a little dull, Miss Dorrit?" he inquired in a low voice.

"No, thank you, sir," said Little Dorrit.

"Busy, I see," observed Mr Pancks, stealing into the room by inches. "What are those now, Miss Dorrit?"

"Handkerchiefs."

"Are they, though!" said Pancks. "I shouldn't have thought it." Not in the least looking at them, but looking at Little Dorrit. "Perhaps you wonder who I am. Shall I tell you? I am a fortune-teller."

Little Dorrit now began to think he was mad.

"I belong body and soul to my proprietor," said Pancks; "you saw my proprietor having his dinner below. But I do a little in the other way, sometimes; privately, very privately, Miss Dorrit. I am a fortune-teller. Pancks the gipsy. I haven't told you your fortune yet, Miss Dorrit."

With that he rubbed his hands, panted away to the door, and urbanely nodded himself out again.

He began to pervade her daily life. She saw him in the street, constantly. When she went to Mr Casby's, he was always there. When she went to Mrs Clennam's, he came there on any pretence, as if to keep her in his sight. A week had not gone by, when she found him to her astonishment in the Lodge one night, conversing with the turnkey on duty, and to all appearance one of his familiar companions. Her next surprise was to find him equally at his ease within the prison and acquainted with Tip in some unknown manner, and taking a Sunday saunter into the College on that gentleman's arm.

Little Dorrit worked and strove as usual, wondering at all this, but keeping her wonder, as she had from her earliest years kept many heavier loads, in her own breast. A change had stolen, and was stealing yet, over the patient heart. Every day found her something more retiring than the day before. To pass in and out of the prison unnoticed, and elsewhere to be overlooked and forgotten, were, for herself, her chief desires.

To her own garret room too, she was glad to retreat as often as she could without desertion of any duty. For this poor place she showed an increasing love; and to sit in it alone became her favourite rest. Insomuch, that on a certain afternoon during the Pancks mysteries, when she was seated at her window, and heard Maggy's well-known step coming up the stairs, she was very much disturbed by the apprehension of being summoned away.

"Please, Little Mother," said Maggy, panting for breath, "you must come down and see him. He's here."

"Who, Maggy?"

"Who, o' course Mr Clennam. He's in your father's room, and he says to me, Maggy, will you be so kind and go and say it's only me."

84

"I am not very well, Maggy. I had better not go."

So away went Maggie, muttering her message all the way to keep it in her mind, and, soon, came back.

"He was very sorry, I can tell you," she announced, "and wanted to send a doctor. And he's coming again tomorrow he is and I don't think he'll have a good sleep tonight along o' hearing about your health, Little Mother. Oh my! Ain't you been a-crying!"

"I think I have, a little, Maggy."

"A little! Oh!"

"But it's all over now – all over for good, Maggy. And my head is much better and cooler, and I am quite comfortable. I am very glad I did not go down."

Her great staring child tenderly embraced her and smoothed her hair and bathed her forehead and eyes with cold water. Then Maggie dragged the box which was her seat on story-telling occasions, sat down upon it, hugged her own knees, and said, with a voracious appetite for stories, and with widely opened eyes: "Now, Little Mother, let's have a good 'un!"

"What shall it be about, Maggy?"

"Oh, let's have a princess," said Maggy, "and let her be a reg'lar one. Beyond all belief, you know!"

Little Dorrit considered for a moment; and with a rather sad smile upon her face, which was flushed by the sunset, she began.

The sunset flush was still bright on Little Dorrit's face when she came to the end of her story. Maggie sat so long with her eyes wide open, that at length Little Dorrit, to entice her from her box, rose and looked out of window. As she glanced down into the yard, she saw Pancks come in and leer up with the corner of his eye as he went by.

"Who's he, Little Mother?" said Maggy. She had joined her at the window and was leaning on her shoulder. "I see him come in and out often."

"I have heard him called a fortune-teller," said Little Dorrit, with the sunset very bright upon her. "But I doubt if he could tell many people even their past or present fortunes. Enough, let us come away from the window."

CHAPTER 23

Conspirators and Others

The private residence of Mr Pancks was in Pentonville, where he lodged on the second floor of a professional gentleman's residence, who wrote up in the fan-light, RUGG, GENERAL AGENT, ACCOUNTANT, DEBTS RECOVERED.

The tenancy of Mr Pancks was limited to one airy bedroom; he covenanting and agreeing with Mr Rugg his landlord, that in consideration of a certain scale of payments accurately defined, and on certain verbal notice duly given, he should be at liberty to elect to share the Sunday breakfast, dinner, tea, or supper, or each or any or all of those repasts or meals of Mr and Miss Rugg (his daughter) in the back-parlour.

Up to this time, Mr Pancks had transacted little or no business at his quarters in Pentonville, except in the sleeping line; but now that he had become a fortune-teller, he was often closeted after midnight with Mr Rugg in his little front-parlour office, and even after those untimely hours, burnt tallow in his bedroom.

He also made a personal acquaintance with the elder Mr Chivery, his amiable wife and his disconsolate son. He particularly addressed himself to the cultivation of a good understanding with Young John. In this endeavour he so prospered as to lure that pining shepherd forth from the groves, and tempt him to undertake mysterious missions; on which he began to disappear at uncertain intervals for as long a space as two or three days together. The prudent Mrs Chivery wondered greatly at this change until Mr Pancks confidentially agreed to pay her, for the occupation of her son's time, at the handsome rate of seven and sixpence per day.

He invited Young John to dinner, and even brought him within range of the dangerous (because expensive) fascinations of Miss Rugg. Mr Pancks presented him to the yellow-haired Ruggs as the young man he had so often mentioned who loved Miss Dorrit.

Young John said, with acknowledgements, that he only hoped he did what was right, and what showed how entirely he was devoted to Miss Dorrit. He wished to be unselfish; and he hoped he was. He wished to do anything as laid in his power to serve Miss Dorrit, altogether putting himself out of sight; and he hoped he did.

"Sir," said Mr Rugg, taking him by the hand, "you are a young man that it does one good to come across."

At the end of the feast Pancks took out his note-book. He looked over it and picked out little extracts, which he wrote on separate slips of paper on the table then held them up like a hand of cards.

"Now, there's a churchyard in Bedfordshire," said Pancks. "Who takes it?"

"I'll take it, sir," returned Mr Rugg, "if no one bids."

Mr Pancks dealt him his card, and looked at his hand again.

"Now, there's an enquiry in York," said Pancks. "Who takes it?"

"I'm not good for York," said Mr Rugg.

"Then perhaps," pursued Pancks, "you'll be so obliging, John Chivery?" Young John assenting, Pancks dealt him his card, and consulted his hand again.

"There's a church in London; I may as well take that. And a family Bible; I may as well take that, too. Here's a clerk at Durham for you, John, and an old seafaring gentleman at Dunstable for you, Mr Rugg."

When he had thus disposed of his cards, all being done very quietly and in a suppressed tone, Mr Pancks puffed his way into his own breast-pocket and tugged out a canvas bag; from which, with a sparing hand, he told forth money for travelling expenses in two little portions. "Cash goes out fast," he said anxiously, as he pushed a portion to each of his male companions, "very fast."

"I can only assure you, Mr Pancks," said Young John, "that I deeply regret my circumstances being such that I can't afford to pay my own charges, or that it's not advisable to allow me the time necessary for my doing the distances on foot; because nothing would give me greater satisfaction than to walk myself off my legs without fee or reward."

Such was the dinner without precedent, given by Pancks at Pentonville; and such was the busy and strange life Pancks led.

The only waking moments at which he appeared to relax from his cares were when he showed a dawning interest in the lame foreigner with the stick, down Bleeding Heart Yard.

The foreigner, by name John Baptist – they called him Mr Baptist in the Yard – was such a chirping, easy, hopeful little fellow, that his attraction for Pancks was probably in the force of contrast. Solitary, weak, and scantily acquainted with the most necessary words of the only language in which he could communicate with the people about him, he went with the stream of his fortunes, in a brisk way that was new in those parts. With little to eat, and less to drink, and nothing to wear but what he wore upon him, or had brought tied up in one of the smallest bundles that ever were seen, he put as bright a face upon it as if he were in the most flourishing circumstances when he first hobbled up and down the yard, humbly propitiating the general good-will with his white teeth.

The lame foreigner with the stick had to make head as well as he could; not absolutely single-handed, because Mr Arthur Clennam had recommended him to the Plornishes (he lived at the top of the same house), but still at heavy odds.

However, the Bleeding Hearts were kind hearts; and when they saw the little fellow cheerily limping about with a good-humoured face, doing no harm, drawing no knives, committing no outrageous immoralities, they began to accommodate themselves to his level, calling him "Mr Baptist," but treating him like a baby, and laughing immoderately at his lively gestures and his childish English.

It was in this stage of his progress, and in about the third week of his occupation, that Mr Pancks's fancy became attracted by the little man. Mounting to his attic, attended by Mrs Plornish as interpreter, he found Mr Baptist with no furniture but his bed on the ground, a table, and a chair, carving with the aid of a few simple tools, in the blithest way possible.

"Now, old chap," said Mr Pancks, "pay up!"

He had his money ready, folded in a scrap of paper, and laughingly handed it in; then with a free action, threw out as many fingers of his right hand as there were shillings, and made a cut crosswise in the air for an odd sixpence.

"Oh!" said Mr Pancks, watching him, wonderingly. "That's it, is it? You're a quick customer. It's all right. I didn't expect to receive it, though."

From that time it became a frequent custom with Pancks the gipsy, as he went home jaded at night, to pass round by Bleeding Heart Yard, go quietly up the stairs, look in at Mr Baptist's door, and, finding him in his room, to say, "Hallo, old chap!" then go his way with an appearance of being lightened and refreshed.

CHAPTER 24

Nobody's State of Mind

If Arthur Clennam had not arrived at that wise decision firmly to restrain himself from loving Pet, he would have lived on in a state of much perplexity, involving difficult struggles with his own heart. Not the least of these would have been a contention, always waging within it, between a tendency to dislike Mr Henry Gowan, if not to regard him with positive repugnance, and a whisper that the inclination was unworthy. As it was, Mr Gowan seemed transferred to Daniel Doyce's mind with a similar dislike.

"I want to present you to my mother," said Mr Henry Gowan, calling on Clennam one morning. There was nothing Clennam would have desired less, or would have been more at a loss how to avoid.

"My mother lives in a most primitive manner down in that dreary red-brick dungeon at Hampton Court," said Gowan. "If you would make your own appointment, suggest your own day for permitting me to take you there to dinner, you would be bored and she would be charmed. Really that's the state of the case."

On the appointed day, Mrs Gowan received Arthur with condescension. He found her a courtly old lady, formerly a Beauty, and still sufficiently well-favoured to have dispensed with the powder on her nose and a certain impossible bloom under each eye. She was a little lofty with him; so was another old lady, dark-browed and high-nosed, and a grey old gentleman of dignified and sullen appearance; both of whom had come to dinner.

The dignified old gentleman turned out to be Lord Lancaster Stiltstalking, who had been maintained by the Circumlocution Office for many years as a representative of the Britannic Majesty abroad.

There was only one other person in the room: a microscopically small footboy who, if his jacket could have been unbuttoned and his heart laid bare, would have been seen, as a distant adherent of the Barnacle family, ready to aspire to a situation under Government.

Mr Henry Gowan seemed to have a malicious pleasure in playing off the three talkers against each other, and in seeing Clennam startled by what they said.

"Mr Clennam," said Mrs Gowan, "apart from the happiness I have in becoming known to you, though in this odiously inconvenient place – a mere barrack – there is a subject on which I am dying to speak to you. It is the subject in connection with which my son first had, I believe, the pleasure of cultivating your acquaintance. Is she really pretty, this flame of Henry's? I am pretty sure he picked her up at Rome; but never mind where – somewhere. Now (this is entirely between ourselves), is she very plebeian?"

"Really, ma'am," returned Clennam, "I am so undoubtedly plebeian myself, that I do not feel qualified to judge."

Mrs Gowan glanced at the other end of the room, where her son was playing écarté on a sofa with the old lady.

"Henry," she resumed, "is self-willed and resolute; and as these people naturally strain every nerve to catch him, I can entertain very little hope, Mr Clennam, that the thing will be broken off."

As she shrugged her shoulders, Clennam stiffly bowed then said in a lower tone than he had adopted yet:

"Mrs Gowan – a misconception on your part, a very great misconception if I may venture to call it so, seems to require setting right. You have supposed Mr Meagles and his family to strain every nerve, I think you said, to secure Mr Henry Gowan?"

The lady placidly assented.

"Now that is so far," said Arthur, "from being the case, that I know Mr Meagles to be unhappy in this matter; and to have interposed all reasonable obstacles with the hope of putting an end to it."

Mrs Gowan shut up her great green fan, tapped him on the arm with it, and tapped her smiling lips. "Why, don't I know my son, and don't I know that this is exactly the way to hold him?" she said contemptuously.

At this opportune moment the cards were thrown up, and Mr Henry Gowan came across the room, saying, "Mother, we have a long way to go, and it's getting late." Mr Clennam rose.

"You have had a portentously long audience of my mother," said Gowan, as the door closed upon them. "I fervently hope she has not bored you?"

"Not at all," said Clennam.

They had a little open phaeton for the journey, and were soon in it on the road home. Clennam maintained a thoughtful silence.

"You are evidently out of spirits," said Gowan; "I am very much afraid my mother must have bored you dreadfully."

"Believe me, not at all," said Clennam. "It's nothing – nothing at all!"

CHAPTER 25

Five-and-Twenty

What Mr Pancks already knew about the Dorrit family, what more he really wanted to find out, and why he should trouble his busy head about them at all, were questions that often perplexed Arthur Clennam. It was not a selfish fear or hesitation that rendered him uneasy, but a mistrust lest Pancks might not observe his part of the understanding between them, and, making any discovery, might take some course upon it without imparting it to him.

He returned home one evening from an interview with Little Dorrit's father, who had mentioned that she was out visiting – which was what he always said when she was hard at work to buy his supper – and found Mr Meagles in an excited state walking up and down his room. On Arthur's opening the door, Mr Meagles stopped, faced round, and said: "Clennam! – Tattycoram!"

"What's the matter?"

"Lost!"

"Why, bless my heart alive!" cried Clennam in amazement. "What do you mean?"

"Wouldn't count five-and-twenty, sir; couldn't be got to do it; stopped at eight, and took herself off."

"Left your house?"

"Never to come back," said Mr Meagles, shaking his head. "You don't know that girl's passionate and proud character. A team of horses couldn't draw her back now; the bolts and bars of the old Bastille couldn't keep her."

"How did it happen? Pray sit down and tell me."

"Well!" continued Mr Meagles in an apologetic way, "I admit as a practical man, and I am sure Mother would admit as a practical woman,

91

that we do, in families, magnify our troubles and make mountains of our molehills in a way that is calculated to be rather trying to people who look on. Still, Pet's happiness or unhappiness is quite a life or death question with us; and we may be excused, I hope, for making much of it. At all events, it might have been too much for Tattycoram, don't you think so?"

"I do indeed think so," returned Clennam, in most emphatic recognition of this very moderate expectation.

"No, sir," said Mr Meagles, shaking his head ruefully. "she couldn't stand it. The chafing and firing of that girl, the wearing and tearing of that girl within her own breast, has been such that I have softly said to her again and again in passing her, 'Five-and-twenty, Tattycoram, five-and-twenty.' But, do what we would, it seems as if it was to be; she broke out violently one night. We had said good-night to Pet in her presence (very affectionately, I must allow), and she had attended Pet upstairs – you remember she was her maid. Perhaps Pet, having been out of sorts, may have been a little more inconsiderate than usual in requiring services of her: but I don't know that I have any right to say so; she was always thoughtful and gentle."

"The gentlest mistress in the world."

"Thank you, Clennam," said Mr Meagles, shaking him by the hand; "you have often seen them together. Well! We presently heard this unfortunate Tattycoram loud and angry, and before we could ask what was the matter, Pet came back in a tremble, saying she was frightened of her. Close after her came Tattycoram in a flaming rage. 'I hate you all three,' says she, stamping her foot at us. 'I am bursting with hate of the whole house.'"

"Upon which you – ?"

"I?" said Mr Meagles, with a plain good faith that might have commanded the belief of Mrs Gowan herself. "I said, count five-and-twenty, Tattycoram."

"And you know no more of her?"

"No more," returned Mr Meagles. "I have been hunting about all day. She must have gone very early and very silently. I have found no trace of her down about us."

"Stay!" said Clennam, after a moment's reflection. "You want to see her? I assume that?"

"Yes, assuredly; I want to give her another chance; Mother and Pet want to give her another chance; come! You yourself," said Mr Meagles, persuasively, as if the provocation to be angry were not his own at all, "want to give the poor passionate girl another chance, I know, Clennam."

"It would be strange and hard indeed if I did not," said Clennam, "when you are all so forgiving. What I was going to ask you was, have you thought of that Miss Wade?"

"I have. I did not think of her until I had pervaded the whole of our neighbourhood, and I don't know that I should have done so then but for finding Mother and Pet, when I went home, full of the idea that Tattycoram must have gone to her."

"Have you any idea where Miss Wade is to be found?"

Mr Meagles handed him a slip of paper, on which was written the name of one of the dull by-streets in the Grosvenor region, near Park Lane.

"Here is no number," said Arthur looking over it.

"No number, my dear Clennam?" returned his friend.

"However, it's worth an inquiry. Will you accompany me?"

It happened that in the street where Miss Wade lived, they had several times passed a dingy house, apparently empty, with bills in the windows, announcing that it was to let.

They knocked once, and they rang once, without any response.

"Empty," said Mr Meagles, listening.

"Once more," said Clennam, and knocked again. After that knock they heard a movement below and somebody shuffling up towards the door.

The confined entrance was so dark that it was impossible to make out distinctly what kind of person opened the door; but it appeared to be an old woman.

"Excuse our troubling you," said Clennam. "Pray can you tell us where Miss Wade lives?"

The voice in the darkness unexpectedly replied, "Lives here."

"Is she at home?"

"I suppose she is," said the voice abruptly; "you had better come in, and I'll ask."

"This is odd, Clennam," said Mr Meagles, softly.

"Odd enough," assented Clennam in the same tone, "but we have succeeded; that's the main point. Here's a light coming!"

The light was a lamp, and the bearer was the old woman: very dirty, very wrinkled and dry. "She's at home," she said, "she'll come directly."

Having set the lamp down on the table, the old woman dusted her hands on her apron, which she might have done for ever without cleaning them, looked at the visitors with a dim pair of eyes, and backed out. At the same time Miss Wade came in.

She was exactly the same as when they had parted, just as handsome, just as scornful, just as repressed. She manifested no surprise in seeing them, nor any other emotion.

"I apprehend," she said, "that I know the cause of your favouring me with this visit. We may come to it at once."

"The cause then, ma'am," said Mr Meagles, "is Tattycoram."

"So I supposed."

"Miss Wade," said Mr Meagles, "will you be so kind as to say whether you know anything of her?"

"Surely. I know she is here with me."

"Then, ma'am," said Mr Meagles, "allow me to make known to you that I shall be happy to have her back, and that my wife and daughter will be happy to have her back. I hope we know how to make allowances."

"You hope to know how to make allowances?" she returned, in a level, measured voice. "For what?"

"I think my friend would say, Miss Wade," Arthur Clennam interposed, seeing Mr Meagles rather at a loss, "for the passionate sense that sometimes comes upon the poor girl, of being at a disadvantage. Which occasionally gets the better of better remembrances."

The lady broke into a smile as she turned her eyes upon him.

"Indeed?" was all she answered.

Arthur said: "Perhaps it would be well if Mr Meagles could see her, Miss Wade?"

"That is easily done," said she. "Come here, child." She had opened a door while saying this, and now led the girl in by the hand.

"See here," she said, in the same level way as before. "Here is your master. He is willing to take you back, my dear, if you are sensible of the favour and choose to go. You can be, again, a foil to his pretty daughter, a slave to her pleasant wilfulness, and a toy in the house showing the goodness of the family. You can have your droll name again, playfully pointing you out and setting you apart, as it is right that you should be pointed out and set apart. What do you say, Harriet? Will you go?"

The girl raised her lustrous black eyes. "I'd die sooner!"

Miss Wade, who had released her hold, laid her hand protectingly on the girl's neck for a moment, and then said, looking round with her former smile and speaking exactly in her former tone, "Gentlemen! What do you do upon that?"

"Oh, Tattycoram, Tattycoram!" cried Mr Meagles, adjuring her besides with an earnest hand. "Think what a future lies before you."

"Gentlemen!" said Miss Wade, calmly. "When you have concluded – Mr Clennam, perhaps you will induce your friend – "

"Not without another effort," said Mr Meagles, stoutly. "Tattycoram, my poor dear girl, count five-and-twenty."

"Do not reject the hope, the certainty, this kind man offers you," said Clennam in a low, emphatic voice. "Turn to the friends you have not forgotten. Think once more!"

"I won't! Miss Wade," said the girl, with her bosom swelling high, and speaking with her hand held to her throat, "take me away!"

"Tattycoram," said Mr Meagles. "Once more yet! The only thing I ask of you in the world, my child! Count five-and-twenty!"

There was a visible triumph in Miss Wade's face as she turned to dismiss the visitors.

Mr Meagles sorrowfully went out and Mr Clennam followed.

CHAPTER 26

Nobody's Disappearance

Not resting satisfied with the endeavours he had made to recover his lost charge, Mr Meagles addressed a letter of remonstrance, breathing nothing but goodwill, not only to Tattycoram, but to Miss Wade too. There was no answer so Mr Meagles besought Arthur to see once more what he could do. Arthur discovered that the empty house was left in charge of the old woman and that Miss Wade was gone. Mr Meagles, for six successive days, published a discreetly covert advertisement in the morning papers, to the effect that if a certain young person who had lately left home without reflection, would at any time apply to his address at Twickenham, everything would be as it had been before, and no reproaches need be apprehended. Still no answer. Mr Meagles and his family, under these combined discouragements, had begun reluctantly to give up Tattycoram as irrecoverable, when the new and active firm of Doyce and Clennam, in their private capacities, went down on a Saturday to stay at the cottage until Monday. The senior partner took the coach, and the junior partner took his walking-stick.

A tranquil summer sunset shone upon him as he approached the end of his walk, when he saw a figure in the path before him.

Minnie was there, alone. There was a flutter in her manner, which Clennam had never seen in it before; and as he came near her, it entered his mind all at once that she was there of a set purpose to speak to him.

She gave him her hand, and said, "You wonder to see me here by myself? But the evening is so lovely, I have strolled further than I meant at first. I thought it likely I might meet you, and that made me more confident. Mr Doyce arrived more than an hour ago, and told us you were walking down.

"Mr Clennam," she said, hesitating more timidly yet, and speaking so low that he bent his head to hear her. "I should very much like to give you my confidence, if you would not mind having the goodness to receive it. I should have very much liked to have given it to you long ago, because – I felt that you were becoming so much our friend."

"Pray give it to me. Pray trust me."

"I could never have been afraid of trusting you," she returned, raising her eyes frankly to his face. "I think I would have done so some time ago, if I had known how. But I scarcely know how, even now. I and Mr Gowan are to be married."

"Mr Gowan," said Arthur Clennam, "has reason to be very happy!"

She wept, as she tried to thank him as they walked on slowly and almost silently under the darkening trees.

"You know how I am loved at home," she said, "and how I love home – "

Pet's affectionate heart was overcharged, and she sobbed while she pictured what would happen.

"I know what a change Papa will feel at first, and I know that at first I cannot be to him anything like what I have been these many years. And it is then, Mr Clennam, then more than at any time, that I beg and entreat you to remember him, and sometimes to keep him company when you can spare a little while; and to tell him that you know I was fonder of him when I left him, than I ever was in all my life. And Mama, you know what a dear, devoted mother she is, and you will remember her too; will you not?"

Let Minnie trust him, Clennam said, let Minnie trust him to do all she wished.

"Oh, as you are a kind, true man! When I am first separated from home try to reconcile Papa to him a little more. Will you do this for me?"

They came out of the avenue next moment, arm-in-arm as they had entered it: and the trees seemed to close up behind them in the darkness, like their own perspective of the past.

The voices of Mr and Mrs Meagles and Doyce were audible directly, speaking near the garden gate. Pet glided away and Mr Meagles and Clennam walked up and down together.

"Arthur," said Mr Meagles, using that familiar address for the first time in their communication, "do you remember my telling you, as we walked up and down one hot morning, looking over the harbour at Marseilles, that Pet's baby sister who was dead seemed to Mother and me to have grown as she had grown, and changed as she had changed?"

"Very well."

"You remember my saying that our thoughts had never been able to separate those twin sisters, and that, in our fancy, whatever Pet was, the other was?"

"Yes, very well."

"Arthur," said Mr Meagles, much subdued, "I carry that fancy further tonight. I feel tonight, my dear fellow, as if you had loved my dead child very tenderly, and had lost her when she was like what Pet is now."

"Thank you!" murmured Clennam, "thank you!" And pressed his hand.

"Will you come in?" said Mr Meagles, presently.

"In a little while."

97

CHAPTER 27

Mrs Flintwinch in the Storm

The house in the city preserved its heavy dullness through all these transactions, and the invalid within it turned the same unvarying round of life.

There was a fair stroke of business doing, as Mistress Affery made out, for her husband had abundant occupation in his little office, and saw more people than had been used to come there for some years. This might easily be, the house having been long deserted; but he did receive letters and keep books, and correspond. Moreover, he went about to other counting-houses and other establishments. At some period of every day, he and Mrs Clennam held a council on matters of business; and it appeared to Affery, who was always groping about, listening and watching, that the two clever ones were making money.

The state of mind into which Mr Flintwinch's dazed lady had fallen had now begun to be so expressed in all her looks and actions that she was held in very low account by the two clever ones.

Little Dorrit had finished a long day's work in Mrs Clennam's room, and was neatly gathering up her shreds and odds and ends before going home, while Mr Pancks, whom Affery had just shown in, was addressing an inquiry to Mrs Clennam on the subject of her health.

"I bear what I have to bear," she answered. "You are often in this direction, are you not?"

"Why, yes, ma'am," said Pancks, "rather so lately."

"You have no need to trouble yourself to come."

"Not the least trouble, ma'am," said Mr Pancks. "You really are looking uncommonly nicely, ma'am."

"Thank you. Good evening."

Slowly and thoughtfully, Mrs Clennam's eyes turned from the door by which Pancks had gone out, to Little Dorrit, rising from the carpet.

"Little Dorrit," she said, when she at last broke silence, "what do you know of that man?"

"I don't know anything of him, ma'am, except that I have seen him about, and that he has spoken to me."

"What has he said to you?"

"I don't understand what he has said, he is so strange. But nothing rough or disagreeable."

"Why does he come here to see you?"

"I don't know, ma'am," said Little Dorrit, with perfect frankness.

"You know that he does come here to see you?"

"I have fancied so," said Little Dorrit. "But why he should come here or anywhere for that, ma'am, I can't think."

"Tell me, Little Dorrit," said Mrs Clennam, "have you many friends now?"

"Very few, ma'am. Besides you, only Miss Flora and – one more."

"Well!" said Mrs Clennam, almost smiling. "It is no affair of mine. I ask, because I take an interest in you; and because I believe I was your friend when you had no other who could serve you. Is that so?"

"Yes, ma'am; indeed it is."

"Are there many of you?" Mrs Clennam, looking towards the watch, once her dead husband's, which always lay upon her table.

"Only father and I, now. I mean, only father and I to keep regularly out of what we get."

"Have you undergone many privations? You and your father?"

"Sometimes it has been rather hard to live," said Little Dorrit, in her soft voice, and timid uncomplaining way; "but I think not harder – as to that – than many people find it."

"That's well said!" Mrs Clennam quickly returned. "That's the truth! You are a good, thoughtful girl. You are a grateful girl too, or I much mistake you."

"It is only natural to be that. There is no merit in being that," said Little Dorrit. "I am indeed."

"Now go, little Dorrit," said Mrs Clennam, "or you will be late, poor child."

A storm had blown up and Mrs Affery attended her going so that the house door might be safely shut. On opening it to let out Little Dorrit, she found Mr Pancks. The moment he saw Little Dorrit, he said with his finger to his nose (as Mrs Affery distinctly heard), "Pancks the gipsy, fortune-telling," and went away.

"Lord save us, here's a gipsy and a fortune-teller in it now!" cried Mistress Affery. She stood at the open door and watched the thunderstorm fly across the sky. Then the house door blew shut and in this dilemma, she ran crying up and down the solitary paved enclosure several times. She stooped down and looked in at the keyhole of the door as if an eye would open it, and from this posture started up suddenly, with a half scream, feeling something on her shoulder. It was the touch of a hand; of a man's hand.

The man was dressed like a traveller, in a foraging cap with fur about it, and a heap of cloak.

"What's the matter?" he asked in plain English. "What are you frightened at?"

"At you," panted Affery.

"Me, madam? Hah!" said the gentleman, who took that very coolly. "Indeed! Do you know such a name as Clennam about here?"

"Lord bless us, I should think I did, I should think I did!" cried Affery.

"Where about here?"

"Where!" cried Affery, goaded into another inspection of the keyhole. "Where but here in this house? And she's all alone in her room, and lost the use of her limbs and can't stir to help herself or me, and t'other clever one's out, and Lord forgive me! She's up there! Them two windows."

"Business-hours, I apprehend, are over for the day?"

"Yes, yes, yes," cried Affery. "Long ago."

"Let me make, then, a fair proposal. Fairness is a part of my character. I am just landed from the packet-boat and have been delayed by the infernal weather! In consequence of this, madam, some necessary business that I should otherwise have transacted here within the regular hours still remains to be done. Now, if you will fetch any authorised neighbouring somebody to do it, in return for my opening the door, I'll open the door."

At this moment Flintwinch appeared and saw the gentleman standing in the dark, and heard Mrs Clennam calling from her room.

CHAPTER 28

The Word of a Gentleman

The voice from upstairs called again and Affery cried: "It's all right. Affery is coming with a light."

"Be so good," said Jeremiah, closing the house door, and taking a pretty sharp survey of the smiling visitor in his turn, "as to step into my counting-house." Mr Flintwinch led the way into his own office, which presented a sufficiently business-like appearance. Here he put the light on his desk, and said to the stranger, with his wryest twist upon him, "Your commands."

"My name is Blandois."

"Blandois. I don't know it," said Jeremiah.

"I thought it possible," resumed the other, "that you might have been advised from Paris – "

"We have had no advice from Paris respecting anybody of the name of Blandois," said Jeremiah.

Mr Blandois, not at all put out by this omission on the part of the correspondents of the house of Clennam and Co., took his pocket-book from his breast-pocket, selected a letter from that receptacle, and handed it to Mr Flintwinch. "No doubt you are well acquainted with the writing. Perhaps the letter speaks for itself, and requires no advice. You are a far more competent judge of such affairs than I am. It is my misfortune to be, not so much a man of business, as a gentleman."

Mr Flintwinch took the letter, and read, under date of Paris, "We have to present to you, on behalf of a highly esteemed correspondent of our Firm, M. Blandois, of this city," &c. &c.

"Such facilities as he may require and such attentions as may lie in your power," &c. &c. "Also have to add that if you will honour M. Blandois' drafts at sight to the extent of, say Fifty Pounds sterling (£50)," &c. &c.

"Very good, sir," said Mr Flintwinch. "Take a chair. To the extent of anything that our House can do – we are in a retired, old-fashioned, steady way of business, sir – we shall be happy to render you our best assistance."

Mr Flintwinch had already begun to think this a highly gentlemanly personage and said, what could he have the honour of doing for Mr Blandois tonight, out of business hours?

"Faith!" returned that gentleman, shrugging his cloaked shoulders, "I must change, and eat and drink, and be lodged somewhere. Have the kindness to advise me, a total stranger, where, and money is a matter of perfect indifference until tomorrow. The nearer the place, the better. Next door, if that's all."

"There is," said Mr Flintwinch, with more than his usual deliberation, as he met, for a moment, Mr Blandois' shining eyes, which were restless; "there is a coffee-house and tavern close here, which, so far, I can recommend; but there's no style about it."

"I dispense with style!" said Mr Blandois, waving his hand. "Do me the honour to show me the house, and introduce me there, and I shall be infinitely obliged. And oblige me, by presenting my card of visit and adding that I shall be happy to wait on Mrs Clennam if it should suit her convenience to endure the presence of a stranger for a few minutes.

Jeremiah made all despatch, and said, on his return, "She'll be glad to see you, sir; but, being conscious that her sick room has no attractions, wishes me to say that she won't hold you to your offer, in case you should think better of it."

"To think better of it," returned the gallant Blandois, "would be to slight a lady." Thus expressing himself, he threw the draggled skirt of his cloak over his shoulder, and accompanied Mr Flintwinch to the tavern. Here, in dry clothes and scented linen, with sleeked hair, a great ring on each forefinger and a massive show of watch-chain, Mr Blandois waited for his dinner.

When he had finished he went straight back to the house of Clennam and Co. and was introduced to Mrs Clennam, who had his letter lying before her. She bent her head and requested him to sit. "I thank you, sir, for thinking of a disabled woman like me. Few who come here on business have any remembrance to bestow on one so removed from observation. My husband being dead and my son preferring another pursuit, our old House has no other representative in these days than Mr Flintwinch. You are English, sir?"

"Faith, madam, no; I am neither born nor bred in England. In effect, I am of no country," said Mr Blandois, stretching out his leg and smiting it: "I descend from half-a-dozen countries."

"You have been much about the world?"

"It is true. By Heaven, madam, I have been here and there and everywhere!"

"You have no ties, probably. Are not married?"

"Madam," said Mr Blandois, with an ugly fall of his eyebrows, "I adore your sex, but I am not married – never was."

Mistress Affery, who stood at the table near him, pouring out the tea, happened in her dreamy state to look at him as he said these words, and to fancy that she caught an expression in his eyes which attracted her own eyes so that she could not get them away.

"You'll excuse her, Mr Blandois," said Jeremiah, pouring out the tea himself, "she's failing and breaking up; that's what she's about. Do you take sugar, sir?"

"Thank you, no tea for me. – Pardon my observing it, but that's a very remarkable watch!"

The tea-table was drawn up near the sofa, with a small interval between it and Mrs Clennam's own particular table. Mr Blandois in his gallantry had risen to hand that lady her tea, and it was in placing the cup within her reach that the watch, lying before her as it always did, attracted his attention.

"May I be permitted? Thank you. A fine old-fashioned watch," he said, taking it in his hand. "May I remove it from the outer case? Thank you. An old silk watch-lining, worked with beads! I have seen these among old Dutch people and Belgians. Extraordinary how they used to complicate these ciphers. Now is this D.N.F.? It might be almost anything."

"Those letters are not intended, I believe, for the initials of any name," intervened Mrs Clennan.

"Of a motto, perhaps," said Mr Blandois, casually.

"Of a sentence. They have always stood, I believe, for Do Not Forget!"

"And naturally," said Mr Blandois, replacing the watch and stepping backward to his former chair, "you do not forget."

Mrs Clennam replied in a firm voice, "I do not forget. Hence I am contented, and say it is better with me than with millions."

As she spoke these words, she put her hand upon the watch, and restored it to the precise spot on her little table which it always occupied. With her touch lingering upon it, she sat for some moments afterwards, looking at it steadily and half-defiantly.

"This is an old room," Mr Blandois remarked, with a sudden sprightliness of manner, looking round when he got near the door, "I have been so interested that I have not observed it. But it's a genuine old room."

"It is a genuine old house," said Mrs Clennam, with her frozen smile. "A place of no pretensions, but a piece of antiquity."

"Faith!" cried the visitor. "If Mr Flintwinch would do me the favour to take me through the rooms on my way out, he could hardly oblige me more."

"I tell you beforehand, Mr Blandois, that you'll find it very dingy and very bare," said Jeremiah, taking up the candle. "It's not worth your looking at."

But Mr Blandois only laughed, kissed Mrs Clennam's hand and followed Jeremiah out of the room.

"You don't care to go upstairs?" said Jeremiah, on the landing.

"On the contrary, Mr Flintwinch; if not tiresome to you, I shall be ravished!"

Mr Flintwinch, therefore, wormed himself up the staircase, and Mr Blandois followed close. They ascended to the great garret bedroom which Arthur had occupied on the night of his return. "There, Mr Blandois!" said Jeremiah, showing it, "I hope you may think that worth coming so high to see. I confess I don't."

Mr Blandois being enraptured, they walked through other garrets and passages, and came down the staircase again. By this time Mr Flintwinch had remarked that he never found the visitor looking at any room, after throwing one quick glance around, but always found the visitor looking at him, Mr Flintwinch. With this discovery in his thoughts, he turned about on the staircase for another experiment. He met his eyes directly; and on the instant of their fixing one another, the visitor, with that ugly play of nose and moustache, laughed again, a diabolically silent laugh.

"A most admirable old house. So mysterious. Do you never hear any haunted noises here?"

"Noises," returned Mr Flintwinch. "No."

"Haha! A portrait here, I see." (Still looking at Mr Flintwinch, as if he were the portrait.) "May I ask the subject, Mr Flintwinch?"

"Mr Clennam, deceased. Her husband."

"Former owner of the remarkable watch, perhaps?" said the visitor.

Mr Flintwinch, who had cast his eyes towards the portrait, twisted himself about again, and again found himself the subject of the same look and smile. "Yes, Mr Blandois," he replied tartly. "It was his, and his uncle's before him, and Lord knows who before him; and that's all I can tell you of its pedigree."

"They must have been very happy," said Blandois.

"Who?" demanded Mr Flintwinch, with another screw at him.

Mr Blandois shook his right forefinger towards the sick room, and his left forefinger towards the portrait, and then, putting his arms akimbo and striding his legs wide apart, stood smiling down at Mr Flintwinch with the advancing nose and the retreating moustache.

"As happy as most other married people, I suppose," returned Mr Flintwinch. "I can't say. I don't know. There are secrets in all families."

"Secrets!" cried Mr Blandois, quickly. "Say it again, my son."

"I say," replied Mr Flintwinch, "I say there are secrets in all families."

"Favour me with the candle a moment," said Mr Blandois. "Let us have another look at the husband of the remarkable lady. Hah!" holding up the light at arm's length. "A decided expression of face here too, though not of the same character. Looks as if he were saying, what is it – Do Not Forget – does he not, Mr Flintwinch?"

"By Heaven, sir, he does!"

They had brought their survey to a close in the little room at the side of the hall, and he stood there, eyeing Mr Blandois.

"I am glad you are so well satisfied, sir," was his calm remark. "I didn't expect it. You seem to be quite in good spirits."

"In admirable spirits," returned Blandois. "Word of honour! Never more refreshed in spirits. Do you ever have presentiments, Mr Flintwinch?"

"I am not sure that I know what you mean by the term, sir," replied that gentleman.

"Say, in this case, Mr Flintwinch, undefined anticipations of pleasure to come."

"I can't say I'm sensible of such a sensation at present," returned Mr Flintwinch with the utmost gravity. "If I should find it coming on, I'll mention it."

"Now I," said Blandois, "I, my son, have a presentiment tonight that we shall be well acquainted. Do you find it coming on?"

"N-no," returned Mr Flintwinch, deliberately inquiring of himself. "I can't say I do."

"I have a strong presentiment that we shall become intimately acquainted. – You have no feeling of that sort yet?"

"Not yet," said Mr Flintwinch.

Mr Blandois, taking him by both shoulders again, rolled him about a little in his former merry way, then drew his arm through his own, and invited him to come off and drink a bottle of wine like a dear deep old dog as he was.

Without a moment's indecision, Mr Flintwinch accepted the invitation, and they went out to the quarters where the traveller was lodged, through a heavy rain which had rattled on the windows, roofs, and pavements, ever since nightfall. As time passed Mr Blandois grew indistinctly conscious of swaggering too fiercely and boastfully. He therefore terminated the entertainment at the end of the third bottle.

"You will draw upon us tomorrow, sir," said Mr Flintwinch, with a business-like face at parting.

"I'll draw upon you; have no fear. Adieu, my Flintwinch. By a thousand Thunders, you shall see me again!"

He did not present himself next day, though the letter of advice came duly to hand. Inquiring after him at night, Mr Flintwinch found, with surprise, that he had paid his bill and gone back to the Continent by way of Calais. Nevertheless, Jeremiah thought that Mr Blandois would keep his word and would be seen again.

CHAPTER 29

Spirit

Mrs Plornish's father – a poor little reedy piping old gentleman, like a worn-out bird; who had been in what he called the music-binding business, and met with great misfortunes, and who had seldom been able to make his way, or to see it or to pay it, or to do anything at all with it but find it no thoroughfare, had retired of his own accord to the Workhouse which was appointed by law to be the Good Samaritan of his district, on the settlement of that execution which had carried Mr Plornish to the Marshalsea College.

But no poverty in him, and no coat on him that never was the mode, and no Old Men's Ward for his dwelling-place, could quench his daughter's admiration. Mrs Plornish was as proud of her father's talents as she could possibly have been if they had made him Lord Chancellor. The poor little old man knew some pale and vapid little songs, long out of date, and Mrs Plornish declared she did believe there never was such a singer as Father, and wipe her eyes. Old Nandy, as he was called, had a patron. Mr Dorrit was in the habit of receiving him as if the old man held of him in vassalage under some feudal tenure.

It was Old Nandy's birthday, and they let him out. He said nothing about its being his birthday, or they might have kept him in; for such old men should not be born. He passed along the streets as usual to Bleeding Heart Yard, and had his dinner with his daughter and son-in-law, and gave them a song. He had hardly concluded, when Little Dorrit looked in to see how they all were.

"Miss Dorrit," said Mrs Plornish, "here's Father! Ain't he looking nice? And such voice he's in!"

Little Dorrit gave him her hand, and smilingly said she had not seen him this long time.

"No, they're rather hard on poor Father," said Mrs Plornish with a lengthening face, "and don't let him have half as much change and fresh air as would benefit him. But he'll soon be home for good, now. Won't you, Father?"

"Yes, my dear, I hope so. In good time, please God."

Mrs Plornish, who had been turning her face a little away with a corner of her apron in her hand, brought herself back to the conversation again by telling Miss Dorrit that Father was going over the water to pay his respects, unless she knew of any reason why it might not be agreeable.

Her answer was, "I am going straight home, and if he will come with me I shall be so glad to take care of him – so glad of his company."

"There, Father!" cried Mrs Plornish. "Ain't you a spritely young man to be going for a walk along with Miss Dorrit!"

They walked at a slow pace, and Little Dorrit took him by the Iron Bridge and sat him down there for a rest, and they looked over at the water and talked about the shipping. They were within five minutes of

107

their destination, when, at the corner of her own street, they came upon Fanny in her new bonnet, bound for the same port.

"Why, good gracious me, Amy!" cried that young lady, starting. "You never mean it!"

"Mean what, Fanny dear?"

"Oh! Don't Fanny me, you mean little thing, don't! The idea of coming along the open streets, in the broad light of day, with a Pauper!" (firing off the last word as if it were a ball from an air-gun).

"Oh Fanny!"

"I tell you not to Fanny me, for I'll not submit to it! I never knew such a thing. The way in which you are resolved and determined to disgrace us on all occasions, is really infamous. You bad little thing!"

"Does it disgrace anybody," said Little Dorrit, very gently, "to take care of this poor old man?"

"Yes, miss," returned her sister, "and you ought to know it does."

As they came to the Lodge they saw the Father of the Marshalsea sauntering towards it. As the spectacle of their approach met his view, he turned about and hurried in at his own doorway and up the staircase.

Leaving the old unfortunate, whom in an evil hour she had taken under her protection, with a hurried promise to return to him directly, Little Dorrit hastened after her father, and, on the staircase, found Fanny following her, and flouncing up with offended dignity. The three came into the room almost together; and when Fanny told him how she had seen Amy with a pauper, the Father sat down in his chair, buried his face in his hands, and uttered a groan.

"What is it, father?" cried Little Dorrit, bending over him. "Have I made you unhappy, father? Not I, I hope!"

"You hope, indeed! You common-minded little Amy! You complete prison-child! I have endured everything here but humiliation. That I have happily been spared – until this day."

Here his convulsive grasp unclosed itself, and he put his pocket-handkerchief to his eyes. Little Dorrit, on the ground beside him, with her imploring hand upon his arm, watched him remorsefully. Coming out of his fit of grief, he clenched his pocket-handkerchief once more.

Fanny, with a partly angry and partly repentant sob, began to cry herself, and to say that she wished she were dead.

The Father of the Marshalsea in the meantime took his younger daughter to his breast, and patted her head.

"There, there! I will forget it as soon as I can." His excited feelings might have found some further painful utterance, but for a knock at the door, which had been already twice repeated and to which Fanny (still wishing herself dead, and indeed now going so far as to add, buried) cried "Come in!"

"Ah, Young John!" said the Father, in an altered and calmed voice. "What is it, Young John?"

"A letter for you, sir, being left in the Lodge just this minute, and a message with it, I thought, happening to be there myself, sir, I would bring it to your room." The speaker's attention was much distracted by the piteous spectacle of Little Dorrit at her father's feet, with her head turned away.

"Indeed, John? Thank you."

"The letter is from Mr Clennam, sir – it's the answer – and the message was, sir, that Mr Clennam also sent his compliments, and word that he would do himself the pleasure of calling this afternoon, hoping to see you, and likewise," attention more distracted than before, "Miss Amy."

"Oh!" As the Father glanced into the letter (there was a bank-note in it), he reddened a little, and patted Amy on the head afresh.

"Thank you, Young John. Quite right. Much obliged to you for your attention. No one waiting?"

"No, sir, no one waiting."

"Thank you, John. How is your mother, Young John?"

"Thank you, sir, she's not quite as well as we could wish – in fact, we none of us are, except father – but she's pretty well, sir."

"Say we sent our remembrances, will you? Say kind remembrances, if you please, Young John. And send Old Nandy up to join us."

"Thank you, sir, I will." And Mr Chivery junior went his way.

"There, there, Amy!" said the Father, when Young John had closed the door, "let us say no more about it."

Nandy arrived and a little after Clennam presented himself. Mr Dorrit most graciously received him and besought him to join their meal.

"Amy, my love, you know Mr Clennam even better than I have the happiness of doing. This, Mr Clennam, you must know, is an old pensioner of mine, Old Nandy, a very faithful old man." (He always spoke of him as an object of great antiquity, but he was two or three years younger than himself.) "Let me see. You know Plornish, I think? I think my daughter Amy has mentioned to me that you know poor Plornish?"

"Oh yes!" said Arthur Clennam.

"Well, sir, this is Mrs Plornish's father."

"Indeed? I am glad to see him."

After supper, as Clennam had a purpose in remaining, he stood at the window while Maggy and her Little Mother washed the tea-service and cleared it away. He noticed that his companion stood at the window with the air of an affable and accessible Sovereign, and that, when any of his people in the yard below looked up, his recognition of their salutes just stopped short of a blessing.

When Little Dorrit had her work on the table, and Maggy hers on the bedstead, Fanny fell to tying her bonnet as a preliminary to her departure. Arthur, still having his purpose, remained. At this time the door opened, without any notice, and Mr Tip came in.

He kissed Amy as she started up to meet him, nodded to Fanny, nodded to his father, gloomed on the visitor without further recognition, and sat down.

"Tip, dear," said Little Dorrit, shocked by this, "don't you see – "

"Yes, I see, Amy. If you refer to the presence of any visitor you have here – I say, if you refer to that," answered Tip, jerking his head with emphasis towards his shoulder nearest Clennam, "I see!"

"Is that all you say?"

"That's all I say. And I suppose," added the lofty young man, after a moment's pause, "that visitor will understand me, when I say that's all I say. In short, I suppose the visitor will understand that he hasn't used me like a gentleman."

"I do not understand that," observed the obnoxious personage referred to with tranquillity.

"No? Why, then, to make it clearer to you, sir, I beg to let you know that when I address what I call a properly-worded appeal, and an urgent appeal, and a delicate appeal, to an individual, for a small temporary accommodation, easily within his power – easily within his power, mind! – and when that individual writes back word to me that he begs to be excused, I consider that he doesn't treat me like a gentleman."

The Father of the Marshalsea, who had surveyed his son in silence, no sooner heard this sentiment, than he began in angry voice: –

"How dare you – "

But his son stopped him.

"Now, don't ask me how I dare, father, because that's bosh. As to the fact of the line of conduct I choose to adopt towards the individual present, you ought to be proud of my showing a proper spirit."

"I should think so!" cried Fanny.

"A proper spirit?" said the Father. "Is it come to this that my son teaches me – *me* – !"

"Now, don't let us bother about it, father, or have any row on the subject. I have fully made up my mind that the individual present has not treated me like a gentleman. And there's an end of it. All I can do is to cut. Good-night, Amy. Don't be vexed. I am very sorry it happens here, and you here, upon my soul I am; but I can't altogether part with my spirit, even for your sake, old girl."

With those words he put on his hat and went out, accompanied by Miss Fanny.

When they were gone, the Father of the Marshalsea was at first inclined to sink into despondency again, and would have done so, but that a gentleman opportunely came up within a minute or two to attend him to the Snuggery. It was the gentleman Clennam had seen on the night of his own accidental detention there, who had come to escort the Father to the Chair, it being an occasion on which he had promised to preside over the assembled Collegians in the enjoyment of a little Harmony.

So, at last, Clennam's purpose in remaining was attained, and he could speak to Little Dorrit with nobody by, for Maggy, who was by, counted as nobody.

CHAPTER 30

More Fortune-telling

Arthur Clennam moved to sit down by the side of Little Dorrit, who trembled so much that he took hold of one of her hands.

"How seldom I have seen you lately, Little Dorrit!"

"I have been busy, sir."

"But I heard only today," said Clennam, "by mere accident, of your having been with those good people close by me. Why not come to me, then?"

"I – I don't know. Or rather, I thought you might be busy too. You generally are now, are you not?"

He saw her trembling little form and her downcast face, and the eyes that drooped the moment they were raised to his – he saw them almost with as much concern as tenderness.

"My child, your manner is so changed!"

The trembling was now quite beyond her control. Softly withdrawing her hand, and laying it in her other hand, she sat before him with her head bent and her whole form trembling.

"My own Little Dorrit," said Clennam, compassionately. She burst into tears. Maggy looked round of a sudden, and stared for at least a minute; but did not interpose. Clennam waited some little while before he spoke again.

"I cannot bear," he said then, "to see you weep; but I hope this is a relief to an overcharged heart."

She had taken courage now, and answered, far more in her usual manner, "You are so good! But even if there was nothing else in it to be sorry for and ashamed of, it is such a bad return to you – "

"Hush!" said Clennam, smiling and touching her lips with his hand.

In raising her eyes she observed his face more nearly than she had done yet, and said, with a quick change of tone, "You have not been ill, Mr Clennam?"

"No."

"Nor tried? Nor hurt?" she asked him, anxiously.

It fell to Clennam now, to be not quite certain how to answer. He said in reply: "To speak the truth, I have been a little troubled, but it is over. Do I show it so plainly? I ought to have more fortitude and self-control. Let me confess then, that I fancied I loved someone."

If he had known the sharpness of the pain he caused the patient heart, in speaking thus! While doing it, too, with the purpose of easing and serving her.

"I found that the day when any such thing would have been graceful in me, or good in me, or hopeful or happy for me or any one in connection with me, was gone, and would never shine again."

O! If he had known, if he had known! If he could have seen the dagger in his hand, and the cruel wounds it struck in the faithful bleeding breast of his Little Dorrit!

"All that is over, and I have turned my face from it. Now tell me, child, why have you kept so retired from me? Tell me."

"I am better here. My place and use are here. I am much better here," said Little Dorrit, faintly.

"So you said that day upon the bridge. I thought of it much afterwards. Have you no secret you could entrust to me, with hope and comfort, if you would!"

"Secret? No, I have no secret," said Little Dorrit in some trouble.

Arthur entreated her to see him oftener, and to remember that it was impossible to have a stronger interest in her welfare than he had, or to be more set upon promoting it than he was.

"Little Dorrit," he said, taking her hand again, and speaking lower than he had spoken yet, "you may have an interest – I will not say, now, though even that might be – may have, at another time, an interest in someone else; an interest not incompatible with your affection here."

She was very, very pale, and silently shook her head.

"It may be, dear Little Dorrit."

"No. No. No."

"Then you will trust me fully? Will have no secret unhappiness, or anxiety, concealed from me?"

"Almost none."

"And you have none now?"

She shook her head. But she was very pale.

"When I lie down tonight, and my thoughts come back – as they will, for they do every night, even when I have not seen you – to this sad place, I may believe that there is no grief beyond this room, now, and its usual occupants, which preys on Little Dorrit's mind?"

She seemed to catch at these words – that he remembered, too, long afterwards – and said, more brightly, "Yes, Mr Clennam; yes, you may!"

There was a knock at the door and there stood Mr Pancks without a hat and with his bare head in the wildest condition.

"Pancks the gipsy," he observed out of breath, "fortune-telling. How d'ye do, Miss Dorrit? I thought you wouldn't mind my running round, and looking in for a moment. Mr Clennam I heard was here, from Mr Dorrit. How are you, sir?"

Clennam thanked him, and said he was glad to see him.

"Capital company here," said Pancks. – "Eh, Miss Dorrit?"

She was half afraid of him, and irresolute what to say. He laughed, with a nod towards Clennam.

"Don't mind him, Miss Dorrit. He's one of us. We agreed that you shouldn't take on to mind me before people, but we didn't mean Mr Clennam. He's one of us. He's in it. An't you, Mr Clennam? – Eh, Miss Dorrit?"

The excitement of this strange creature was fast communicating itself to Clennam. Little Dorrit with amazement, saw this, and observed that they exchanged quick looks.

"I'm coming into my property, that's the fact," he went on. "But I shall be missed; and I don't want 'em to miss me. Mr Clennam, you and I made a bargain. I said you should find me stick to it. You shall find me stick to it now, sir, if you'll step out of the room a moment. Miss Dorrit, I wish you good-night. Miss Dorrit, I wish you good fortune."

He rapidly shook her by both hands, and puffed downstairs with Arthur following him.

"What is it, for Heaven's sake!" Arthur demanded, when they burst out there both together.

"Stop a moment, sir. Mr Rugg. Let me introduce him." With those words he presented another man without a hat, and with a cigar.

"Mr Clennam, Mr Rugg," said Pancks. "Stop a moment. Come to the pump."

Then and there, on that Marshalsea pavement, in the shades of evening, did Mr Pancks, of all mankind, fly over the head and shoulders of Mr Rugg of Pentonville, General Agent, Accountant, and Recoverer of Debts. Alighting on his feet, he took Clennam by the button-hole, led him behind the pump, and pantingly produced from his pocket a bundle of papers. Mr Rugg, also, pantingly produced from his pocket a bundle of papers.

"Stay!" said Clennam in a whisper. "You have made a discovery."

Mr Pancks answered, with an unction which there is no language to convey, "We rather think so."

"Does it implicate any one?"

"How implicate, sir?"

"In any suppression or wrong dealing of any kind?"

"Not a bit of it."

"Thank God!" said Clennam to himself. "Now show me."

"You are to understand" – snorted Pancks, feverishly unfolding papers, "that we are this very day virtually complete. We shan't be legally for a day or two. Call it at the outside a week. We've been at it night and day for I don't know how long. Mr Rugg, you know how long? Never mind. Don't say. You'll only confuse me. You shall tell her, Mr Clennam. Not till we give you leave. Where's that rough total, Mr Rugg? Oh! Here we are! There sir! That's what you'll have to break to her. That man's your Father of the Marshalsea!"

CHAPTER 31

What was Behind Mr Pancks on Little Dorrit's Hand

Resigning herself to inevitable fate, Mrs Gowan handsomely resolved not to oppose her son's marriage. In her progress to, and happy arrival at, this resolution, she was possibly influenced, not only by her maternal affections but by three politic considerations.

Of these, the first may have been that her son had never signified the smallest intention to ask her consent, or any mistrust of his ability to dispense with it; the second, that the pension bestowed upon her by a grateful country (and a Barnacle) would be freed from any little filial inroads, when her Henry should be married to the darling only child of a man in very easy circumstances; the third, that Henry's debts must clearly be paid down upon the altar-railing by his father-in-law.

Among her connections and acquaintances, however, she maintained her individual dignity and the dignity of the blood of the Barnacles, by diligently nursing the pretence that it was a most unfortunate business; that she had opposed it for a long time, but what could a mother do? She had a particularly long conversation with Mrs Merdle who was obsessed by Society and grieved capaciously with Mrs Gowan over this unfortunate match.

It was at this momentous time that another far greater change was to be announced. Mr Pancks, in discharge of his compact with Clennam, revealed to him the whole of his gipsy story, and told him Little Dorrit's fortune. Her father was heir-at-law to a great estate that had long lain

115

unknown of, unclaimed, and accumulating. His right was now clear, nothing interposed in his way, the Marshalsea gates stood open, the Marshalsea walls were down, a few flourishes of his pen, and he was extremely rich.

In his tracking out of the claim to its complete establishment, Mr Pancks had shown a sagacity that nothing could baffle, and a patience and secrecy that nothing could tire. "I little thought, sir," said Pancks, "when you and I crossed Smithfield that night, and I told you what sort of a Collector I was, that this would come of it. I little thought, sir, when I told you you were not of the Clennams of Cornwall, that I was ever going to tell you who were of the Dorrits of Dorsetshire." He then went on to detail. How, having that name recorded in his note-book, he was first attracted by the name alone. How, having often found two exactly similar names, even belonging to the same place, to involve no traceable consanguinity, near or distant, he did not at first give much heed to this, except in the way of speculation as to what a surprising change would be made in the condition of a little seamstress, if she could be shown to have any interest in so large a property.

How he rather supposed himself to have pursued the idea into its next degree, because there was something uncommon in the quiet little seamstress, which pleased him and provoked his curiosity.

How he had felt his way inch by inch, and "Moled it out, sir" (that was Mr Pancks's expression), grain by grain.

How he had made acquaintances in the Prison, expressly that he might come and go there as all other comers and goers did; and how his first ray of light was unconsciously given him by Mr Dorrit himself and by his son; to both of whom he easily became known; with both of whom he talked much, casually ("but always Moleing you'll observe," said Mr Pancks): and from whom he derived, without being at all suspected, two or three little points of family history which, as he began to hold clues of his own, suggested others. How it had at length become plain to Mr Pancks that he had made a real discovery of the heir-at-law to a great fortune, and that his discovery had but to be ripened to legal fullness and perfection. How he had, thereupon, sworn his landlord, Mr Rugg, to secrecy in a solemn manner, and taken him into Moleing partnership.

How they had employed John Chivery as their sole clerk and agent, seeing to whom he was devoted. And how, until the present hour, when authorities mighty in the Bank and learned in the law declared their successful labours ended, they had confided in no other human being.

"So if the whole thing had broken down, sir," concluded Pancks, "at the very last, say the day before the other day when I showed you our papers in the Prison yard, or say that very day, nobody but ourselves would have been cruelly disappointed, or a penny the worse."

Clennam, who had been almost incessantly shaking hands with him throughout the narrative, was reminded by this to say, in an amazement which even the preparation he had had for the main disclosure smoothed down, "My dear Mr Pancks, this must have cost you a great sum of money."

"Pretty well, sir," said the triumphant Pancks. "No trifle, though we did it as cheap as it could be done. And the outlay was a difficulty, let me tell you."

"A difficulty!" repeated Clennam. "But the difficulties you have so wonderfully conquered in the whole business!" shaking his hand again.

"I'll tell you how I did it," said the delighted Pancks, putting his hair into a condition as elevated as himself. "First, I spent all I had of my own. That wasn't much."

"I am sorry for it," said Clennam: "not that it matters now, though. Then, what did you do?"

"Then," answered Pancks, "I borrowed a sum of my proprietor."

"Of Mr Casby?" said Clennam. "He's a fine old fellow."

"Noble old boy; an't he?" said Mr Pancks, entering on a series of the dryest snorts. "Generous old buck. Confiding old boy. Philanthropic old buck. Benevolent old boy! Twenty per cent. I engaged to pay him, sir. But we never do business for less at our shop."

Arthur felt an awkward consciousness of having, in his exultant condition, been a little premature.

"I said to that boiling-over old Christian," Mr Pancks pursued, appearing greatly to relish this descriptive epithet, "that I had got a little project on hand; a hopeful one; I told him a hopeful one; which wanted a certain small capital. I proposed to him to lend me the money on my note. Which he did, at twenty. If I had broken down after that, I should have been his grubber for the next seven years at half wages and double grind. When that was gone, sir and it did go, though I dribbled it out like so much blood, I had taken Mr Rugg into the secret. I proposed to borrow of

117

Mr Rugg (or of Miss Rugg; it's the same thing; she made a little money by a speculation in the Common Pleas once). He lent it at ten, and thought that pretty high. But Mr Rugg's a red-haired man, sir, and gets his hair cut. And as to the crown of his hat, it's high. And as to the brim of his hat, it's narrow. And there's no more benevolence bubbling out of him, than out of a ninepin."

"Your own recompense for all this, Mr Pancks," said Clennam, "ought to be a large one."

"I don't mistrust getting it, sir," said Pancks. "I have made no bargain. I owed you one on that score; now I have paid it. Money out of pocket made good, time fairly allowed for, and Mr Rugg's bill settled, a thousand pounds would be a fortune to me. That matter I place in your hands. I authorise you now to break all this to the family in any way you think best. Miss Amy Dorrit will be with Mrs Finching this morning. The sooner done the better. Can't be done too soon."

This conversation took place in Clennam's bedroom, while he was yet in bed, for Mr Pancks had knocked up the house and made his way in, very early in the morning.

He now said he would "go and look up Mr Rugg", from whom his excited state of mind appeared to require another back; and bundling up his papers, and exchanging one more hearty shake of the hand with Clennam, he went at full speed downstairs, and steamed off.

Clennam, of course, resolved to go direct to Mr Casby's. He dressed and got out so quickly that he found himself at the corner of the patriarchal street nearly an hour before her time; but he was not sorry to have the opportunity of calming himself with a leisurely walk.

When he returned to the street, and had knocked at the bright brass knocker, he was shown upstairs to Flora's breakfast-room. Little Dorrit was not there herself, but Flora was, and testified the greatest amazement at seeing him.

"Good gracious, Arthur – Doyce and Clennam!" cried that lady, "who would have ever thought of seeing such a sight!"

She was making the tea when Arthur came in, and now hastily finished that operation.

Arthur then told her, in the fewest words, that it was their little friend he came to see; and what he had to announce to their little friend. At which astounding intelligence, Flora clasped her hands, fell into a tremble, and shed tears of sympathy and pleasure, like the good-natured creature she really was.

"For goodness sake let me get out of the way first," said Flora, putting her hands to her ears and moving towards the door, "or I know I shall go off dead and screaming and make everybody worse!"

Arthur nodded his free permission, since Flora shut out all verbal communication. Flora nodded in return to thank him, and hurried out of the room.

Little Dorrit's step was already on the stairs, and in another moment she was at the door. Do what he could to compose his face, he could not convey so much of an ordinary expression into it, but that the moment she saw it she dropped her work, and cried, "Mr Clennam! What's the matter?"

"Nothing, nothing. That is, no misfortune has happened. I have come to tell you something, but it is a piece of great good-fortune."

They stood in a window, and her eyes, full of light, were fixed upon his face. He put an arm about her, seeing her likely to sink down and repeated loudly, "Wonderful fortune. Dear Little Dorrit! Your father. Your father can be free within this week. He does not know it; we must go to him from here, to tell him of it. Your father will be free within a few days. Your father will be free within a few hours. Remember we must go to him from here, to tell him of it!"

That brought her back. Her eyes were closing, but they opened again.

"This is not all the good-fortune. This is not all the wonderful good-fortune, my dear Little Dorrit. Shall I tell you more?"

Her lips shaped "Yes."

"Your father will be no beggar when he is free. He will want for nothing. Shall I tell you more? Remember! He knows nothing of it; we must go to him, from here, to tell him of it! He will be a rich man. He is a rich man. A great sum of money is waiting to be paid over to him as his inheritance; you are all henceforth very wealthy. Bravest and best of children, I thank Heaven that you are rewarded!"

As he kissed her, she turned her head towards his shoulder, and raised her arm towards his neck; cried out "Father! Father! Father!" and swooned away.

But Little Dorrit's solicitude to get to her father, and to carry the joyful tidings to him, and not to leave him in his jail a moment with this

119

happiness in store for him and still unknown to him, did more for her speedy restoration than all the skill and attention on earth could have done. "Come with me to my dear father. Pray come and tell my dear father!" were the first words she said. Her father, her father. She spoke of nothing but him, thought of nothing but him. Kneeling down and pouring out her thankfulness with uplifted hands, her thanks were for her father.

Flora, who had by now returned, was quite overcome by this, and she launched out among the cups and saucers into a wonderful flow of tears and speech.

Little Dorrit thanked her, and embraced her, over and over again; and finally came out of the house with Clennam, and took coach for the Marshalsea.

When Mr Chivery, who was on duty, admitted them into the Lodge, he saw something in their faces which filled him with astonishment. He stood looking after them while they hurried into the prison, as though he perceived that they had come back accompanied by a ghost a-piece. Two or three Collegians whom they passed, looked after them too, and presently joining Mr Chivery, formed a little group on the Lodge steps, in the midst of which there spontaneously originated a whisper that the Father was going to get his discharge. Within a few minutes, it was heard in the remotest room in the College.

Little Dorrit opened the door from without, and they both entered.

He was sitting in his old grey gown and his old black cap, in the sunlight by the window, reading his newspaper. His glasses were in his hand, and he had just looked round; surprised at first, no doubt, by her step upon the stairs, not expecting her until night; surprised again, by seeing Arthur Clennam in her company. As they came in, the same unwonted look in both of them which had already caught attention in the yard below, struck him.

"Father!" cried Little Dorrit, "I have been made so happy this morning!"

"What surprise," he asked, keeping his left hand over his heart, and there stopping in his speech, while with his right hand he put his glasses exactly level on the table: "What such surprise can be in store for me?"

He looked steadfastly at Clennam, and, so looking at him, seemed to change into a very old haggard man. The sun was bright upon the wall beyond the window, and on the spikes at top. He slowly stretched out the hand that had been upon his heart, and pointed at the wall.

"It is down," said Clennam. "Gone!"

He remained in the same attitude, looking steadfastly at him.

"And in its place," said Clennam, slowly and distinctly, "are the means to possess and enjoy the utmost that they have so long shut out. Mr Dorrit, there is not the smallest doubt that within a few days you will be free, and highly prosperous. I congratulate you with all my soul on this change of fortune, and on the happy future into which you are soon to carry the treasure you have been blest with here – the best of all the riches you can have elsewhere – the treasure at your side."

With those words, he pressed his hand and released it; and his daughter, laying her face against his, encircled him in the hour of his prosperity with her arms, as she had in the long years of his adversity encircled him with her love and toil and truth; and poured out her full heart in gratitude, hope, joy, blissful ecstasy, and all for him.

"I shall see him as I never saw him yet. I shall see my dear love, with the dark cloud cleared away. I shall see him, as my poor mother saw him long ago. Oh my dear, my dear! Oh father! Oh thank God, thank God!"

He yielded himself to her kisses and caresses, but did not return them, except that he put an arm about her. Neither did he say one word. His steadfast look was now divided between her and Clennam. After this had lasted a while Clennam thought it a good reason for diverting his attention from the main surprise, by relating its details. Slowly, therefore, and in a quiet tone of voice, he explained them as best he could, and enlarged on the nature of Pancks's service.

"He shall be – ha – he shall be handsomely recompensed, sir," said the Father, starting up and moving hurriedly about the room. "Assure yourself, Mr Clennam, that everybody concerned shall be – ha – shall be nobly rewarded. No one, my dear sir, shall say that he has an unsatisfied claim against me. I shall repay the – hum – the advances I have had from you, sir, with peculiar pleasure. I beg to be informed at your earliest convenience, what advances you have made my son."

He had no purpose in going about the room, but he was not still a moment.

"Everybody," he said, "shall be remembered. I will not go away from here in anybody's debt. Chivery shall be rewarded. Young John shall be rewarded. I particularly wish, and intend, to act munificently, Mr Clennam."

"Will you allow me," said Arthur, laying his purse on the table, "to supply any present contingencies, Mr Dorrit? I thought it best to bring a sum of money for the purpose."

"Thank you, sir, thank you. I accept with readiness, at the present moment, what I could not an hour ago have conscientiously taken. I am obliged to you for the temporary accommodation. Exceedingly temporary, but well timed – well timed." His hand had closed upon the money, and he carried it about with him. "Be so kind, sir, as to add the amount to those former advances to which I have already referred; being careful, if you please, not to omit advances made to my son. A mere verbal statement of the gross amount is all I shall – ha – all I shall require."

His eye fell upon his daughter at this point, and he stopped for a moment to kiss her, and to pat her head.

"It will be necessary to find a milliner, my love, and to make a speedy and complete change in your very plain dress. Something must be done with Maggy too, who at present is – ha – barely respectable, barely respectable. And your sister, and your brother. And my brother, your uncle – poor soul, I trust this will rouse him – messengers must be despatched to fetch them. They must be informed of this. We must break it to them cautiously, but they must be informed directly."

This was the first intimation he had ever given, that he was privy to the fact that they did something for a livelihood.

He was still jogging about the room, with the purse clutched in his hand, when a great cheering arose in the yard. "The news has spread already," said Clennam, looking down from the window. "Will you show yourself to them, Mr Dorrit? They are very earnest, and they evidently wish it."

"I – hum – ha – I confess I could have desired, Amy my dear," he said, jogging about in a more feverish flutter than before, "to have made some change in my dress first, and to have bought a – hum – a watch and chain. But if it must be done as it is, it – ha – it must be done. Fasten the collar of my shirt, my dear. Mr Clennam, would you oblige me – hum – with a blue neckcloth you will find in that drawer at your elbow. Button my coat across at the chest, my love. It looks – ha – it looks broader, buttoned."

With his trembling hand he pushed his grey hair up, and then, taking Clennam and his daughter for supporters, appeared at the window leaning

122

on an arm of each. The Collegians cheered him very heartily, and he kissed his hand to them with great urbanity and protection.

Little Dorrit was deeply anxious that he should lie down to compose himself. On Arthur's speaking to her of his going to inform Pancks that he might now appear as soon as he would, and pursue the joyful business to its close, she entreated him in a whisper to stay with her until her father should be quite calm and at rest. He needed no second entreaty so she took her faithful place beside him, fanning him and cooling his forehead.

BOOK THE SECOND

RICHES

CHAPTER 1

Fellow Travellers

In the autumn of the year, Darkness and Night were creeping up to the highest ridges of the Alps.

Three parties had made their way to the monastic hostelry of the St Bernard Pass. In the travellers' book they wrote their names:

William Dorrit, Esquire	Miss Dorrit	*And Suite.*
Frederick Dorrit, Esquire	Miss Amy Dorrit	*(From France*
Edward Dorrit, Esquire	Mrs General	*to Italy.)*

Mr and Mrs Henry Gowan   *(From France to Italy.)*

To which was added, in a small complicated hand, ending with a long lean flourish, not unlike a lasso thrown at all the rest of the names:

Blandois   *(Paris. From France to Italy.)*

There were gloomy vaulted sleeping-rooms within, intensely cold, but clean and hospitably prepared for guests, and a parlour for guests to sit in and sup in, where a table was already laid, and where a blazing fire shone red and high.

In this room, after having had their quarters for the night allotted to them by two young Fathers, the travellers presently drew round the hearth eyeing each other drily, and waiting for supper. They exchanged news and it was thus they became familiar with each other. After supper Mrs Gowan went to lie down to recover from a fainting fit after a fall and Amy went to find her. Pet lay with closed eyes on the outside of the bed, protected from the cold by the blankets and wrappers with which she had been covered when she fainted. Amy timidly stepped to the bed, and said in a soft whisper, "Are you better?"

Pet had fallen into a slumber, and the whisper was too low to awake her. Her visitor, standing quite still, looked at her attentively.

"She is very pretty," she said to herself. "I never saw so beautiful a face. Oh how unlike me!"

It was a curious thing to say, but it had some hidden meaning, for it filled her eyes with tears.

With a quiet and tender hand she put aside a straying fold of the sleeper's hair, and then touched the hand that lay outside the covering.

"I like to look at her," she breathed to herself. "I like to see what has affected him so much."

She had not withdrawn her hand, when the sleeper opened her eyes and started.

"Pray don't be alarmed. I am only one of the travellers from downstairs. I came to ask if you were better, and if I could do anything for you."

"I think you have already been so kind as to send your servants to my assistance?"

"No, not I; that was my sister. Are you better?"

"Much better. It is only a slight bruise, and has been well looked to, and is almost easy now. It made me giddy and faint in a moment."

"May I stay with you until someone comes? Would you like it?"

"I should like it, for it is lonely here; but I am afraid you will feel the cold too much."

"I don't mind cold. I am not delicate, if I look so." She quickly moved one of the two rough chairs to the bedside, and sat down.

The other as quickly moved a part of some travelling wrapper from herself, and drew it over her, so that her arm, in keeping it about her, rested on her shoulder.

"You have so much the air of a kind nurse," said Pet, smiling on her, "that you seem as if you had come to me from home."

"I am very glad of it."

"I was dreaming of home when I woke just now. Of my old home, I mean, before I was married."

"And before you were so far away from it."

"I have been much farther away from it than this; but then I took the best part of it with me, and missed nothing. I felt solitary as I dropped asleep here, and, missing it a little, wandered back to it." There was a sorrowfully affectionate and regretful sound in her voice, which made Amy refrain from looking at her for the moment.

"It is a curious chance which at last brings us together," said Amy after a pause; "for do you know, I think I have been looking for you some time."

"Looking for me?"

"I believe I have a little note here from Arthur which I was to give to you whenever I found you. This is it. Unless I greatly mistake, it is addressed to you? Is it not?"

Pet took it, and said yes, and read it. Amy watched her as she did so. It was very short. She flushed a little as she put her lips to her visitor's cheek, and pressed her hand.

"The dear young friend to whom he presents me, may be a comfort to me at some time, he says. She is truly a comfort to me the first time I see her."

"Perhaps you don't – " said Amy, hesitating – "perhaps you don't know my story? Perhaps he never told you my story?"

"No."

"Oh no, why should he! I have scarcely the right to tell it myself at present, because I have been entreated not to do so. There is not much in it, but it might account to you for my asking you not to say anything about the letter here. You saw my family with me, perhaps? Some of them – I only say this to you – are a little proud, a little prejudiced."

"You shall take it back again," said Pet; "and then my husband is sure not to see it. He might see it and speak of it, otherwise, by some accident. Will you put it in your bosom again, to be certain?"

She did so with great care. Her small, slight hand was still upon the letter, when they heard someone in the gallery outside.

"I promised," said Amy, rising, "that I would write to him after seeing you (I could hardly fail to see you sooner or later), and tell him if you were well and happy. I had better say you were well and happy."

"Yes, yes, yes! Say I was very well and very happy. And that I thanked him affectionately, and would never forget him."

"I shall see you in the morning. After that we are sure to meet again before very long. Good-night!"

"Good-night. Thank you, thank you. Good-night, my dear!"

Both of them were hurried and fluttered as they exchanged this parting. As Amy came out of the door a man outside turned round – for he was walking away in the dark.

His politeness, which was extreme, meant he took her lamp, held it so as to throw the best light on the stone steps, and followed her all the way to the supper-room. She went with him, not easily hiding how much she was inclined to shrink and tremble; for the appearance of this traveller was particularly disagreeable to her.

He followed her down with his smiling politeness and resumed his seat in the best place in the hearth. There with the wood-fire, which was beginning to burn low, rising and falling upon him in the dark room, he sat with his legs thrust out to warm, drinking the hot wine down to the lees, with a monstrous shadow imitating him on the wall and ceiling.

The tired company had broken up, and all the rest were gone to bed except Mr Dorrit, who dozed in his chair by the fire.

The traveller had been at the pains of going upstairs to his sleeping-room to fetch his pocket-flask of brandy. He told them so, as he poured its contents into what was left of the wine, and drank with a new relish.

"May I ask, sir, if you are on your way to Italy?"

The grey-haired gentleman had roused himself, and was preparing to withdraw. He answered in the affirmative.

"I also!" said the traveller. "I shall hope to have the honour of offering my compliments in fairer scenes, and under softer circumstances, than on this dismal mountain."

Amy's father bowed, distantly enough, and said he was obliged to him.

"We poor gentlemen, sir," said the traveller, pulling his moustache dry with his hand, for he had dipped it in the wine and brandy; "we poor gentlemen do not travel like princes, but the courtesies and graces of life are precious to us. To your health, sir!"

"Sir, I thank you."

"To the health of your distinguished family – of the fair ladies, your daughters!"

"Sir, I thank you again, I wish you good-night. My dear, are our – ha – our people in attendance?"

"They are close by, father."

"Permit me!" said the traveller, rising and holding the door open, as the gentleman crossed the room towards it with his arm drawn through his daughter's. "Good repose! To the pleasure of seeing you once more! To tomorrow!"

As he kissed his hand, with his best manner and his daintiest smile, the young lady drew a little nearer to her father, and passed him with a dread of touching him.

"Humph!" said the insinuating traveller, whose manner shrunk, and whose voice dropped when he was left alone. "If they all go to bed, why I must go. They are in a devil of a hurry. One would think the night would be long enough, in this freezing silence and solitude, if one went to bed two hours hence."

CHAPTER 2

On the Road

When Mrs General lost her husband it occurred to her, that she might "form the mind," and eke the manners of some young lady of distinction. Or, that she might harness the proprieties to the carriage of some rich young heiress or widow. Testimonials representing Mrs General as a prodigy of piety, learning, virtue, and gentility, were lavishly contributed from influential quarters.

At the same time Mr Dorrit, who had lately succeeded to his property, mentioned to his bankers that he wished to discover a lady, well-bred, accomplished, well connected, well accustomed to good society, who was qualified at once to complete the education of his daughters, and to be their matron or chaperon. Mr Dorrit's bankers, as bankers of the county-widower, instantly said, "Mrs General." He took the trouble of going down to the county of the county-widower to see Mrs General, in whom he found a lady of a quality superior to his highest expectations and an agreement was arrived at which led to her presence on their journeys across Europe.

As they set out for Venice, the bright morning sun dazzled the courier of the Dorrit family, who was making tea for his party.

Mr Gowan and Blandois of Paris had already breakfasted, and were walking up and down by the lake, smoking their cigars.

"Gowan, eh?" muttered Tip, otherwise Edward Dorrit, Esquire. "How's his wife, Amy?"

"She is better, Edward. But they are not going today."

"Oh! They are not going today! Fortunately for that fellow too," said Tip, "or he and I might have come into collision."

"It is thought better here that she should lie quiet today, and not be fatigued and shaken by the ride down until tomorrow."

"You talk as if you had been nursing her. You haven't been relapsing into old habits, have you, Amy?"

He asked her the question with a sly glance of observation at Miss Fanny, and at his father too.

"I have only been in to ask her if I could do anything for her, Tip," said Little Dorrit.

"You needn't call me Tip, Amy child," returned that young gentleman with a frown; "because that's an old habit, and one you may as well lay aside."

"And my dear Amy, you must lay aside waiting on people," instructed Miss Fanny arrogantly.

"I don't so much mind that once in a way," remarked Mr Edward. "But your Clennan, as he thinks proper to call himself, is another thing."

"He is part of the same thing," returned Miss Fanny, "and of a piece with all the rest. He obtruded himself upon us in the first instance. We never wanted him."

"Fanny," returned her father, grandiloquently, "give me leave, my dear. I am free to say that I do not, Amy, share your sister's sentiments – that is to say altogether – hum – altogether – in reference to Mr Clennam. I am content to regard that individual in the light of – ha – generally – a well-behaved person. Hum. A well-behaved person. Ha! Mrs General!"

The entrance of the lady whom he announced, to take her place at the breakfast-table, terminated the discussion. Shortly afterwards, the courier announced that the valet, and the footman, and the two maids, and the four guides, and the fourteen mules, were in readiness; so the breakfast party went out to the convent door to join the cavalcade.

Mr Gowan stood aloof with his cigar and pencil, but Mr Blandois was on the spot to pay his respects to the ladies. Little Dorrit thought he had even a more sinister look, standing swart and cloaked in the snow, than he had in the fire-light over-night.

More treacherous than snow, perhaps, colder at heart, and harder to melt, Blandois of Paris by degrees passed out of her mind, as they came down into the softer regions.

They stopped briefly at Martigny where Mr Dorrit had a row over his room that was already occupied by none other than Mrs Merdle who was travelling with her son, Mr Sparkler.

When the procession was again in motion Little Dorrit sat opposite her father in the travelling-carriage, and recalling the old Marshalsea room, her present existence was a dream. All that she saw was new and wonderful, but it was not real; it seemed to her as if those visions of mountains and picturesque countries might melt away at any moment, and the carriage, turning some abrupt corner, bring up with a jolt at the old Marshalsea gate.

On their journey there were places where they stayed the week together in splendid rooms, where they rode out among heaps of wonders, walked through miles of palaces, and rested in dark corners of great churches.

Through such scenes, the family procession moved on to Venice. And here it dispersed for a time, as they were to live in Venice some few months in a palace (itself six times as big as the whole Marshalsea) on the Grand Canal.

Little Dorrit, quite lost by her new life, often sat down to muse. Social people in other gondolas began to ask each other who the little solitary girl was whom they passed, looking so pensively and wonderingly about her. Little Dorrit, in her quiet, scared, lost manner, went about the city none the less.

As she did so she would think of that old gate, and of herself sitting at it in the dead of the night, pillowing Maggy's head; and of other places and of other scenes associated with those different times. And then she would lean upon her balcony, and look over at the water, as though they all lay underneath it. She would musingly watch its running, as if, in the general vision, it might run dry, and show her the prison again, and herself, and the old room, and the old inmates, and the old visitors: all lasting realities that had never changed.

CHAPTER 3

Something Wrong Somewhere

The family had been a month or two at Venice, when Mr Dorrit, who was much among Counts and Marquises, and had but scant leisure, set an hour of one day apart, beforehand, for the purpose of holding some conference with Mrs General.

The time he had reserved in his mind arriving, he sent Mr Tinkler, his valet, to Mrs General's apartment to present his compliments to that lady, and represent him as desiring the favour of an interview.

"Mrs General," said Mr Dorrit, when she came " – I took the liberty to solicit the favour of a little private conversation with you, because I feel rather worried respecting my – ha – my younger daughter. You will have observed a great difference of temperament, madam, between my two daughters?"

"Fanny," returned Mrs General, "has force of character and self-reliance. Amy, none."

"You are aware, my dear madam," said Mr Dorrit, "that my daughters had the misfortune to lose their lamented mother when they were very young; and that, in consequence of my not having been until lately the recognised heir to my property, they have lived with me as a comparatively poor, though always proud, gentleman, in – ha hum – retirement! There is adaptability of character in Fanny. But my younger daughter, Mrs General, rather worries and vexes my thoughts. I must inform you that she has always been my favourite."

"There is no accounting," said Mrs General, "for these partialities."

"How would you advise me?"

"I am happy," returned Mrs General, "to be so corroborated. I would therefore the more confidently recommend that Mr Dorrit should speak to

130

Amy himself, and make his observations and wishes known to her. Being his favourite, besides, and no doubt attached to him, she is all the more likely to yield to his influence."

"I had anticipated your suggestion, madam," said Mr Dorrit, "but – ha – was not sure that I might – hum – not encroach on – "

"On my province, Mr Dorrit?" said Mrs General, graciously. "Do not mention it."

"Then, with your leave, madam," resumed Mr Dorrit, ringing his little bell to summon his valet, "I will send for her at once."

"Does Mr Dorrit wish me to remain?"

"Perhaps, if you have no other engagement, you would not object for a minute or two – "

"Not at all."

"Amy," said Mr Dorrit, when she came in, "you have just now been the subject of some conversation between myself and Mrs General. We agree that you scarcely seem at home here. Ha – how is this?"

A pause.

"I think, father, I require a little time."

"Pray, my child," said Mr Dorrit, "attend to the – hum – precepts of Mrs General."

Poor Little Dorrit, with a rather forlorn glance at that eminent varnisher, promised to try.

"I do beg," said Mr Dorrit, "that you will seriously take pains and try to conduct yourself in a manner both becoming your position as – ha – Miss Amy Dorrit, and satisfactory to myself and Mrs General."

That lady shut her eyes, on being again referred to; then, slowly opening them and rising, added these words:

"May I take this opportunity of remarking, as an instance in point, that it is scarcely delicate to look at vagrants with the attention which I have seen bestowed upon them by a very dear young friend of mine? They should not be looked at. Nothing disagreeable should ever be looked at."

Little Dorrit, whether speaking or silent, had preserved her quiet earnestness and her loving look. It had not been clouded, except for a passing moment, until now. But once she was left alone with her father, the fingers of her lightly folded hands were agitated, and there was repressed emotion in her face.

Not for herself. She felt that, in what he had just now said to her and in his whole bearing towards her, there was the well-known shadow of the Marshalsea wall. It took a new shape, but it was the old sad shadow. She began with sorrowful unwillingness to acknowledge to herself that she was not strong enough to keep off the fear that no space in the life of man could overcome that quarter of a century behind the prison bars. She had no blame to bestow upon him, therefore: nothing to reproach him with, no emotions in her faithful heart but great compassion and unbounded tenderness.

This is why it was, that, even as he sat before her on his sofa, in the brilliant light of a bright Italian day, the wonderful city without and the splendours of an old palace within, she saw him at the moment in the long-familiar gloom of his Marshalsea lodging, and wished to take her seat beside him, and comfort him, and be again full of confidence with him, and of usefulness to him.

At breakfast, Mr Frederick Dorrit, who had been out earlier with Amy, referred to their having seen in a gallery, on the previous day, the lady and gentleman whom they had encountered on the Great Saint Bernard.

"I should have mentioned our having met Mr and Mrs Gowan, Fanny," said Little Dorrit. "I should like to pay a visit to Mrs Gowan, and to become better acquainted with her, if Papa and Mrs General do not object."

At this remark the face of Mr Dorrit gloomed considerably. He was about (connecting the accrediting with an obtrusive person of the name of Clennam, whom he imperfectly remembered in some former state of existence) to black-ball the name of Gowan finally, when Edward Dorrit, Esquire, came into the conversation.

"Perhaps it's a matter of policy to let you all know that these Gowans – in whose favour, or at least the gentleman's, I can't be supposed to be much prepossessed myself – are known to people of importance, such as the Merdles who you will remember were at Martigny when we were there."

"Under these circumstances," said Mr Dorrit, "I believe I express the sentiments of – ha – Mrs General, no less than my own, when I say that there is no objection, but – ha hum – quite the contrary – to your gratifying your desire, Amy."

CHAPTER 4

Something Right Somewhere

It always soon came to be understood, wherever he and his wife went, that Henry Gowan had married against the wishes of his exalted relations, and had had much ado to prevail on them to countenance her. From the days of their honeymoon, Minnie Gowan felt sensible of being usually regarded as the wife of a man who had made a descent in marrying her, but whose chivalrous love for her had cancelled that inequality.

To Venice they had been accompanied by Monsieur Blandois of Paris, and at Venice Monsieur Blandois of Paris was very much in the society of Gowan.

It chanced, however, that his wife expressed a dislike to the engaging Blandois, and that the balance of feeling in the hotel was against him. Upon it, Gowan resolved to encourage him.

He found a pleasure in declaring that a courtier with the refined manners of Blandois ought to rise to the greatest distinction in any polished country, thus he had glided into a way of having him for a companion.

In the meanwhile Little Dorrit would have been glad to make her visit to Mrs Gowan, alone; but as Fanny decided to go, the two sisters stepped together into one of the gondolas under Mr Dorrit's window, and, with the courier in attendance, were taken in high state to Mrs Gowan's lodging.

The house, on a little desert island, looked as if it had broken away from somewhere else, and had floated by chance into its present anchorage in company with a vine almost as much in want of training as the poor wretches who were lying under its leaves.

On the first-floor of the house was a Bank and above the Bank was Mrs Gowan's residence.

The door was opened by a smiling man like a reformed assassin – a temporary servant – who ushered them into the room where Mrs Gowan sat, with the announcement that two beautiful English ladies were come to see the mistress.

"We have been," said Fanny, "charmed to understand that you know the Merdles. We hope it may be another means of bringing us together."

"They are friends," said Mrs Gowan, "of Mr Gowan's family. I have

133

not yet had the pleasure of a personal introduction to Mrs Merdle, but I suppose I shall be presented to her at Rome."

"Indeed?" returned Fanny, with an appearance of amiably quenching her own superiority. "I think you'll like her."

"You know her very well?"

"Why, you see," said Fanny, with a frank action of her pretty shoulders, "in London one knows every one."

Although the visit had as yet given Little Dorrit no opportunity of conversing with Mrs Gowan, there was a silent understanding between them, which did as well.

"You have been quite well," she now said, "since that night?"

"Quite, my dear. And you?"

"Oh! I am always well," said Little Dorrit, timidly. "I – yes, thank you."

"You don't know that you are a favourite of my husband's, and that I am almost bound to be jealous of you?" said Mrs Gowan. "I must tell him you are here. I should never be forgiven, if I were to let you – and Miss Dorrit – go, without doing so. May I? You can excuse the disorder and discomfort of a painter's studio?"

The inquiries were addressed to Miss Fanny, who graciously replied that she would be beyond anything interested and enchanted.

The first object that confronted Little Dorrit on entering into Henry Gowan's studio, was Blandois of Paris in a great cloak and a furtive slouched hat, standing on a throne platform in a corner. She recoiled from this figure, as it smiled at her. Once attracted by his peculiar eyes, she could not remove her own. She trembled now and Gowan, supposing her to be alarmed by the large, agitated dog beside him, threw down his brush, and seized the dog with both hands by the collar.

"Blandois! How can you be such a fool as to provoke him! By Heaven, and the other place too, he'll tear you to bits! Lie down! Lion!" He was up on his hind legs, and it was a wrestle between master and dog. "Get out of his sight, Blandois! What devil have you conjured into the dog? By my soul, he'll kill you!"

The dog, with a ferocious bark, made one other struggle as Blandois vanished; then, in the moment of the dog's submission, the master felled him with a blow, and standing over him, struck him many times severely with the heel of his boot, so that his mouth was presently bloody.

134

"Now get you into that corner and lie down," said Gowan, "or I'll take you out and shoot you."

Minnie was very much disturbed and Little Dorrit was already occupied in soothing her; Fanny, who had cried out twice or thrice, held Gowan's arm for protection; Lion, deeply ashamed of having caused them this alarm, came trailing himself along the ground to the feet of his mistress.

"You furious brute," said Gowan, striking him with his foot again. "You shall do penance for this." And he struck him again, and yet again.

"O, pray don't punish him any more," cried Little Dorrit. "Don't hurt him. See how gentle he is!"

In such further communication as passed among them before the sisters took their departure, Little Dorrit fancied it was revealed to her that Mr Gowan treated his wife, even in his very fondness, too much like a beautiful child.

Gowan attended them down the staircase, leaving the two together under the scrap of vine upon the causeway from which the sisters were paddled away in state as they had come. They had not glided on for many minutes, when Little Dorrit became aware that another gondola was evidently in waiting on them. It was Mr Sparkler, Mrs Merdle's son.

"Here he is again," cried Fanny. "Look at him. Oh, you simpleton!"

Mr Sparkler had, undeniably, a weak appearance; with his eye in the window like a knot in the glass.

"Do you mean to encourage Mr Sparkler, Fanny?"

"Encourage him, my dear?" said her sister, smiling contemptuously, "that depends upon what you call encourage. No, I don't mean to encourage him. But I'll make a slave of him. I shall make him fetch and carry, my dear, and I shall make him subject to me. And if I don't make his mother subject to me, too, it shall not be my fault."

Miss Fanny made as if she had no recollection of having ever seen him before, and was passing on, with a distant inclination of her head, when he announced himself by name. Even then she was in a difficulty from being unable to call it to mind, until he explained that he had had the honour of seeing her at Martigny. Then she remembered him, and hoped his lady-mother was well.

"Thank you," stammered Mr Sparkler, "she's uncommonly well."

"In Venice?" said Miss Fanny.

135

"In Rome," Mr Sparkler answered. "I am here by myself. I came to call upon Mr Edward Dorrit myself. Indeed, upon Mr Dorrit likewise. In fact, upon the family."

When he arrived at their palace, Mr Dorrit welcomed the visitor with the highest urbanity, and most courtly manners. He inquired particularly after Mrs Merdle. He expressed his hope that Mr Sparkler would shortly dine with them and would he like to accompany the ladies to the Opera in the evening.

At dinner-time Mr Sparkler rose out of the sea, like Venus's son taking after his mother, and made a splendid appearance ascending the great staircase. If Fanny had been charming in the morning, she was now thrice charming, very becomingly dressed in her most suitable colours, and with an air of negligence upon her that doubled Mr Sparkler's fetters, and riveted them.

"I hear you are acquainted, Mr Sparkler," said his host at dinner, "with – ha – Mr Gowan. Mr Henry Gowan?"

"Perfectly, sir," returned Mr Sparkler. "His mother and my mother are cronies in fact."

"If I had thought of it, Amy," said Mr Dorrit, with a patronage as magnificent as that of Lord Decimus himself, "you should have despatched a note to them, asking them to dine today."

He enquired as to whether Mr Gowan painted portraits. Mr Sparkler opined that he painted anything, if he could get the job.

"Well!" said Mr Dorrit. "I think I must engage Mr Gowan to paint my picture."

That evening they took a boat to attend the Opera. Among the loiterers by the river was Blandois of Paris who handed Fanny into the boat.

"Gowan has had a loss," he said, "since he was made happy today by a visit from fair ladies."

"A loss?" repeated Fanny, relinquished by the bereaved Sparkler, and taking her seat.

"A loss," said Blandois. "His dog Lion."

Little Dorrit's hand was in his, as he spoke.

"He is dead," said Blandois.

"Dead?" echoed Little Dorrit. "That noble dog?"

"Faith, dear ladies!" said Blandois, smiling and shrugging, "somebody has poisoned that noble dog. He is as dead as the Doges!"

CHAPTER 5

Mostly Prunes and Prism

"Amy," said Fanny to her one night when they were alone, after a day so tiring that Little Dorrit was quite worn out, though Fanny would have taken another dip into society with the greatest pleasure in life, "I am going to put something into your little head. You won't guess what it is, I suspect."

"I don't think that's likely, dear," said Little Dorrit.

"Come, I'll give you a clue, child," said Fanny. "Mrs General."

Prunes and Prism, in a thousand combinations, having been wearily in the ascendant all day, Little Dorrit looked as if she hoped that Mrs General was safely tucked up in bed.

"Has it never struck you, Amy, that Pa is monstrously polite to Mrs General?"

Amy, murmuring, "No," looked quite confounded.

"No, I dare say not. But he is," said Fanny. "And remember my words. Mrs General has designs on Pa!"

"Dear Fanny," said Amy thoughtfully, "do you think it possible that Mrs General has designs on anyone?"

"Do I think it possible?" retorted Fanny. "My love, I know it. I tell you she has designs on Pa. And more than that, I tell you Pa considers her such a wonder, such a paragon of accomplishment, and such an acquisition to our family, that he is ready to get himself into a state of perfect infatuation with her at any moment."

"You may be mistaken, Fanny. Now, may you not?"

"Oh yes, I *may* be," said Fanny, "but I am not. However, I am glad you can contemplate such an escape, my dear, and I am glad that you can take this for the present with sufficient coolness to think of such a chance. It makes me hope that you may be able to bear the connection. I should not be able to bear it, and I should not try. I'd marry young Sparkler first."

"Oh, you would never marry him, Fanny, under any circumstances."

"Upon my word, my dear," rejoined that young lady with exceeding indifference, "I wouldn't positively answer even for that. There's no knowing what might happen."

Blandois called to pay his respects and accepted the commission to ask his Gowan whether he would paint Mr Dorrit's portrait. His imparting the news to Gowan, that Master gave Mr Dorrit to the Devil with great liberality some round dozen of times (for he resented patronage almost as much as he resented the want of it). Yet he added with feeling: "We journeymen must take jobs when we can get them. Shall we go and look after this job?"

Mr Dorrit received them in the presence of his daughters and of Mr Sparkler, who happened, by some surprising accident, to be calling there.

"How are you, Sparkler?" said Gowan carelessly. "When you have to live by your mother wit, old boy, I hope you may get on better than I do."

Mr Dorrit then mentioned his proposal. "Sir," said Gowan, "I'll do the best I can for the money. I hear you are going to Rome. I am going to Rome, having friends there. Let me begin to do you the injustice I have conspired to do you, there – not here."

These remarks were the prelude to the first reception of Mr and Mrs Gowan at dinner, and they skilfully placed Gowan on his usual ground in the new family.

His wife, too, they placed on her usual ground. Miss Fanny understood, with particular distinctness, that Mrs Gowan's good looks had cost her husband very dear. Of honest Mr Meagles no mention was made; except that it was natural enough that a person of that sort should wish to raise his daughter out of his own obscurity, and that no one could blame him for trying his best to do so.

Little Dorrit could see that it had its part in throwing upon Mrs Gowan the touch of a shadow under which she lived. There was a sympathetic understanding already established between the two, which would have carried them over greater difficulties, and made a friendship out of a more restricted intercourse. Also each perceived that the other felt towards Blandois of Paris an aversion amounting to the repugnance and horror of a natural antipathy towards an odious creature of the reptile kind. There was a passive congeniality between them, besides this active one. To both of them, Blandois behaved in exactly the same manner; and to both of them his manner had uniformly something in it, which they both knew to be different from his bearing towards others. The difference was too minute in its expression to be perceived by others, but they knew it to be there.

This had never been felt by them both in so great a degree, and never by each so perfectly to the knowledge of the other, as on a day when he came to Mr Dorrit's to take his leave before quitting Venice. Mrs Gowan was herself there for the same purpose, and he came upon the two together, the rest of the family being out. The two had not been together five minutes when Blandois's peculiar manner seemed to convey to them, "You were going to talk about me. Ha! Behold me here to prevent it!"

"Gowan is coming here?" said Blandois, with a smile.

Mrs Gowan replied he was not coming.

"Not coming!" said Blandois. "Then permit your devoted servant, when you leave here, to escort you home."

"Thank you: I am not going home."

"Not going home!" said Blandois. "Then I am forlorn."

That he might be; but he was not so forlorn as to roam away and leave them together. He sat entertaining them with his finest compliments, and his choicest conversation; but he conveyed to them, all the time, "No, no, no, dear ladies. Behold me here expressly to prevent Mrs Gowan staying!"

He conveyed it to them with so much meaning, and he had such a diabolical persistency in him, that at length, Mrs Gowan rose to depart. On his offering his hand to Mrs Gowan to lead her down the staircase, she retained Little Dorrit's hand in hers, with a cautious pressure, and said, "No, thank you. But, if you will please to see if my boatman is there, I shall be obliged to you."

It left him no choice but to go down before them. As he did so, hat in hand, Mrs Gowan whispered:

"He killed the dog."

"Does Mr Gowan know it?" Little Dorrit whispered.

"No one knows it. Don't look towards me; look towards him. He will turn his face in a moment. No one knows it, but I am sure he did. You are?"

"I – I think so," Little Dorrit answered.

"Henry likes him, and he will not think ill of him; he is so generous and open himself. But you and I feel sure that we think of him as he deserves. He argued with Henry that the dog had been already poisoned when he changed so, and sprang at him. Henry believes it, but we do not. I see he is listening, but can't hear. Good-bye, my love! Good-bye!"

The last words were spoken aloud, as the vigilant Blandois stopped, turned his head, and looked at them from the bottom of the staircase. He handed Mrs Gowan to her boat, and stood there until it had shot out of the narrow view; when he handed himself into his own boat and followed.

The period of the family's stay at Venice came, in its course, to an end, and they moved, with their retinue, to Rome.

Here it seemed to Little Dorrit that Prunes and Prism got the upper hand. Nobody said what anything was, but everybody said what the Mrs Generals said it was. Mrs General was in her pure element. Nobody else had an opinion.

They received an early visit from Mrs Merdle. "So delighted," said she, "to resume an acquaintance so inauspiciously begun at Martigny."

"At Martigny, of course," said Fanny. "Charmed, I am sure!"

"I understand," said Mrs Merdle, "my son Edmund Sparkler has already improved that chance occasion. He has returned quite transported with Venice."

"Mr Merdle," observed Fanny, as a means of dismissing Mr Sparkler into the background, "is quite a theme of Papa's, you must know, Mrs Merdle."

"I trust," said Mr Dorrit, "that if I have not the – hum – great advantage of becoming known to Mr Merdle on this side of the Alps or Mediterranean, I shall have that honour on returning to England. It is an honour I particularly desire and shall particularly esteem."

"Mr Merdle," said Mrs Merdle, who had been looking admiringly at Fanny through her eye-glass, "will esteem it, I am sure, no less."

CHAPTER 6

The Dowager Mrs Gowan is Reminded that "It Never Does"

While the waters of Venice and the ruins of Rome were sunning themselves for the pleasure of the Dorrit family, the firm of Doyce and Clennam hammered away in Bleeding Heart Yard, and the vigorous clink of iron upon iron was heard there through the working hours. The younger partner had, by this time, brought the business into sound trim; and the elder, left free to follow his own ingenious devices, had done much to enhance the character of the factory. As an ingenious man, he had necessarily to encounter every discouragement from the Circumlocution Office, (that warned every ingenious British subject to be ingenious at his peril,) by harassing him, obstructing him, inviting robbers (by making his remedy uncertain, and expensive) to plunder him, and at the best by confiscating his property after a short term of enjoyment, as though invention were on a par with felony.

Daniel Doyce faced his condition with its pains and penalties attached to it, and soberly worked on for the work's sake. Clennam, cheering him with a hearty co-operation, was a moral support to him, besides doing good service in his business relation. The concern prospered, and the partners were fast friends.

But Daniel could not forget the old design of so many years ago. It was not in reason to be expected that he should; if he could have lightly forgotten it, he could never have conceived it, or had the patience and perseverance to work it out. So Clennam, knowing much explanation would be necessary, resumed the long and hopeless labour of striving to make way with the Circumlocution Office.

With sufficient occupation on his hands, now that he had this additional task – such a task had many and many a serviceable man died of before his day – Arthur Clennam led a life of slight variety. Regular visits to his mother's dull sick room, and visits scarcely less regular to Mr Meagles at Twickenham, were its only changes during many months.

He sadly and sorely missed Little Dorrit. The old interest he had had in her, and her old trusting reliance on him, were tinged with melancholy in his mind.

One wintry Saturday when Clennam was at the cottage, the Dowager Mrs Gowan drove up.

"And how do you both do, Papa and Mama Meagles?" said she, encouraging her humble connections. "And when did you last hear from or about my poor fellow?"

My poor fellow was her son; and this mode of speaking of him politely kept alive, without any offence in the world, the pretence that he had fallen a victim to the Meagles' wiles.

"Ah! Yes, to be sure!" said Mrs Gowan. "You must remember that my poor fellow has always been accustomed to expectations. They may have been realised, or they may not have been realised – "

"Let us say, then, may not have been realised," observed Mr Meagles. The Dowager for a moment gave him an angry look.

"Come, Mrs Gowan, come!" returned Mr Meagles. "Let us try to be sensible; let us try to be good-natured; let us try to be fair. Don't you pity Henry, and I won't pity Pet. And don't be one-sided, my dear madam; it's not considerate, it's not kind. Don't let us say that we hope Pet will make Henry happy, or even that we hope Henry will make Pet happy," (Mr Meagles himself did not look happy as he spoke the words,) "but let us hope they will make each other happy."

"It is in vain," said Mrs Gowan, "for people to attempt to get on together who have such extremely different antecedents; who are jumbled against each other in this accidental, matrimonial sort of way; and who cannot look at the untoward circumstance which has shaken them together in the same light. It never does. I assure you it never does. I will therefore, if you please, go my way, leaving you to yours."

After further argument the haughty Dowager made a smiling obeisance, rather to the room than to any one in it, and therewith bade farewell to Papa and Mama Meagles. Clennam stepped forward to hand her to the Pill-Box which was at the service of all the Pills in Hampton Court Palace; and she got into that vehicle with apparent serenity, and was driven away.

CHAPTER 7

Appearance and Disappearance

"Arthur, my dear boy," said Mr Meagles, on the evening of the following day, "Mother and I have been talking this over, and we don't feel comfortable in remaining as we are. We are very much disposed to pack up bags and baggage and strike right through France and into Italy to see our Pet. The fact is, Arthur," said Mr Meagles, the old cloud coming over his face, "that my son-in-law is already in debt again, and that I suppose I must clear him again."

"All perfectly true," observed Arthur, "and all sufficient reasons for going."

"If you would come down and stay here for a change, when it wouldn't trouble you," Mr Meagles resumed, "I should be glad to think – and so would Mother too, I know."

Within a few days Father and Mother were gone; Mrs Ticket the housekeeper was posted behind the parlour blind, and Arthur's solitary feet were rustling among the dry fallen leaves in the garden walks.

· On one of his visits Mrs Tickit received him with the words, "I have something to tell you, Mr Clennam, that will surprise you."

"What is it, Mrs Tickit?" said he.

· "Sir," returned that faithful housekeeper, having taken him into the parlour and closed the door; "if ever I saw the led away and deluded child in my life, I saw her identically in the dusk of yesterday evening."

"You don't mean Tatty – "

"Coram, yes, I do!" quoth Mrs Tickit, clearing the disclosure at a leap. "I saw her actual form and figure looking in at the gate. But sir, when I quivered my eyes again she wasn't there."

Later Arthur was passing at nightfall along the Strand, when a stoppage on the pavement brought him to a standstill. Immediately, he saw in advance, Tattycoram and a strange swaggering man with a black moustache.

Clennam followed them, resolved to see where they went. They turned short into the Adelphi, – the girl evidently leading, – and went straight on, as if they were going to the Terrace which overhangs the river.

Clennam stopped at the corner, observing the girl and the strange man as they went down the street. When he rounded the dark corner, they were walking along the terrace towards a figure coming towards them, whom he recognised at once as Miss Wade. As they came down to the corner and turned, he heard Miss Wade say, "If I pinch myself for it, sir, that is my business. Confine yourself to yours, and ask me no question."

Whether the girl hung behind because she was not to hear the business, or as already knowing enough about it, Clennam could not determine. Now Miss Wade and the man came back again, and he heard her saying, "You must wait until tomorrow."

"A thousand pardons?" he returned. "My faith! Then it's not convenient tonight?"

"No. I tell you I must get it before I can give it to you."

She stopped in the roadway, as if to put an end to the conference.

He of course stopped too. And the girl stopped.

"It's a little inconvenient," said the man. "I am without money tonight, by chance. I have a good banker in this city, but I would not wish to draw upon the house until the time when I shall draw for a round sum."

"Harriet," said Miss Wade, "arrange with him – this gentleman here – to send him some money tomorrow."

They walked slowly on and Arthur followed them into the Gray's Inn Road. Clennam was quite at home here, in right of Flora, not to mention the Patriarch and Pancks. He was beginning to wonder where they might be going next, when he saw them stop at the Patriarchal door. There was a brief pause for inquiry and answer and the door was shut, and they were housed.

Then Arthur too knocked at the door.

There was no one with Flora but Mr F's Aunt.

"My goodness Arthur!" cried Flora, rising to give him a cordial reception. "And now pray tell me something all you know about the good dear quiet little thing and all the changes of her fortunes." Arthur's increasing wish to speak of something very different was, after a long while, so plainly written on his face, that Flora stopped and asked him what it was.

"I have the greatest desire, Flora, to speak to someone who is now in this house – with Mr Casby no doubt. Someone whom I saw come in, and who, in a misguided and deplorable way, has deserted the house of a friend of mine."

With great good will, Flora accompanied Arthur into the room, where the Patriarch sat alone, twirling his thumbs.

"Mr Clennam, I am glad to see you. I hope you are well, sir, I hope you are well. Please to sit down, please to sit down."

"I had hoped, sir," said Clennam, doing so, and looking round with a face of blank disappointment, "not to find you alone."

"Ah, indeed?" said the Patriarch, sweetly. "Ah, indeed?"

"I beg your pardon, Mr Casby – "

"Not so, not so," said the Patriarch, "not so."

" – But, Miss Wade had an attendant with her – a young woman brought up by friends of mine, over whom her influence is not considered very salutary, and to whom I should be glad to have the opportunity of giving the assurance that she has not yet forfeited the interest of those

144

protectors. Will you therefore be so good as to give me the address of Miss Wade?"

"I have no address. Miss Wade mostly lives abroad, Mr Clennam. She has done so for some years, and as she is fitful and uncertain to a fault I may not see her again for a long, long time. I may never see her again. What a pity, what a pity!"

Casby sat, twirling and twirling, and making his polished head and forehead look largely benevolent in every knob.

With this spectacle before him, Arthur had risen to go, when Mr Pancks arrived. Clennam took his leave of Mr Casby and waited outside, but it was only a short time before Mr Pancks appeared.

Knowing Pancks would understand he spoke without any preface:

"I suppose they were really gone, Pancks?"

"Yes," replied Pancks. "They were really gone."

"Does he know where to find that lady?"

"Can't say."

Did Mr Pancks know anything about her?

"I expect," rejoined that worthy, "I know as much about her as she knows about herself. She is somebody's child – anybody's – nobody's."

"Mr Casby could enlighten her, perhaps?"

"May be," said Pancks. "I expect so, but don't know. He has long had money (not overmuch as I make out) in trust to dole out to her. Sometimes she's proud and won't touch it for a length of time; sometimes she's so poor that she must have it. She writhes under her life. A woman more angry, passionate, reckless, and revengeful never lived. The wonder is to me that she has never done for my proprietor, as the only person connected with her story she can lay hold of!" Mr Pancks, with a countenance of grave import, snorted several times and steamed away.

CHAPTER 8

The Dreams of Mrs Flintwinch Thicken

The shady waiting-rooms of the Circumlocution Office had afforded Arthur Clennam ample leisure, in three or four successive days, to exhaust the subject of his late glimpse of Miss Wade and Tattycoram. He had been able to make no more of it and no less of it, and in this unsatisfactory condition he was fain to leave it.

During this space he had not been to his mother's dismal old house. Now he resolved to go and as he turned into the narrow and steep street from which the court of enclosure, wherein the house stood, opened, another footstep turned into it behind him, and so close upon his own that he was jostled to the wall. The man who strode on before him was the man he had followed in company with the girl, and whom he had overheard talking to Miss Wade.

With no defined intention of following him, but with an impulse to keep the figure in view a little longer, Clennam quickened his pace to pass the twist in the street which hid him from his sight. On turning it, he saw the man no more.

Standing now, close to the gateway of his mother's house, he looked down the street but it was empty. Then he turned into the courtyard and as he looked, by mere habit, towards the feebly lighted windows of his mother's room, his eyes encountered the figure he had just lost ascending the unevenly sunken steps, and knocking at the door. He went up to the door too, and ascended the steps.

The sound of Mistress Affery cautiously chaining the door before she opened it, caused both the visitors to look that way. Affery opened it a very little, with a flaring candle in her hands and asked who was that, at that time of night, with that knock!

"Why, Arthur!" she added with astonishment, seeing him first. "Not you sure? Ah, Lord save us! No," she cried out, seeing the other. "Him again!"

"It's true! Blandois again, dear Mrs Flintwinch," cried the stranger. "Open the door, and let me take my dear friend Jeremiah to my arms! Open the door, and let me hasten myself to embrace my Flintwinch!"

"He's not at home," cried Affery.

To Arthur's increased surprise, Mistress Affery, stretching her eyes wide at himself, as if in warning that this was not a gentleman for him to interfere with, drew back the chain, and opened the door. The stranger, without ceremony, walked into the hall, leaving Arthur to follow him.

The voice of Mrs Clennam opportunely called from her chamber above, "Affery, let them both come up. Arthur, come straight to me!"

"Arthur?" exclaimed Blandois, taking off his hat at arm's length, and

146

bringing his heels together from a great stride in making him a flourishing bow. "The son of my lady? I am the all-devoted of the son of my lady!" Arthur did not reply and they climbed the stairs together in silence.

"Madame," said Blandois, when they had entered Mrs Clennam's room "It appears to me, that Monsieur, your son, is disposed to complain of me. He is not polite."

"Sir," said Arthur, "whoever you are, and however you come to be here, if I were the master of this house I would lose no time in placing you on the outside of it."

"But you are not," said his mother, without looking at him. "Unfortunately for the gratification of your unreasonable temper, you are not the master, Arthur. The gentleman is acquainted with Flintwinch – "

The key of the door below was now heard in the lock, and the door was heard to open and close. In due sequence Mr Flintwinch appeared; on whose entrance the visitor rose from his chair, laughing loud, and folded him in a close embrace.

"How goes it, my cherished friend!" said he. "How goes the world, my Flintwinch? Rose-coloured?"

The amazement, suspicion, resentment, and shame, with which Arthur looked on at all this, struck him dumb. As Mrs Clennam never removed her eyes from Blandois (on whom they had some effect, as a steady look has on a lower sort of dog), so Jeremiah never removed his from Arthur. Thereupon Mrs Clennam said, moving one of her hands for the first time, and moving it very slightly with an action of dismissal:

"Please to leave us to our business, Arthur."

"Mother, I do so with reluctance."

Disdaining to speak, and indeed not very well able, for he was half-choking, Clennam only glanced at the visitor as he passed out.

The visitor saluted him with another parting snap. His nose came down over his moustache and his moustache went up under his nose, in an ominous and ugly smile.

"For Heaven's sake, Affery," whispered Clennam, as she opened the door for him in the dark hall, and he groped his way to the sight of the night-sky, "what is going on here?"

CHAPTER 9

A Letter from Little Dorrit

Dear Mr Clennam,

I write from Rome. We left Venice before Mr and Mrs Gowan did, but they were not so long upon the road as we were, and did not travel by the same way, and so when we arrived we found them in a lodging here, in a place called the Via Gregoriana. I dare say you know it. Now I am going to tell you all I can about them, because I know that is what you most want to hear.

On account of Mr Gowan's painting Papa's picture (which I am not quite convinced I should have known from the likeness if I had not seen him doing it), I have had more opportunities of being with her since then than I might have had without this fortunate chance.

She is very much alone. Very much alone indeed.

Owing (as I think, if you think so too) to Mr Gowan's unsettled and dissatisfied way, he applies himself to his profession very little.

He does nothing steadily or patiently; but equally takes things up and throws them down, and does them, or leaves them undone, without caring about them. But what I particularly want you to know, and why I have resolved to tell you so much while I am afraid it may make you a little uncomfortable without occasion, is this. She is so true and so devoted, and knows so completely that all her love and duty are his for ever, that you may be certain she will love him, admire him, praise him, and conceal all his faults, until she dies. I believe she conceals them, and always will conceal them, even from herself.

You may wish to know that when she began to call me Amy, I told her my short story, and that you had always called me Little Dorrit. I told her that the name was much dearer to me than any other, and so she calls me Little Dorrit too.

Perhaps you have not heard from her father or mother yet, and may not know that she has a baby son. He was born only two days ago, and just a week after they came. It has made them very happy.

We are all quite well, and Fanny improves every day. You can hardly think how kind she is to me now, and what pains she takes with me. She has a lover, Mr Sparkler, son of Mrs Merdle, who has followed her, first all the way from Switzerland, and then all the way from Venice, and who has just confided to me that he means to follow her everywhere. I have no lover, of course.

Dear Mr Clennam, it is possible that I have thought of you – and others – so much by day, that I have no thoughts left to wander round you by night. For I must now confess to you that I suffer from home-sickness and that I long ardently and earnestly for home. I have tried to get on a little better under Mrs General's instruction, and I hope I am not quite so dull as I used to be. I have begun to speak and understand, almost easily, the hard languages I told you about. God bless you, dear Mr Clennam.

Do not forget your ever grateful and affectionate

LITTLE DORRIT.

P.S. – Particularly remember that Minnie Gowan deserves the best remembrance in which you can hold her. You cannot think too generously or too highly of her. And if you see Mr Pancks, please give him your Little Dorrit's kind regard. He was very good to Little D.

CHAPTER 10

In Which a Great Patriotic Conference is Holden

The famous name of Merdle became, every day, more famous in the land. His influence was immense over those of influence. They sat at his feasts, and he sat at theirs. For in Mrs Merdle's absence abroad, Mr Merdle still kept the great house open for the passage through it of a stream of visitors. At one of his opulent banquets, Lord Decimus, who was an overpowering peer, a bashful young member of the Lower House and a friend of the Barnacles of the Circumlocution office, enquired of Ferdinand Barnacle, who happened to sit beside him, "What is this story I have heard of a gentleman long confined in a debtors' prison proving to be of a wealthy family, and having come into the inheritance of a large sum of money? I have met with a variety of allusions to it. Do you know anything of it, Ferdinand?"

"I only know this much," said Ferdinand, "that he has given the Department with which I have the honour to be associated with, no end of trouble, and has put us into innumerable fixes."

"What," said Lord Decimus, "was the character of his business; what was the nature of these – a – Fixes, Ferdinand?"

"Oh, it's a good story, as a story," returned that gentleman; "as good a thing of its kind as need be. This Mr Dorrit (his name is Dorrit) had incurred a responsibility to us, ages before the fairy came out of the Bank and gave him his fortune, under a bond he had signed for the performance of a contract which was not at all performed. He was a partner in a house in some large way – spirits, or buttons, or wine or blacking or oatmeal, or woollen, or pork, or hooks and eyes or iron or treacle, or shoes and so on, and the house burst, and we being among the creditors, detainees were lodged on the part of the Crown in a scientific manner, and all the rest of it. When the fairy had appeared and he wanted to pay us off, Egad we had got into such an exemplary state of checking and counter-checking, signing and counter-signing, that it was six months before we knew how to take the money, or how to give a receipt for it. It was a triumph of public business," said this handsome young Barnacle, laughing heartily, "you never saw such a lot of forms in your life."

Mr Tite Barnacle's view of the business was of a less airy character. He took it ill that Mr Dorrit had troubled the Department by wanting to pay the money, and considered it a grossly informal thing after so many years.

"May I ask," said Lord Decimus, "if Mr Darrit – or Dorrit – has any family?"

Nobody else replying, the host said, "He has two daughters, my lord."

"Oh! you are acquainted with him?" asked Lord Decimus.

"Mrs Merdle is. Mr Sparkler is, too. In fact," said Mr Merdle, "I rather believe that one of the young ladies has made an impression on Edmund Sparkler. He is susceptible, and – I – think – the conquest – " Here Mr Merdle stopped, and looked at the table-cloth, as he usually did when he found himself observed or listened to.

In a day or two it was announced to all the town, that Edmund Sparkler, Esquire, son-in-law of the eminent Mr Merdle of worldwide renown, was made one of the Lords of the Circumlocution Office; and proclamation was issued that this admirable appointment was to be hailed as a gracious mark of homage, rendered by the gracious Decimus, to that commercial interest which must ever in a great commercial country – and all the rest of it, with blast of trumpet. So bolstered by the mark of Government homage, Mr Merdle's wonderful affairs went up and up.

150

CHAPTER 11

The Progress of an Epidemic

Down in Bleeding Heart Yard, where there was not one unappropriated halfpenny, as lively an interest was taken in Mr Merdle – this paragon of men – as on the Stock Exchange. Mrs Plornish, now established in the small grocery and general trade in a snug little shop at the crack end of the yard, at the top of the steps, with her little old father and Maggy acting as assistants, habitually held forth about him over the counter in conversation with her customers.

So rife and potent was the fever in Bleeding Heart Yard, that Mr Pancks's rent-days caused no interval in the patients. The disease took the singular form, on those occasions, of causing the infected to find an unfathomable excuse and consolation in allusions to the magic name.

The Defaulter would make answer, "Ah, Mr Pancks. If I was the rich gentleman whose name is in everybody's mouth – if my name was Merdle, sir – I'd soon pay up, and be glad to do it."

Mr Pancks could only bite his nails and puff away to the next Defaulter.

From one of the many such defeats of one of many rent-days, Mr Pancks, having finished his day's collection, repaired with his note-book under his arm to Mrs Plornish's corner.

Warned of a visitor by the bell at the shop-door, Mrs Plornish came out to see who it might be. "I guessed it was you, Mr Pancks," said she, "for it's quite your regular night; ain't it? Here's father, come out to serve at the sound of the bell, like a brisk young shopman. Ain't he looking well? Father's more pleased to see you than if you was a customer, for he dearly loves a gossip; and when it turns upon Miss Dorrit, he loves it all the more. You never heard father in such voice as he is at present," said Mrs Plornish, her own voice quavering, she was so proud and pleased.

Mr Pancks snorted at Nandy in his friendliest manner and casually asked whether that lively chap, John Baptist, sole lodger of Mrs Plornish, had come in yet? Mrs Plornish answered no, not yet, though he had gone to the West-End with some work. Nandy disappeared into the shop and Pancks said, "How is your business getting on, Mrs Plornish?"

"Very steady, indeed, sir," returned Mrs Plornish. "The only thing that stands in its way, sir, is the Credit."

This drawback, rather severely felt by most people who engaged in commercial transactions with the inhabitants of Bleeding Heart Yard, was a large stumbling-block in Mrs Plornish's trade. When Mr Dorrit had established her in the business, the Bleeding Hearts pledged themselves, with great feeling, to deal with Mrs Plornish.

If the Bleeding Hearts had but paid, the undertaking would have been a complete success; whereas, by reason of their exclusively confining themselves to owing, the profits actually realised had not yet begun to appear in the books.

Mr Pancks was making a very porcupine of himself by sticking his hair up in the contemplation of this state of accounts, when old Mr Nandy, re-entering the cottage with an air of mystery, entreated them to come and look at the strange behaviour of Mr Baptist, who seemed to have met with something that had scared him. All three going into the shop, and watching through the window, then saw Mr Baptist, pale and agitated, go through the following extraordinary performances. First, he was observed hiding at the top of the steps leading down into the yard, and peeping up and down the street with his head cautiously thrust out close to the side of the shop-door. After very anxious scrutiny, he came out of his retreat, and went briskly down the street as if he were going away altogether; then, suddenly turned about, and went, at the same pace, and with the same feint, up the street then back again.

"Hallo, old chap!" said Mr Pancks. "What's the matter?"

They all went into the cottage.

"I have seen someone," said Baptist, "a bad man. A baddest man. I have hoped that I should never see him again. I have fear of this man. I do not wish to see him, I do not wish to be known of him – never again."

Mr Baptist, by degrees began to chirp a little; but never stirred from the seat he had taken behind the door and close to the window, though it was not his usual place. As often as the little bell rang, he started and peeped out secretly, with the end of the little curtain in his hand and the rest before his face; evidently not at all satisfied but that the man he dreaded had tracked him through all his doublings and turnings, with the certainty of a terrible bloodhound.

The bell rang again, and Mr Clennam came in. Clennam had been poring late over his books and letters; for the waiting-rooms of the Circumlocution Office ravaged his time sorely. Over and above that, he was depressed and made uneasy by the late occurrence at his mother's. He looked worn and solitary. He felt so, too; but, nevertheless, was returning home from his counting-house by that end of the Yard to give them the intelligence that he had received a letter from Miss Dorrit.

The news made a sensation in the cottage which drew off the general attention from Mr Baptist. "Let me make you a cup of tea," said Mrs Plornish, "if you'd condescend to take such a thing in the cottage; and many thanks to you, too, I am sure, for bearing us in mind so kindly."

Arthur expressed himself gratified by their high appreciation of so very slight an attention on his part; and explained that he was going straight home to refresh himself after a long day's labour. As Mr Pancks was somewhat noisily getting his steam up for departure, he concluded by asking that gentleman if he would walk with him. Clennam had long had a growing belief that Mr Pancks, in his own odd way, was becoming attached to him. All these strings intertwining made Pancks a very cable of anchorage that night.

"You didn't take particular notice of little Baptist just now; did you?" said Pancks.

"No. Why?"

"He's a bright fellow, and I like him," said Pancks. "something has gone amiss with him today. Have you any idea of any cause that can have overset him?"

"You surprise me! None whatever."

"Perhaps you'll ask him," said Pancks, "what he has on his mind."

"I ought first to see for myself that he has something on his mind, I think," said Clennam. "I have found him in every way so diligent, so grateful (for little enough), and so trustworthy, that it might look like suspecting him. And that would be very unjust. He keeps the keys of the Factory, watches it every alternate night, and acts as a sort of housekeeper to it generally; but we have little work in the way of his ingenuity, though we give him what we have. Is it not curious, Pancks, that the ventures which run just now in so many people's heads should run even in little John Baptist's head?"

"Ventures?" retorted Pancks, with a snort. "What ventures?"

"These Merdle enterprises."

"Ay! But think of the whole yard having got it."

"Do you mean, my good Pancks," asked Clennam emphatically, "that even you would put that thousand pounds of yours, let us say, for instance, out at this kind of interest?"

"Certainly," said Pancks. "Already done it, sir."

"And you have really invested," Clennam had already passed to that word, "your thousand pounds, Pancks?"

"To be sure, sir!" replied Pancks boldly, with a puff of smoke. "And only wish it ten!"

Quitting the investment subject, Clennan told Pancks how and why he was occupied with the great National Department. "A hard case it has been, and a hard case it is on Doyce, but I do my best, as to duly weighing and considering these new enterprises of which I have had no experience, I doubt if I am fit for it, I am growing old. I am in a very anxious and uncertain state concerning my mother and a particular interview I witnessed. I have many misgivings."

"Brings me back, sir," exclaimed Pancks with a startling touch on Clennam's arm, "brings me back, sir, to the Investments! I don't say anything of your making yourself poor to repair a wrong you never committed. That's you. A man must be himself. But I say this, fearing you may want money to save your own blood from exposure and disgrace – make as much as you can! Be as rich as you honestly can. It's your duty. Not for your sake, but for the sake of others. Take time by the forelock. Poor Mr Doyce (who really is growing old) depends upon you. Your relative depends upon you. You don't know what depends upon you."

"Well, well, well!" returned Arthur. "But what if I invest in the Merdle enterprises and lose?" said Arthur.

"Can't be done, sir," returned Pancks. "I have looked into it. Name up everywhere – immense resources – enormous capital – great position – high connection – government influence. Can't be done!"

They said little more and Arthur ended the evening feeling he might implicitly rely on Pancks, if he ever should come to need assistance; either in any of the matters of which they had spoken that night, or any other subject that could in any way affect himself.

CHAPTER 12

Taking Advice

When it became known to the Britons on the shore of the yellow Tiber that their intelligent compatriot, Mr Sparkler, was made one of the Lords of their Circumlocution Office, they congratulated Mrs Merdle while Henry Gowan, whom Decimus had thrown away, went through the whole round of his acquaintance vowing, almost (but not quite) with tears in his eyes, that Edmund Sparkler was the sweetest-tempered, simplest-hearted, altogether most lovable jackass that ever grazed on the public common. Miss Fanny was now sufficiently identified with Sparkler to feel compromised by his being more than usually ridiculous; and hence, being by no means deficient in quickness, she sometimes came to his rescue against Gowan, and did him very good service. But, while doing this, she was ashamed of him, undetermined whether to get rid of him or more decidedly encourage him, distracted with apprehensions that she was every day becoming more and more immeshed in her uncertainties, and tortured by misgivings that Mrs Merdle triumphed in her distress. With this tumult in her mind, she burst into violent weeping, and, when her sister came and sat close at her side to comfort her, after many outpourings, she said, "Amy, you're an Angel!"

"My love," Fanny went on, "our characters and points of view are sufficiently different (kiss me again, my darling), to make it very probable that I shall surprise you by what I am going to say. What I am going to say, my dear, is, that notwithstanding our property, we labour, socially speaking, under disadvantages so it becomes a question with me whether I shall make up my mind to take it upon myself to carry the family through."

"How?" asked her sister, anxiously.

"I will not," said Fanny, without answering the question, "submit to be step-mothered by Mrs General; and I will not submit to be, in any respect whatever, either patronised or tormented by Mrs Merdle."

Little Dorrit laid her hand upon the hand that held a bottle of sweet water, with a still more anxious look.

"Oh, my dear Fanny!" expostulated Little Dorrit, upon whom a kind of terror had been stealing as she perceived what her sister meant.

"Let me say first, that I would far rather we worked for a scanty living again than I would see you rich and married to Mr Sparkler. You know that you have qualities to make you the wife of one very superior to him."

"It wouldn't be an unhappy life, Amy. It would be the life I am fitted for. Whether by disposition, or whether by circumstances, is no matter; I am better fitted for such a life than for almost any other."

There was something of a desolate tone in those words; but, with a short proud laugh she took another walk, and after passing a great looking-glass came to another stop. Meeting an earnest and imploring look in Amy's face, she brought her hands down, and laid one on Amy's lips.

"Now, don't argue with me, child," she said in a sterner way, "because it is of no use. I understand these subjects much better than you do. I have not nearly made up my mind, but it may be. Now we have talked this over comfortably, and may go to bed. You best and dearest little mouse, good-night!"

It might have been about a month or six weeks after the night of the new advice, when Little Dorrit began to think she detected some new understanding between Mr Sparkler and Fanny. Mr Sparkler, as if in attendance to some compact, scarcely ever spoke without first looking towards Fanny for leave. Moreover, it became plain whenever Henry Gowan attempted to perform the friendly office of drawing him out, that he was not to be drawn. And not only that, but Fanny would presently, without any pointed application in the world, chance to say something with such a sting in it that Gowan would draw back as if he had put his hand into a bee-hive.

Then one day Fanny announced to Amy her engagement to Mr Sparkler.

"Oh Fanny, Fanny!" cried Little Dorrit, and turning to her sister in the bright window, fell upon her bosom and cried there. Fanny laughed at first; but soon laid her face against her sister's and cried too – a little. It was the last time Fanny ever showed that there was any hidden, suppressed, or conquered feeling in her on the matter. From that hour the way she had chosen lay before her, and she trod it with her own imperious self-willed step.

CHAPTER 13

No Just Cause or Impediment why these Two Persons Should Not be Joined Together

Mr Dorrit, on being informed by his elder daughter that she had accepted matrimonial overtures from Mr Sparkler, to whom she had plighted her troth, received the communication at once with great dignity and with a large display of parental pride. He thanked Mr Sparkler for the compliment rendered to himself and to his family.

Mrs Merdle had heard of this affair from Edmund and had openly said to Mr Dorrit that personally she was charmed and gratified.

"I cannot," said Mrs Merdle, "take upon myself to answer positively for Mr Merdle, but I should think that he too would be quite charmed."

Mr Dorrit wrote with many flourishes to Mr Merdle and Mr Merdle replied accordingly, upon which Mr Dorrit decided to formally inform Mrs General.

"Papa," said Fanny, taking him up short upon that name, "I don't see what Mrs General has got to do with it."

"My dear," said Mr Dorrit, "it will be an act of courtesy to – hum – a lady, well bred and refined – "

"Oh! I am sick of Mrs General's good breeding and refinement, Papa," said Fanny. "I am tired of Mrs General."

At this, Mr Dorrit rose from his chair with a fixed look of severe reproof, and remained standing in his dignity before his daughter.

Shortly after this he asked his valet, to summon Mrs General.

"Madame," he said when she arrived, "take a chair. I wish to announce to you that my daughter Fanny is – ha – contracted to be married to Mr Sparkler. Hence, madam, you will be relieved of half your difficult charge." Mr Dorrit repeated it with his angry eye on Fanny.

"Mr Dorrit," returned Mrs General, with her gloved hands resting on one another in exemplary repose, "allow me to offer my sincere congratulations."

The winter passed on towards the spring and soon it became necessary for Mr Sparkler to repair to England.

It followed that the question was rendered pressing when, where, and how Mr Sparkler should be married to the foremost girl in all this world with no nonsense about her. Its solution, after some little mystery and secrecy, Miss Fanny herself announced to her sister.

"That woman," she spoke of Mrs Merdle, of course, "remains here until after Easter; so, in the case of my being married here and going to London with Edmund, I should have the start of her. Further Amy, that woman being out of the way, I don't know that I greatly object to Mr Merdle's proposal to Pa that Edmund and I should take up our abode in his house until our own can be chosen and fitted up. Further still, Amy, Mr Merdle has entreated Pa to stay nearby and I suppose he will. Little Owl, on the whole do you advise me to make the arrangements?"

"It – seems so, love," said Little Dorrit.

"Very well," cried Fanny with an air of resignation, "then I suppose it must be done. And now, my pet, I am going to give you a word of advice. When you are left alone here with Mrs General – till Papa comes back, Amy, don't you let her slide into any sort of artful understanding with you that she is looking after Pa, or that Pa is looking after her. She will if she can. And if Pa should tell you when he comes back, that he has it in contemplation to make Mrs General your Mama (which is not the less likely because I am going away), my advice to you is, that you say at once, 'Papa, I beg to object most strongly.'"

Having stated her plans to her sister, Fanny proceeded with characteristic ardour to prepare for her marriage. Cards of breakfast-invitation were sent out to half the English in the city and eventually the celebration went off with admirable pomp.

Afterwards, the Bride mounted into her handsome chariot, incidentally accompanied by the Bridegroom, and set off for Florence.

If Little Dorrit found herself left a little lonely and a little low that night, nothing would have done so much against her feeling of depression as the being able to sit at work by her father, as in the old time, and help him to his supper and his rest. But that was not to be until the all-pervasive Mrs General retired for the night. Then Little Dorrit put her arm round her father's neck, to bid him good-night.

"Amy, my dear," said Mr Dorrit, taking her by the hand, "this is the close of a day, that has – ha – greatly impressed and gratified me." He smiled lovingly at her. "I trust that the time is not far distant when some – ha – eligible partner may be found for you."

"Oh no!" cried Little Dorrit in alarm. "Let me stay with you. I want nothing but to stay and take care of you!"

"Amy," said Mr Dorrit, "I merely wish that we should – ha – understand each other. Hum. Good-night, my dear and sole remaining daughter. Good-night. God bless you!"

CHAPTER 14

Getting on

The newly married pair, on their arrival in Harley Street, Cavendish Square, London, were received by the Chief Butler who said, in a very handsome way, to one of his men, "Thomas, help with the luggage." He escorted the Bride upstairs into Mr Merdle's presence.

Mrs Sparkler, installed in the rooms of state – the innermost sanctuary of down, silk, chintz, and fine linen – felt that so far her triumph was good, and her way made, step by step.

In the meanwhile Mr Merdle ordered his carriage to be ready early in the morning that he might wait upon Mr Dorrit immediately after breakfast. As he arrived at the hotel in Brook Street, Grosvenor Square, people were already posted on the lower stairs, that his shadow might fall upon them when he came down.

The Courier, with agitation in his voice, announced, "Miss' Mairdale!" Mr Dorrit's overwrought heart bounded as he leaped up.

"Mr Merdle, this is – ha – indeed an honour. Permit me to express the – hum – sense, the high sense, I am well aware, sir, of the many demands upon your time, and its – ha – enormous value. You are well, I hope?"

"I am as well as I – yes, I am as well as I usually am," said Mr Merdle.

There were black traces on his lips where they met, as if a little train of gunpowder had been fired there; and he looked like a man who, if his natural temperament had been quicker, would have been very feverish that morning. This, and his heavy way of passing his hand over his forehead, had prompted Mr Dorrit's solicitous inquiries.

"Mrs Merdle," Mr Dorrit insinuatingly pursued, "was looking wonderfully well when I quitted Rome."

"Mrs Merdle," said Mr Merdle, "is generally considered a very attractive woman. And she is, no doubt. I am sensible of her being so. But," he said, looking Mr Dorrit in the face for the first time, "if we speak of attractions, your daughter ought to be the subject of our conversation. She is extremely beautiful. Both in face and figure, she is quite uncommon. When the young people arrived last night, I was really surprised to see such charms. I thought I would drive round the first thing," continued Mr Merdle, "to offer my services, in case I can do anything for you; and to say that I hope you will at least do me the honour of dining with me today, and every day when you are not better engaged during your stay in town."

Mr Dorrit was enraptured by these attentions.

"Do you stay long, sir?"

"I have not at present the intention," said Mr Dorrit, "of – ha – exceeding a fortnight."

"That's a very short stay, after so long a journey," returned Mr Merdle.

"Hum. Yes," said Mr Dorrit. "But the truth is – ha – my dear Mr Merdle, that I find a foreign life so well suited to my health and taste, that I – hum – have but two objects in my present visit to London. First, the – ha – the distinguished happiness and – ha – privilege which I now enjoy and appreciate; secondly, the arrangement – hum – the laying out, that is to say, in the best way, of – ha, hum – my money."

"Well, sir," said Mr Merdle, "if I can be of any use to you in that respect, you may command me."

Greatly relieved by Mr Merdle's affable offer of assistance, he caught at it directly, and heaped acknowledgements upon him.

"However," said Mr Merdle, "I do generally retain in my own hands the power of exercising some preference – people in general would be pleased to call it favour – as a sort of compliment for my care and trouble."

"And public spirit and genius," Mr Dorrit suggested.

"Therefore," said Mr Merdle, "I can only give you a preference to a certain extent."

"I perceive. To a defined extent," observed Mr Dorrit.

"Defined extent. And perfectly above-board. As to my advice, however," said Mr Merdle, "that is another matter. That shall be at your command whenever you think proper."

New acknowledgements from Mr Dorrit. New passages of Mr Merdle's hand over his forehead. Calm and silence. Contemplation of Mr Dorrit's waistcoat buttons by Mr Merdle.

"My time being rather precious," said Mr Merdle, suddenly getting up, as if he had been waiting in the interval for his legs and they had just come, "I must be moving towards the City. Can I take you anywhere, sir? I shall be happy to set you down, or send you on. My carriage is at your disposal."

Mr Dorrit bethought himself that he had business at his banker's. His banker's was in the City. That was fortunate; Mr Merdle would take him into the City.

At dinner that day, although the occasion was not foreseen and provided for, a brilliant company of such as are not made of the dust of the earth, but of some superior article for the present unknown, shed their lustrous benediction upon Mr Dorrit's daughter's marriage. And Mr Dorrit's daughter that day began, in earnest, her competition with that woman not present; and began it so well that Mr Dorrit could all but have taken his affidavit, if required, that Mrs Sparkler had all her life been lying at full length in the lap of luxury, and had never heard of such a rough word in the English tongue as Marshalsea.

Next day, and the day after, and every day, all graced by more dinner company, cards descended on Mr Dorrit like theatrical snow. As the friend and relative by marriage of the illustrious Merdle, everybody wanted to make or improve Mr Dorrit's acquaintances. So the dream increased in rapture every hour, as Mr Dorrit felt increasingly sensible that this connection had brought him forward indeed.

Only one thing concerned him. It was the Chief Butler. That stupendous character looked at him, in the course of his official looking at the dinners, in a manner that Mr Dorrit considered questionable. He looked at him, as he passed through the hall and up the staircase, going to dinner, with a glazed fixedness that Mr Dorrit did not like. Seated at table, Mr Dorrit still saw him through his wine-glass, regarding him with a cold and ghostly eye. It misgave him that the Chief Butler must have known a Collegian, and must have seen him in the College – perhaps had been presented to him. Let him think what he would, the Chief Butler had him in his supercilious eye, even when that eye was on the plate and other table-garniture; and he never let him out of it.

CHAPTER 15

Missing

The term of Mr Dorrit's visit was within two days of being out when one of the servants of the hotel presented himself bearing a card. Mr Dorrit, taking it, read:

"Mrs Finching."

On announcing a connection to Little Dorrit, Flora, putting aside her veil with a bashful tremor upon her, proceeded to introduce herself lengthily in her usual confused speech which she ended with the insightful words, "I am roving off again."

"The object of my intruding," she continued, "is my own without the slightest consultation with any human being and most decidedly not with Arthur – pray excuse me Doyce and Clennam I don't know what I am saying."

"State your pleasure, madam."

"There's a foreigner from Italy who disappeared in the City as no doubt you have read in the papers equally with myself," said Flora.

She produced from her pocket a police handbill, setting forth that a foreign gentleman of the name of Blandois, last from Venice, had unaccountably disappeared on such a night in such a part of the city of London; that he was known to have entered such a house, at such an hour; that he was stated by the inmates of that house to have left it, about so many minutes before midnight; and that he had never been beheld since.

Mr Dorrit read the bill.

"Blandois!" he said. "Venice! And this description! I know this gentleman. He has been in my house. He is intimately acquainted with a gentleman of good family (but in indifferent circumstances), of whom I am a – hum – patron."

"Then my humble and pressing entreaty is the more," said Flora, "that in travelling back you will have the kindness to look for this foreign gentleman."

"Pray, madam," said Mr Dorrit, referring to the handbill again, "who is Clennam and Co?"

"He has the grimmest of women for a mother and is an old man besides," said Flora.

"I would not detain you one moment longer," said Flora, "if you would have the goodness to give your promise as a gentleman that both in going back to Italy and in Italy too you would look for this Mr Blandois high and low and if you found or heard of him make him come forward for the clearing of all parties."

By that time Mr Dorrit had so far recovered from his bewilderment, as to be able to say, in a tolerably connected manner, that he should consider that his duty. Flora was delighted with her success, and rose to take her leave.

Mr Dorrit found that the interview had summoned back discarded reminiscences which jarred with the Merdle dinner-table. He wrote and sent off a brief note excusing himself for that day, for he thought it behoved his importance to pursue some direct inquiry into the Blandois disappearance, and be in a condition to carry back to Mr Henry Gowan the result of his own personal investigation.

Having dined as plainly as the establishment and the Courier would let him, he set out in a hackney-cabriolet alone for Mrs Clennam's gloomy house. A watch was evidently kept upon the place. As Mr Dorrit paused, a man passed in from over the way, and another man passed out from some dark corner within; and both looked at him in passing, and both remained standing about.

The door gave back a dreary, vacant sound, and a woman with her apron thrown over her face and head stood in the aperture.

"Who is it?" said the woman.

Mr Dorrit, much amazed by this appearance, replied that he was from Italy, and that he wished to ask a question relative to the missing person, whom he knew.

"Hi!" cried the woman, raising a cracked voice. "Jeremiah!"

Upon this, a dry old man appeared and a strong stern voice, though a woman's, called from above, "Who is it?"

"Who is it?" returned Jeremiah. "More inquiries. A gentleman from Italy."

"Bring him up here!"

Mrs Clennam had her books open on her little table. "Oh!" said she abruptly, as she eyed her visitor with a steady look. "You are from Italy, sir, are you? Well? Where is this missing man? Have you come to give us information?"

"So far from it, I – hum – have come to seek information."

"Is Mr Blandois a friend of yours?"

"No – a – hum – an acquaintance," answered Mr Dorrit.

"You have no commission from him, perhaps?"

"Certainly not. I wished to make myself acquainted with the circumstances at first-hand, because there is – ha hum – an English gentleman in Italy whom I shall no doubt see on my return, who has been in habits of close and daily intimacy with Monsieur Blandois. Mr Henry Gowan. You may know the name."

"Never heard of it."

"Pray, madam," said Mr Dorrit. "Was Monsieur Blandois here on business on the night indicated in this present sheet?"

"On what he called business," returned Mrs Clennam. "I have no doubt that he is travelling somewhere, or hiding somewhere."

"Do you know – ha – why he should hide anywhere?"

"No."

At that moment, Mistress Affery dropped the candlestick she held, and cried out, "There! Oh good Lord! there it is again. Hark, Jeremiah! Now!"

If there were any sound at all, it was so slight that she must have fallen into a confirmed habit of listening for sounds; but Mr Dorrit believed he did hear a something, like the falling of dry leaves. The woman's terror, for a very short space, seemed to touch the three; and they all listened.

Then Jeremiah took another candle from Mrs Clennam's table, and said, "Now, sir; shall I light you down?"

Mr Dorrit professed himself obliged, and went down. Mr Flintwinch shut him out, and chained him out, without a moment's loss of time.

He was again passed by the two men, one going out and the other coming in; got into the vehicle he had left waiting, and was driven away. Before he had gone far, the driver stopped to let him know that he had given his name, number, and address to the two men, on their joint requisition; and also the address at which he had taken Mr Dorrit up, the hour at which he had been called from his stand and the way by which he had come.

CHAPTER 16

A Castle in the Air

The farewell banquet to Mr Dorrit was of a gorgeous nature, and wound up his visit in a most brilliant manner.

"My dear," he told Fanny at parting, "our family looks to you to – ha – assert its dignity and – hum – maintain its importance. I know you will never disappoint it."

"No, Papa," said Fanny, "you may rely upon that, I think. My best love to dearest Amy, and I will write to her very soon."

They parted in an outer drawing-room, where only Mr Sparkler waited on his lady, and dutifully bided his time for shaking hands. When Mr Sparkler was admitted to this closing audience, Mr Merdle came creeping in and insisted on escorting Mr Dorrit downstairs.

The grandeur of his farewell was yet full upon Mr Dorrit when he alighted at his hotel. He was passing through the hall with a serene magnificence, when lo! a sight presented itself that struck him dumb and motionless. John Chivery stood there in his best clothes, and a bundle of cigars in his hand!

Mr Dorrit glared on the young man, choked, and said, in the mildest of tones, "Ah! Young John! It is Young John, I think; is it not? He may come up. Let Young John follow. I will speak to him above."

Young John followed, smiling and much gratified. Mr Dorrit's rooms were reached. Candles were lighted. The attendants withdrew.

"Now, sir," said Mr Dorrit, turning round upon him and seizing him by the collar when they were safely alone. "What do you mean by this?"

The amazement and horror depicted in the unfortunate John's face – for he had rather expected to be embraced next – were of that powerfully expressive nature that Mr Dorrit withdrew his hand and merely glared at him.

"How dare you do this?" said Mr Dorrit. "How do you presume to come here? How dare you insult me?"

"I thought, sir," said Young John, with as pale and shocked a face as ever had been turned to Mr Dorrit's in his life – even in his College life: "I thought, sir, you mightn't object to have the goodness to accept a bundle – "

"Damn your bundle, sir!" cried Mr Dorrit, in irrepressible rage. "I – hum – don't smoke."

"I humbly beg your pardon, sir. You used to."

"Tell me that again," cried Mr Dorrit, quite beside himself, "and I'll take the poker to you!"

John Chivery backed to the door.

"Stop, sir!" cried Mr Dorrit. "stop! Sit down. Confound you, sit down! What else did you come for, sir?"

"Nothing else in the world, sir. Oh dear me! Only to say, sir, that I hoped you was well, and only to ask if Miss Amy was well?"

Mr Dorrit was ashamed. He went back to the window and when he turned, he looked tired and ill.

"Young John, I am very sorry to have been hasty with you. Sit down again, Young John."

"Thank you, sir – but I'd rather stand."

Mr Dorrit sat down instead. After painfully holding his head a little while, he turned it to his visitor, and said, with an effort to be easy:

"And how is your father, Young John? How – ha – how are they all?"

"Thank you, sir, They're all pretty well, sir. They're not any ways complaining. As well as my old business I am in my" – John hesitated a little – "father's business."

"Oh indeed!" said Mr Dorrit. "Do you – ha hum – go upon the ha – "

"Lock, sir? Yes, sir."

"Much to do, John?"

"Yes, sir." He stood up. "I wish you good-night, sir."

"Stay a moment, John – ha – stay a moment. Hum. Leave me the cigars, John, I – ha – beg."

"Certainly, sir." John put them, with a trembling hand, on the table.

"Stay another moment. It would be a – ha – a gratification to me to send a little – hum – Testimonial, by such a trusty messenger, to be divided among – ha hum – them – them – according to their wants. Would you object to take it, John?"

"Not in any ways, sir."

"Thank you, John. I – ha – I'll write it, John."

His hand shook and he wrote in a tremulous scrawl. It was a cheque for one hundred pounds. He folded it up, put it in young John's hand, and pressed the hand in his.

"I hope you'll – ha – overlook – hum – what has passed, John."

"Don't speak of it, sir, on any accounts. I don't in any ways bear malice, I'm sure."

After remaining alone for an hour, Mr Dorrit rang for the Courier, "You can take that bundle of cigars to smoke on the journey, if you like," said Mr Dorrit, with a careless wave of his hand. "Ha – brought by – hum – little offering from – ha – son of old tenant of mine."

Next morning's sun saw Mr Dorrit's equipage upon the Dover road, and another day's sun saw him at Calais. And having now got the Channel between himself and John Chivery, he began to feel safe, and to find that the foreign air was lighter to breathe than the air of England.

On again by the heavy French roads. Arrived at Paris, and resting there, Mr Dorrit strolled about the streets, looking in at the shop-windows, and particularly the jewellers' windows. Ultimately, he went into the most famous jeweller's, and said he wanted to buy a gift for a lady.

What species of gift did Monsieur desire? asked the little woman. A love gift? For example, these ravishing ear-rings and this necklace so superb to correspond, were what one called a love-gift. These brooches and these rings, of a beauty so gracious and celestial, were what one called, with the permission of Monsieur, nuptial gifts.

Perhaps it would be a good arrangement, Mr Dorrit hinted, smiling, to purchase both, and to present the love-gift first, and to finish with the nuptial offering?

Building his castle-in-the-air with all his might, but reserving the plans of his castle exclusively for his own eye, Mr Dorrit posted away for Marseilles and on to Rome.

CHAPTER 17

The Storming of the Castle in the Air

As they neared Rome, Mr Dorrit became tired and ill and disturbed, seeing the past all round him.

Little Dorrit met him with a cry of pleasure. She put her arms about her father's neck, and kissed him again and again.

"I think you look a little tired, love."

"Then you are mistaken," said Mr Dorrit, and spoke in a confused way to his brother who was in the same room to greet him.

"Frederick, you are not well. I beg you to go to bed."

Mr Dorrit took very little supper, but was a long time over it, and often reverted to his brother's declining state. He spoke about the glorious state that Mr Merdle kept, and asked after Mrs Merdle.

Little Dorrit spoke quietly. "She is very well. She is going away next week and is going to have a great farewell Assembly, dear, and a dinner before it. She has invited both you and me to her Dinner the day after tomorrow."

"Write round in the morning, and say that I have returned, and shall – hum – be delighted."

The day came for the farewell banquet and Mrs Merdle received Mr Dorrit with great distinction. The table was long, and the dinner was long and Little Dorrit, overshadowed by a large pair of black whiskers and a large white cravat, lost sight of her father altogether, until a servant put a scrap of paper in her hand, with a whispered request from Mrs Merdle that she would read it directly. Mrs Merdle had written on it in pencil, "Pray come and speak to Mr Dorrit, I doubt if he is well."

She was hurrying to him, unobserved, when he got up out of his chair, and leaning over the table called to her, supposing her to be still in her place:

"Amy, Amy, my child!"

The action was so unusual, to say nothing of his strange eager appearance and strange eager voice, that it instantaneously caused a profound silence.

"Amy, my dear," he repeated. "Will you go and see if Bob is on the lock?"

She was at his side, and touching him, but he still perversely supposed her to be in her seat, and called out, still leaning over the table, "Amy, Amy. I don't feel quite myself. Ha. I don't know what's the matter with me. I particularly want to see Bob."

He looked confusedly about him, and, becoming conscious of the number of faces by which he was surrounded, addressed them:

"Ladies and gentlemen, the duty – ha – devolves upon me of – hum – welcoming you to the Marshalsea."

Little Dorrit was pale and frightened; but she had no other care than to soothe him and get him away, for his own dear sake. She was between him and the wondering faces, imploring him to go away with her.

By this time, the exceeding mortification undergone by Mrs Merdle occasioned the withdrawal of the greater part of the company into another room and soon Little Dorrit and her father were left to the servants who got him into the coach and up to his room, where Little Dorrit laid him down on his bed. And from that hour his poor maimed spirit, only remembering the place where it had broken its wings, cancelled the dream through which it had since groped, and knew of nothing beyond the Marshalsea. As for Little Dorrit and his brother Frederick, they remained there watching him until his last hour.

That night, unable to sustain the anguish of his brother's death, Frederick died too. The two brothers were before their Father; far beyond the twilight judgement of this world; high above its mists and obscurities and strange dreams.

CHAPTER 18

Introduces the Next

The passengers were landing from the packet on the pier at Calais. Clennam, harassed by more anxieties than one, sought out a certain street and number which he kept in his mind.

"So Pancks said," he murmured to himself, as he stopped before a dull house answering to the address. "I suppose his information to be correct and his discovery, among Mr Casby's loose papers, indisputable; but, without it, I should hardly have supposed this to be a likely place."

A strong, cheerful peasant woman stood in a dark doorway, and Clennam said in French, that he wished to see the English lady.

"Enter then and ascend, if you please. What name?"

"Monsieur Blandois," said Clennam.

"With pleasure, Monsieur."

After some pause, a door of communication with another room was opened, and a lady entered. She manifested great surprise on seeing Clennam, and her glance went round the room in search of someone else.

"Pardon me, Miss Wade. I am alone."

"It was not your name that was brought to me."

"No; I know that. Excuse me. I have already had experience that my name does not predispose you to an interview; and I ventured to mention the name of one I am in search of."

"Pray," she returned, motioning him to a chair so coldly that he remained standing, "what name was it that you gave?"

"I mentioned the name of Blandois. Can you give me some little clue by which I can establish what has become of him? This is the favour I ask in a distress of mind for which I hope you will feel some consideration. If you should have any reason for imposing conditions upon me, I will respect it without asking what it is."

"You chanced to see me in the street with the man," she observed. "Then you knew the man before?"

"Not before; afterwards," said Arthur, "on the very night of his disappearance. In my mother's room, in fact. I left him there. You will read in this paper all that is known of him."

He handed her one of the printed police bills, which she read with a steady and attentive face.

"This is more than I knew of him," she said, giving it back. "Come, sir. I will be as open with you as you can desire. I will confess that if I cared for my credit I should regard myself as heavily compromised by having had anything to do with this fellow. Yet he never passed in at *my* door – never sat in colloquy with *me* until midnight. That he is a low, mercenary wretch whom I first saw prowling about Italy (where I was, not long ago), and that I hired him there, as the suitable instrument of a purpose I happened to have, I have no objection to tell you. In short, it was worth my while, for my own pleasure – the gratification of a strong feeling – to pay a spy who would fetch and carry for money. I paid this creature. And I dare say he would have taken any life with as little scruple as he took my money. That, at least, is my opinion of him; and I see it is not very far removed from yours. Your mother's opinion of him, I am to assume, was vastly different."

"My mother, let me remind you," said Clennam, "was first brought into communication with him in the unlucky course of business."

"It appears to have been an unlucky course of business," returned Miss Wade; "and business hours on that occasion were late."

170

"You imply," said Arthur, smarting under these cool-handed thrusts, "that there was something – "

"Mr Clennam," she composedly interrupted, "I have spoken of him as still living," she added, "but he may have been put out of the way for anything I know or care. I have no further occasion for him. He was the chosen associate of your dear friend, Mr Gowan, was he not? Why don't you ask your dear friend to help you?"

"Mr Gowan knows nothing additional about him. He was a chance acquaintance, made abroad."

"A chance acquaintance made abroad!" she repeated. "Yes. Your dear friend has need to divert himself with all the acquaintances he can make, seeing what a wife he has. I hate his wife, sir, and I hate him worse than his wife, because I was once dupe enough, and false enough to myself, almost to love him. Here sir, if you want to know what I mean by hating, read these papers."

She went to the bureau, unlocked it, took from an inner drawer a few folded sheets of paper and gave them to Arthur. "Read those at your leisure, and you will see what I mean by hating! Now! No more of that! Sir, whether you find me temporarily and cheaply lodging in an empty London house, or in a Calais apartment, you will find Harriet with me. You may like to see her before you leave." Arthur nodded and Miss Wade cried out: "Harriet, come in!" She called Harriet again and the second call produced Harriet, once Tattycoram.

"Here is Mr Clennam," said Miss Wade. "Not come in search of you, you see; but still seeking someone. He wants that Blandois man."

"With whom I saw you in the Strand in London," hinted Arthur.

"If you know anything of him, Harriet, except that he came from Venice – which we all know – tell it to Mr Clennam freely."

"I know nothing more about him," said the girl. She looked quickly at Arthur and said: "Are they well, sir?"

"Who?"

She glanced at Miss Wade and said, "Mr and Mrs Meagles."

"They were, when I last heard of them. They are not at home. By the way, let me ask you. Is it true that you were seen there?"

"Where? Where does anyone say I was seen?" returned the girl, sullenly casting down her eyes.

"Looking in at the garden gate of the cottage."

"No," said Miss Wade. "she has never been near it."

"You are wrong, then," said the girl. "I went down there the last time we were in London. I went one afternoon when you left me alone. And I did look in."

As each of the two handsome faces looked at the other, Clennam felt how each of the natures must be constantly tearing the other to pieces.

"Oh!" said Miss Wade, coldly subduing and removing her glance; "if you had any desire to see the place where you led the life from which I rescued you because you had found out what it was, that is another thing. But is that your truth to me? Is that your fidelity to me? Is that the common cause I make with you?"

"If you speak so of them with anyone else by to hear, you'll provoke me to take their part," said the girl.

"Go back to them," Miss Wade retorted. "Go back to them."

"You know very well," retorted Harriet in her turn, "that I won't go back to them. I went to look at the house, because I had often thought that I should like to see it once more. I will ask again how they are, because I once liked them and at times thought they were kind to me."

Hereupon Clennam said that he was sure they would still receive her kindly, if she should ever desire to return.

"Never!" said the girl passionately. "I shall never do that. Nobody knows that better than Miss Wade, though she taunts me because she has made me her dependent."

Arthur Clennam looked at them, standing a little distance asunder in the dull confined room, each proudly cherishing her own anger.

He said a word or two of leave-taking and came down the dark winding stairs into the yard with an increased sense of gloom. Pondering much on what he had seen and heard in that house, as well as on the failure of all his efforts to trace the suspicious character who was lost, he returned to London and to England by the packet that had taken him over. On the way he unfolded the sheets of paper, and read the story of Miss Wade: of her childhood with her grandmother where the other children patronised her and where one of them, Charlotte, whom she liked, tormented her; of how she went on to be a governess to the family of a poor nobleman whose wife patronised her and was jealous of the childrens' affection for her. And how eventually, after one or two short and very similar experiences, she entered another family where she had but one pupil: a girl of fifteen,

172

who was the only daughter. The parents were elderly people of station, and rich. A nephew whom they had brought up was a frequent visitor at the house and began to pay her so much attention it led to their being engaged. They planned to get married in six months and go to India. However he made her feel as if he had bought her for her looks and she did not want him to parade his attachment before the rich people.

His aunt deliberately and wilfully added to her trials and vexations. It was at the time, (Arthur read with interest,) that Mr Gowan appeared at the house. He made Miss Wade feel more and more resentful, and more and more contemptible, by always presenting everything that surrounded her with some new hateful light upon it, laying bare every smarting wound she had. As a result she soon began to like the society of Mr Gowan better than any other.

This went on, until the aunt, her Mistress, took it upon herself to suggest that it might be better if she were a little less companionable with Mr Gowan. It was then Miss Wade told her that Mr Gowan was the only relief she had had in her degradation; that she had borne it too long, and would see none of them more. And she never did.

As for Mr Gowan, it was not very long before he was courting his present wife whom Miss Wade hated. She travelled a little until, among the company she had been frequenting, she found a young girl in whose position there was a singular likeness to her own. She thought she would try to release Harriet from her bondage and sense of injustice but had not succeeded. None the less, they had been together ever since, sharing her small means.

Arthur folded up the papers and pondered for a long time on the frailties of human beings.

CHAPTER 19

Who Passes by this Road so Late?

Arthur Clennam had made his unavailing expedition to Calais in the midst of a great pressure of business. A certain barbaric Power with valuable possessions on the map of the world, had occasion for the services of one or two engineers and Daniel Doyce was one of the chosen. There was no foreseeing at that time whether he would be absent for months or years. The preparations for his departure, and the conscientious arrangement for him of all the details and results of their joint business, had necessitated labour within a short compass of time, which had occupied Clennam day and night. He had slipped across the water in his first leisure, and had slipped as quickly back again for his farewell interview with Doyce.

Arthur now showed him, with pains and care, the state of their gains and losses, responsibilities and prospects.

"It's all beautiful, Clennam," admired Doyce, "in its regularity and order. Nothing can be plainer. Nothing can be better. I have perfect confidence in my partner, and I am satisfied that he will do what is best. If I have a prejudice connected with money and money figures it is against speculating."

"It so happens," said Clennam, "that just now, not half an hour before you came down, I was saying the same thing to Pancks, who looked in here. We both agreed that to travel out of safe investments is one of the most dangerous, as it is one of the most common, of those follies which often deserve the name of vices."

"And now," said Daniel, looking at his watch, "as time and tide wait for no man, my trusty partner, and as I am ready for starting, bag and baggage, at the gate below, let me say a last word. I want you to grant a request of mine, that you will abandon my invention. It has done me harm, my friend. It has aged me, tired me, vexed me, disappointed me. It does no man any good to have his patience worn out, and to think himself ill-used. I fancy, even already, that unavailing attendance on delays and evasions has made you something less elastic than you used to be."

"Private anxieties may have done that for the moment," said Clennam, "but not official harrying. Not yet. I am not hurt yet."

"Then you won't grant my request?"

"Decidedly, no," said Clennam.

As there was no moving him, Daniel Doyce returned the grasp of his hand, and, casting a farewell look round the counting-house, went downstairs with him. Daniel gave them all a hearty "Good-bye, Men!" and the coach disappeared from sight, as if the concussion of the air had blown it out of Bleeding Heart Yard.

Mr Baptist, as a grateful little fellow in a position of trust, was among the workmen, and had done as much towards the cheering as a mere foreigner could, until Clennam beckoned him to follow upstairs.

Arthur's liberated attention soon reverted to the theme that was foremost in his thoughts, namely every circumstance that had impressed itself upon his mind on the mysterious night when he had seen the man at his mother's. He recalled a tune the man had hummed:

"*Who passes by this road so late?*
Compagnon de la Majolaine – "

"*Of all the king's knights 'tis the flower,*
Compagnon de la Majolaine;"

continued John Baptist deferentially. "Such a pretty, innocent song, sir. They all know it in France. I have heard it many times, sung by the little children."

"The last time I heard it," returned Arthur, "was in a voice quite the reverse of pretty, and quite the reverse of innocent." He said it more to himself than to his companion, and added to himself, repeating the man's next words. "Death of my life, sir, it's my character to be impatient!"

"*Eh!*" cried John Baptist, and with his rapid native action, his hands made the outline of a high hook nose, pushed his eyes near together, dishevelled his hair, puffed out his upper lip to represent a thick moustache, and threw the heavy end of an ideal cloak over his shoulder.

"In the name of Fate and wonder," said Clennam, "you have just now described a man who was by when you heard that song; have you not?"

"Yes!" said Mr Baptist, nodding fifty times.

"Stay!" cried Clennam, spreading out the handbill on his desk. "Was this the man? Come here and look over me, while I read."

"It is the man! Behold him!"

"This is of far greater moment to me," said Clennam, in great agitation, "than you can imagine. Tell me where you knew the man."

"At Marsiglia – Marseilles."

"What was he?"

"A prisoner, an assassin!"

Clennam fell back as if the word had struck him a blow: so terrible did it make his mother's communication with the man appear.

John Baptist told Arthur how he was brought into such foul company through a little contraband trading, and how he had in time been released from prison, but one night at the house of entertainment called the Break of Day at Chalons on the Saone, had been awakened in his bed by the same assassin, then assuming the name of Lagnier, though his name had formerly been Blandois; how he held the assassin in such dread that he had fled from him at daylight, and how he had ever since been haunted by the fear of seeing the assassin again and being claimed by him as an acquaintance.

"Listen," said Arthur, very seriously. "This man has wholly disappeared."

"Of it I am well content!" said John Baptist, raising his eyes piously. "A thousand thanks to Heaven! Accursed assassin!"

"Not so," returned Clennam; "for until something more is heard of him, I can never know an hour's peace."

CHAPTER 20

Mistress Affery makes a Conditional Promise, Respecting her Dreams

Clennam entered on a weary day. It was in vain that he tried to control his attention by directing it to any business occupation or train of thought. The fact that his mother had been in communication with such a man, would remain unalterable. That the communication had been of a secret kind, and that she had been submissive to him and afraid of him, he hoped might be known to no one beyond himself; yet, knowing it, how could he separate it from his old vague fears, and how believe that there was nothing evil in such relations? He resolved, if his mother would still admit of no approach, to make a desperate appeal to Affery, and this was the decision he put in practice when the day closed in.

His first disappointment, on arriving at the house, was to find the door open, and Mr Flintwinch smoking a pipe on the steps.

"Have you any news?" said Arthur.

"We have no news," said Jeremiah.

"I mean of the foreign man," Arthur explained.

"*I* mean of the foreign man," said Jeremiah.

He looked so grim, as he stood askew, with the knot of his cravat under his ear, that the thought passed into Clennam's mind, and not for the first time, could Flintwinch for a purpose of his own have got rid of Blandois? Could it have been his secret, and his safety, that were at issue?

"I'll tell you what I do," said Mr Flintwinch, glancing up at the windows; "I see the light of fire and candle in your mother's room!"

"And what has that to do with it?"

"Why, sir, I read by it," said Mr Flintwinch, screwing himself at him, "that if it's advisable (as the proverb says it is) to let sleeping dogs lie, it's just as advisable, perhaps, to let missing dogs lie. Let 'em be. They generally turn up soon enough."

"My mother is alone, I suppose?"

"Not alone," said Mr Flintwinch. "Mr Casby and his daughter are with her."

Clennam decided to speak to his mother without postponement.

"Mother," he said after greeting her and her company, and moving her in the wheelchair to the desk and seating himself on the stool, "I have heard something today which I feel persuaded you don't know, and which I think you should know, of the antecedents of that man I saw here. He has been a prisoner in a French gaol."

She answered with composure, "I should think that very likely."

"But in a gaol for criminals, mother. On an accusation of murder."

She started at the word, and her looks expressed her natural horror. Yet she still spoke aloud, when she demanded: –

"Who told you so?"

"A man who was his fellow-prisoner."

"That man's antecedents, I suppose, were not known to you, before he told you?"

"No."

"Though the man himself was?"

"Yes."

Mrs Clennam's attentive frown expanded by degrees into a severe look of triumph, and she retorted with emphasis, "Take care how you judge others, then. I say to you, Arthur, for your good, take care how you judge!"

"Mother, shall I do nothing to assist you?"

"Nothing."

"Will you entrust me with no confidence, no charge, no explanation? Will you take no counsel with me? Will you not let me come near you?"

"How can you ask me?" she replied. "You separated yourself from my affairs. It was not my act; it was yours. How can you consistently ask me such a question? You know that you left me to Flintwinch, and that he occupies your place. A prisoner, in a French gaol, on an accusation of murder," repeated Mrs Clennam, steadily going over what her son had said. "That is all you know of him from the fellow-prisoner?"

"In substance, all. But I did not mean, mother, that you should repeat what I have communicated. I think you had better not repeat it."

"Do you make that a condition with me?"

"Well! Yes."

"Observe, then! It is you who make this a secret," said she, holding up her hand, "and not I. Now, let me go."

He yielded to her imperious but elated look, and turned her chair back to the place from which he had wheeled it. In doing so he saw elation in the face of Mr Flintwinch, which most assuredly was not inspired by Flora.

Nothing remained but the appeal to his old friend Affery, even though she warded off conversation with a toasting-fork.

Arthur thought of an expedient which Flora might originate so he whispered to her, "Could you say you would like to go through the house?"

Now, poor Flora, being always in fluctuating expectation of the time when Clennam would renew his boyhood and be madly in love with her again, received the whisper with the utmost delight.

"Dear Mrs Clennam," she said with much stuttering and muttering, "would it be inconvenient or asking too much to beg to be permitted to revive scenes that dwell in my mind, and walk through the house?"

Mrs Clennam intimated that all the house was open to her. Flora rose and looked to Arthur for his escort.

"Certainly," said he, aloud; "and Affery will light us, I dare say."

Affery was excusing herself with, "Don't ask nothing of me, Arthur!" when Mr Flintwinch stopped her with, "Why not? Affery, what's the matter with you, woman? Why not, jade?"

She came unwillingly out of her corner, and took the candlestick he offered.

"Go before, you fool!" said Jeremiah. "Are you going up, or down, Mrs Finching?"

Flora answered, "Down."

"Then go before, and down, you Affery," said Jeremiah. "And do it properly, or I'll come rolling down the banisters, and tumbling over you!"

Affery headed the exploring party; Jeremiah closed it. He had no intention of leaving them. Clennam looking back, and seeing him following three stairs behind, in the coolest and most methodical manner, exclaimed in a low voice, "Is there no getting rid of him!"

Flora reassured his mind by replying promptly, "Why though not exactly proper Arthur and a thing I couldn't think of before a younger man or a stranger still I don't mind him if you so particularly wish it and provided you'll have the goodness not to take me too tight."

Wanting the heart to explain that this was not at all what he meant, Arthur extended his supporting arm round Flora's figure.

In this preposterous attitude, unspeakably at variance with his anxious mind, Clennam descended to the basement of the house; finding that wherever it became darker than elsewhere, Flora became heavier, and that when the house was lightest she was too.

Returning from the dismal kitchen regions, which were as dreary as they could be, Mistress Affery passed with the light into his father's old room, and then into the old dining-room; always passing on before like a phantom that was not to be overtaken, and neither turning nor answering when he whispered, "Affery! I want to speak to you!"

In the dining-room, a sentimental desire came over Flora to look into the dragon closet which had so often swallowed Arthur in the days of his boyhood, when a knock was heard at the outer door.

Mistress Affery, with a suppressed cry, threw her apron over her head.

"Is anybody going to the door?" said Arthur.

"I am going to the door, sir," returned Jeremiah savagely. "Stay here the while, all! Affery, my woman, move an inch, or speak a word in your foolishness, and I'll treble your dose!"

The moment he was gone, Arthur released Mrs Finching: with some difficulty, by reason of that lady misunderstanding his intentions, and making arrangements with a view to tightening instead of slackening.

"Affery, speak to me now!"

"Don't touch me, Arthur!" she cried, shrinking from him. "Don't come near me. He'll see you. Jeremiah will. Don't."

"He can't see me," returned Arthur, suiting the action to the word, "if I blow the candle out."

"He'll hear you," cried Affery.

"He can't hear me," returned Arthur, suiting the action to the words again, "if I draw you into this black closet, and speak here. Why do you hide your face?"

"Because I am afraid of seeing something."

"You can't be afraid of seeing anything in this darkness, Affery."

"Yes I am. Much more than if it was light."

"Why are you afraid?"

"Because the house is full of mysteries and secrets; because it's full of whisperings and counsellings; because it's full of noises. There never was such a house for noises. I shall die of 'em, if Jeremiah don't strangle me first. As I expect he will."

"I have never heard any noises here, worth speaking of."

"Ah! But you would, though, if you lived in the house. Here's Jeremiah! You'll get me killed."

"My good Affery, I solemnly declare to you that I can see the light of the open door on the pavement of the hall, and so could you if you would uncover your face and look."

"I durstn't do it," said Affery, "I durstn't never, Arthur. I'm always blind-folded when Jeremiah an't a looking, and sometimes even when he is."

"He cannot shut the door without my seeing him," said Arthur. "You are as safe with me as if he was fifty miles away. Affery, I want to know what is amiss here; I want some light thrown on the secrets of this house."

"I tell you, Arthur," she interrupted, "noises is the secrets, rustlings and stealings about, tremblings, treads overhead and treads underneath."

"But those are not all the secrets."

"I don't know," said Affery. "Don't ask me no more. Your old sweetheart an't far off, and she's a blabber."

His old sweetheart, being in fact so near at hand that she was then reclining against him in a flutter, a very substantial angle of forty-five degrees, here interposed to assure Mistress Affery with greater earnestness than directness of asseveration, that what she heard should go no further, but should be kept inviolate, "if on no other account on Arthur's – "

"I appeal to you, Affery," interrupted Clennam, "for my mother's sake, for your husband's sake, for my own, for all our sakes. I am sure you can tell me something connected with the coming here of this man, if you will."

"I'll tell you then," said Affery, "that the first time he ever come he heard the noises his own self. 'What's that?' he said to me. 'I don't know what it is,' I says to him, catching hold of him, 'but I have heard it over and over again.' While I says it, he stands a looking at me, all of a shake, he do."

"Has he been here often?"

"Only that night, and the last night."

"What did you see of him on the last night, after I was gone?"

"Them two clever ones had him all alone to themselves."

"And did you hear or see no more, Affery?"

"Don't I tell you I was sent to bed, Arthur! Here he is!"

"I assure you he is still at the door. Those whisperings and counsellings, Affery, that you have spoken of. What are they?"

"How should I know? Don't ask me nothing about 'em, Arthur. Get away!"

"But my dear Affery; unless I can gain some insight into these hidden things, in spite of your husband and in spite of my mother, ruin will come of it."

"Don't ask me nothing," repeated Affery. "I have been in a dream for ever so long. Go away, go away!"

"What do you mean by being in a dream?"

"I an't a going to tell you. Get away! I shouldn't tell you, if you was by yourself; much less with your old sweetheart here."

It was equally vain for Arthur to entreat, and for Flora to protest. Affery, who had been trembling and struggling the whole time, turned a deaf ear to all adjuration, and was bent on forcing herself out of the closet.

"I'd sooner scream to Jeremiah than say another word! I'll call out to him, Arthur, if you don't give over speaking to me. Now here's the very last word I'll say afore I call to him – If ever you begin to get the better of them two clever ones your own self, then do you get the better of 'em

181

afore my face; and then do you say to me, Affery tell your dreams! Maybe, then I'll tell 'em!"

The shutting of the door stopped Arthur from replying. They glided into the places where Jeremiah had left them; and Clennam, stepping forward as that old gentleman returned, informed him that he had accidentally extinguished the candle. Mr Flintwinch looked on as he re-lighted it at the lamp in the hall, and took such umbrage at seeing his wife with her apron over her head, that he charged at her.

Flora, now permanently heavy, did not release Arthur from the survey of the house, until it had extended even to his old garret bedchamber. His thoughts were otherwise occupied than with the tour of inspection; yet he took particular notice at the time, as he afterwards had occasion to remember, of a resistance to the opening of one room door, which occasioned Affery to cry out that somebody was hiding inside, and to continue to believe so, though somebody was sought and not discovered. When they at last returned to his mother's room, they found her shading her face with her muffled hand, and talking in a low voice to the Patriarch as he stood benevolently before the fire.

CHAPTER 21

The Evening of a Long Day

That illustrious man and great national ornament, Mr Merdle, continued his shining course. A baronetcy was spoken of with confidence; a peerage was frequently mentioned.

So quietly did the mowing of the old scythe go on, that fully three months had passed unnoticed since the two English brothers had been laid in one tomb in the strangers' cemetery at Rome.

Mr and Mrs Sparkler were established in their own house: a little mansion, quite a triumph of inconvenience, with a perpetual smell in it of soup and coach-horses, but extremely dear, as being exactly in the centre of the habitable globe. In this enviable abode (and envied it really was by many people), Mrs Sparkler attempted to make conversation with Mr Sparkler, who now seemed to be permanently under her influence.

Mr and Mrs Sparkler had been dining alone, with their gloom cast over them, and Mrs Sparkler reclined on a drawing-room sofa. Her conversation turned first to the deaths of her father and uncle, and then to her sister.

"Speaking of Amy; – my poor little pet was devotedly attached to poor Papa, and no doubt will have lamented his loss exceedingly, and grieved very much. I have done so myself. I have felt it dreadfully. But Amy will no doubt have felt it even more, from having been on the spot the whole time, and having been with poor dear Papa at the last; which I unhappily was not."

Here Fanny stopped to weep, and to say, "Dear, dear, beloved Papa! How truly gentlemanly he was! What a contrast to poor Uncle! From the effects of that trying time," she pursued, "my good little Mouse will have to be roused. Also, from the effects of this long attendance upon our brother Edward who has become ill; an attendance which is not yet over, which may even go on for some time longer, and which in the meanwhile unsettles us all by keeping poor dear Papa's affairs from being wound up. Fortunately, however, the papers with his agents here being all sealed up and locked up, as he left them when he providentially came to England, the affairs are in that state of order that they can wait until my brother Edward recovers his health in Sicily. That he contracted Malaria Fever somewhere, either by travelling day and night to Rome, where, after all, he arrived too late to see poor dear Papa before his death – or under some other unwholesome circumstances – is indubitable. Likewise his extremely careless life has made him a very bad subject for it indeed."

A double knock was heard at the door. A very odd knock. Low, as if to avoid making a noise and attracting attention. Long, as if the person knocking were preoccupied in mind, and forgot to leave off. When the candles were brought in, Mr Merdle was discovered standing behind the door, picking his lips. "I thought I'd give you a call," he said. "I am rather particularly occupied just now; and, as I happened to be out for a stroll, I thought I'd give you a call."

As he was in dinner dress, Fanny asked him where he had been dining?

"Well," said Mr Merdle, "I haven't been dining anywhere, particularly."

"Of course you have dined?" said Fanny.

"Why – no, I haven't exactly dined," said Mr Merdle.

183

He had passed his hand over his yellow forehead and considered, as if he were not sure about it. Something to eat was proposed. "No, thank you," said Mr Merdle, "I don't feel inclined for it. I was to have dined out along with Mrs Merdle. But as I didn't feel inclined for dinner, I let Mrs Merdle go by herself just as we were getting into the carriage, and thought I'd take a stroll instead."

Would he have tea or coffee? "No, thank you," said Mr Merdle. "I looked in at the Club, and got a bottle of wine."

"I was speaking of poor Papa when you came in, sir," said Mrs Sparkler.

"Aye! Quite a coincidence," said Mr Merdle.

Fanny did not see that; but felt it incumbent on her to continue talking. "I was saying," she pursued, "that my brother's illness has occasioned a delay in examining and arranging Papa's property."

"Yes," said Mr Merdle; "yes. There has been a delay."

As the topic seemed exhausted, and Mr Merdle too, Fanny inquired if he were going to take up Mrs Merdle and the carriage on his way home?

"No," he answered; "I shall go by the shortest way, and leave Mrs Merdle to – " here he looked all over the palms of both his hands as if he were telling his own fortune – "to take care of herself. I dare say she'll manage to do it."

"Probably," said Fanny.

"But, however," said Mr Merdle, "I am equally detaining you and myself. I thought I'd give you a call, you know."

"Charmed, I am sure," said Fanny.

"So I am off," added Mr Merdle, getting up. "Could you lend me a penknife?"

It was an odd thing, Fanny smilingly observed, for her who could seldom prevail upon herself even to write a letter, to lend to a man of such vast business as Mr Merdle. "Isn't it?" Mr Merdle acquiesced; "but I want one."

"Edmund," said Mrs Sparkler, "open (now, very carefully, I beg and beseech, for you are so very awkward) the mother of pearl box on my little table there, and give Mr Merdle the mother of pearl penknife."

"Thank you," said Mr Merdle; "but if you have got one with a darker handle, I think I should prefer one with a darker handle."

"Tortoise-shell?"

"Thank you," said Mr Merdle; "yes. I think I should prefer tortoise-shell."

Edmund accordingly received instructions to open the tortoise-shell box, and give Mr Merdle the tortoise-shell knife. On his doing so, his wife said to the master-spirit graciously: "I will forgive you, if you ink it."

"I'll undertake not to ink it," said Mr Merdle. "It won't be ink."

CHAPTER 22

The Chief Butler Resigns the Seals of Office

At the physician's dinner-party all the important people were there, including Mrs Merdle, alone, without the company of her illustrious but unwell husband. When the banquet was over, the physician took Mrs Merdle down to her carriage and inquired into Mr Merdle's symptoms.

Mrs Merdle smiled graciously. "Upon my honour, I think Mr Merdle reposes greater confidence in you than in any one."

"On the contrary, he tells me absolutely nothing, even professionally. It is a most provoking situation!"

The physician handed her into her carriage. On his return upstairs, the rest of the guests soon dispersed, and he was left alone until his attention was caught by a ringing at the door bell. He went down, and there found a man without hat or coat, breathing fast as if he had been running.

"I come from the warm-baths, sir, round in the neighbouring street. Would you please to come directly, sir. We found that, lying on the table."

He put into the physician's hand a scrap of paper. The physician looked at it, and read his own name and address written in pencil; nothing more. He looked closer at the writing, looked at the man, took his hat from its peg, put the key of his door in his pocket, and they hurried away together.

When they came to the warm-baths the messenger hurried before him, turning into a little room.

There was a bath in that corner, from which the water had been hastily drained off. Lying in it was the body of a heavily-made man, with an obtuse head, and coarse, mean, common features. The face and figure were clammy to the touch and the white marble at the bottom of the bath was veined with a dreadful red. On the ledge at the side, were an empty laudanum-bottle and a tortoise-shell handled penknife – soiled, but not with ink.

"Separation of jugular vein – death rapid – been dead at least half an hour." This echo of the physician's words ran through the passages and little rooms. He turned his eyes to the dress upon the sofa, and to the watch, money, and pocket-book on the table. A folded note caught his observant glance. "This is addressed to me."

There were no directions for him to give. The people of the house knew what to do; the proper authorities were soon brought. The physician was glad to walk out into the night air towards the house of his lawyer friend who was a near neighbour of his. When he came to the house, he saw a light in the room where he knew his friend often sat late.

The physician's knock astonished the lawyer. "What's the matter?" he asked his friend.

"You asked me once what Merdle's complaint was. I have found it out."

"My God!" said the lawyer, starting back, and clapping his hand upon the other's breast. "And so have I! I see it in your face."

They went together to break the news to Mrs Merdle and spoke first to the Chief Butler.

"Mr Merdle is dead."

"I should wish," said the Chief Butler, "to give a month's notice."

"Mr Merdle has destroyed himself."

The Chief Butler, erect and calm, replied in these memorable words. "Sir, Mr Merdle never was the gentleman, and no ungentlemanly act on Mr Merdle's part would surprise me."

When the physician, after discharging himself of his meeting upstairs, rejoined the lawyer in the street, he said no more of his interview with Mrs Merdle than that he had not yet told her all, but that what he had told her she had borne pretty well.

The report that the great man was dead, got about with astonishing rapidity. The cause of "Pressure" was so entirely satisfactory to the public mind it might have lasted all day, but for the lawyer's having taken the real state of the case into Court at half-past nine. This led to its beginning to be currently whispered all over London by about one, that Mr Merdle had killed himself. Then appalling whispers began to circulate, east, west, north, and south, that the late Mr Merdle's complaint had been simply Forgery and Robbery. He was simply the greatest Forger and the greatest Thief that ever cheated the gallows.

CHAPTER 23

Reaping the Whirlwind

The usual diligence and order of the Counting-house at the Works were overthrown and Arthur sat with his arms crossed on the desk, and his head bowed down upon them.

Mr Pancks rushed in and saw him, and stood still.

"I persuaded you to it, Mr Clennam. Say what you will. You can't say more to me than I say to myself. You can't say more than I deserve."

"I," pursued Clennam, without attending to him, "who have ruined my partner! Pancks, Pancks, I have ruined Doyce."

"Reproach me!" cried Pancks.

"If you had never yielded to this fatal mania, Pancks," said Clennam, more in commiseration than retaliation, "it would have been how much better for you, and how much better for me! Only yesterday, Pancks, Monday, I had the fixed intention of selling, realising, and making an end of it. My course must be taken at once. What wretched amends I can make must be made. I must clear my unfortunate partner's reputation. The sooner the business can pass out of my hands, the better for it."

"We need legal help. Shall I fetch Rugg, Mr Clennam?"

"If you could spare the time, I should be much obliged to you."

"I am sorry to perceive, sir," said Mr Rugg, on arrival, "that you have been allowing your own feelings to be worked upon. These losses are much to be deplored, sir, but we must look 'em in the face. Now, Mr Clennam, by your leave, let us go into the matter. Let us see the state of the case. What can we do for ourself?"

"This is not the question with me, Mr Rugg," said Arthur. "You mistake it in the beginning. It is, what can I do for my partner, how can I best make reparation to him?"

Clennam then told Mr Rugg to clear his partner morally, to the fullest extent, and declare that he, Arthur Clennam, of that Firm, had of his own sole act, and even expressly against his partner's caution, embarked its resources in the swindles that had lately perished. His intention was to print a declaration to the foregoing effect, which he had already drawn up; then he would address a letter to all the creditors, exonerating his partner in a solemn manner. If, through their consideration for his partner's innocence, the affairs could ever be got into such train as that the business could be profitably resumed, and its present downfall overcome, then his own share in it should revert to his partner, and he himself, at as small a salary as he could live upon, would ask to be allowed to serve the business as a faithful clerk.

Upon that statement Mr Rugg fell to work.

The disclosure was made, and the storm raged fearfully. Mr Rugg informed his client within a week that he feared there were writs out.

"I must take the consequences of what I have done," said Clennam. "The writs will find me, and I know the consequence of small writs. However I would rather be taken to the Marshalsea than to any other prison."

On seeing that he would never change Arthur's mind, Mr Rugg sighed. "Shall I accompany you then, Mr Clennam?" he asked politely.

"I would rather go alone, thank you," said Clennam. "Be so good as to send me my clothes."

Mr Chivery was on the Lock, and Young John was in the Lodge; both were astonished on seeing who the prisoner was.

As Clennam knew enough of the place to know that he was required to remain in the Lodge a certain time, he took a seat in a corner, and feigned to be occupied with the perusal of letters from his pocket. They did not so engross his attention, but that he saw, with gratitude, how the elder Mr Chivery kept the Lodge clear of Prisoners, how he made his misery as easy to him as he could.

Arthur was sitting with his eyes fixed on the floor when he felt himself touched upon the shoulder. It was Young John; who said, "You can come now. You want a room. I have got you one."

"I thank you heartily."

Young John turned again, and took him in at the old doorway, up the old staircase, into the old room. He spoke with emotion. "I thought you'd like the room, and here it is for you."

Little Dorrit's absence in his altered fortunes made it, and him in it, so very desolate and so much in need of such a face of love and truth, that he turned against the wall to weep, sobbing out, as his heart relieved itself, "Oh my Little Dorrit!"

CHAPTER 24

The Pupil of the Marshalsea

The day was sunny, and the Marshalsea, with the hot noon striking upon it, was unwontedly quiet. Arthur Clennam dropped into a solitary arm-chair, itself as faded as any debtor in the jail, and yielded himself to his thoughts. It was not remarkable that everything his memory turned upon should bring him round again to Little Dorrit and how much the dear little creature had influenced his better resolutions.

His door was opened, and the head of the elder Chivery was put in a very little way, without being turned towards him.

"I am off the Lock, Mr Clennam, and going out. Your things is come and my son is going to carry 'em up. I should have sent 'em up but for his wishing to carry 'em himself. Indeed he would have 'em himself, and so I couldn't send 'em up." Mr Chivery took his head away, and shut the door. He might have been gone ten minutes, when his son succeeded him.

"How long may it be your intentions, sir, to go without eating and drinking?" asked Young John solicitously.

"I have not felt the want of anything yet," returned Clennam. "I have no appetite just now."

"The more reason why you should take some support, sir," urged Young John. "I'm going to have tea in my own apartment. If it's not a liberty, please to come and take a cup." Arthur rose and expressed his willingness so Young John locked his door for him as they went out, and led the way to his own residence.

It was at the top of the house nearest to the gateway. Young John looked hard at him, biting his fingers.

"I see you recollect the room, Mr Clennam?"

"I recollect it well, Heaven bless her!"

189

Clennam tried to do honour to the meal, but unavailingly.

"I wonder," said Young John at length, "if it's not worth your while to take care of yourself for your own sake, it's not worth doing for some one else's."

"It seems to me just possible," said Arthur, "that you have made some reference to Miss Dorrit."

"It is just possible, sir," returned John Chivery.

"Did you ever hear from Mrs Chivery, your mother, that I went to see her once?"

"No, sir," returned John, shortly. "Never heard of such a thing."

"But I did. Can you imagine why?"

"No, sir," returned John, shortly. "I can't imagine why."

"I will tell you. I was solicitous to promote Miss Dorrit's happiness; and if I could have supposed that Miss Dorrit returned your affection – "

Poor John Chivery turned crimson to the tips of his ears. "Miss Dorrit never did, sir. She was far above me in all respects at all times." Tears glistened in his eyes. "Mr Clennam, do you mean to say that you don't know?"

"What, John?"

"Of Miss Dorrit's love."

"For whom?"

"You," said John.

"Me!"

"Ah!" groaned Young John. "You!"

He had been stunned. Little Dorrit love him! Later the darkness found him occupied with these thoughts. The darkness also found Mr and Mrs Plornish knocking at his door with a basket of choice food. Mrs Plornish was affected to tears.

"The way father has been talking about you, Mr Clennam," she said. "It's made him quite poorly. As to Mr Baptist, whatever he'll do when he knows of it, I can't conceive nor yet imagine. He'd have been here before now, you may be sure, but that he's away on confidential business of your own." She looked round the room. "It's a thing to be thankful for, indeed, that Miss Dorrit is not here to know it. There's nothing I can think of, that would have touched Miss Dorrit so bad as this."

Finally, the worthy couple went away arm in arm.

Little Dorrit, Little Dorrit. Again, for hours. Always Little Dorrit!

CHAPTER 25

An Appearance in the Marshalsea

The opinion of the community outside the prison gates bore hard on Clennam as time went on, and he made no friends among the community within. He kept his own room and was held in distrust.

However, he did have visitors. First there was the sprightly young Barnacle, Ferdinand, who expressed the hope that the Circumlocution Office had nothing to do with his imprisonment and doubts that the invention would ever come to anything. Then there was his lawyer Mr Rugg, who advised his client yet again to quit the Marshalsea and move to the bench.

After him Monsieur Blandois appeared, followed by John Baptist and Mr Pancks.

"You villain of ill-omen!" cried Arthur. "You have purposely cast a dreadful suspicion upon my mother's house. Why have you done it?"

"Signore!" interposed John Baptist, also addressing Arthur: "for to commence, hear me! I received your instructions to find him, and with much difficulty I do."

"It is the truth."

"Many thanks," said Arthur and turned to Blandois. "I want to know how you dare direct a suspicion of murder against my mother's house? I want that suspicion to be cleared away. You shall be taken there, and be publicly seen. I want to know, moreover, what business you had there."

Blandois sat himself down with a threatening swagger, and said:

"You want to know why I played this little trick that you have interrupted? Know then that I had, and that I have – do you understand me? have – a commodity to sell to my lady your respectable mother. I described my precious commodity, and fixed my price. Touching the bargain, your admirable mother was a little too calm, so I conceived the happy idea of disappearing to make her respond. Beyond this; it might have restored her wit to my lady your mother – might have persuaded her at last to announce, covertly, in the journals, that the difficulties of a certain contract would be removed by the appearance of a certain important party to it. But that, you have interrupted. Perhaps you would have done better to leave me alone?"

"No! At least," said Clennam, "you are known to be alive and unharmed. At least you cannot escape from these two witnesses; and they can produce you before any public authorities."

"Have I my commodity on sale, for that? Bah, poor debtor! You have only interrupted my little project. Let it pass. Contrabandist! Give me pen, ink, and paper."

John Baptist got up again, and laid them before him. Blandois wrote, and read aloud, as follows:

"To MRS CLENNAM.
"Wait answer.
"Prison of the Marshalsea.
"At the apartment of your son.
"Dear Madam, – I am in despair to be informed today by our prisoner here that you have had fears for my safety.
"Reassure yourself, dear madam. I am well, I am strong and constant. With the greatest impatience I should fly to your house, but that I foresee it to be possible, under the circumstances, that you will not yet have quite definitively arranged the little proposition I have had the honour to submit to you. I name one week from this day, for a last final visit on my part; when you will unconditionally accept it or reject it, with its train of consequences.
"BLANDOIS.
"A thousand friendships to that dear Flintwinch.
"I kiss the hands of Madame F."

Mr Pancks volunteered to take the letter, upon which Blandois said to Clennam:

"One must talk. She's handsome, sir."

"I neither know nor ask," said Clennam, "of whom you speak."

"Della bella Gowana, sir, as they say in Italy. Of the fair Gowan."

"Of whose husband you were the – follower, I think?"

"Sir? Follower? You are insolent. The friend."

"Do you sell all your friends?"

"I sell anything that commands a price. I perceive you have acquaintance with another lady. Also handsome. A strong spirit. Let us see. How do they call her? Wade."

He received no answer, but could easily discern that he had hit the mark.

"Yes," he went on, "that handsome lady and strong spirit addresses me in the street, and I am not insensible. I respond. She has seen me with Gowan and wishes to know how the fair Gowana is beloved, how the fair Gowana is cherished, and so on. She is not rich, but offers such and such little recompences that I am consent to accept. Whoof! The fair Gowana! Charming, but imprudent! For it was not well of the fair Gowana to hide letters from old lovers, in her bedchamber on the mountain, that her husband might not see them."

"I earnestly hope," cried Arthur aloud, "that Pancks may not be long gone, for this man's presence pollutes the room."

Possibly another quarter of an hour elapsed before Mr Pancks returned, followed by Flintwinch.

"Well, Arthur," said Flintwinch. "Here is a note from your mother."

It was in his mother's maimed writing, on a slip of paper, and contained only these words:

"I hope it is enough that you have ruined yourself. Rest contented without more ruin. Jeremiah Flintwinch is my messenger and representative. Your affectionate M.C."

Clennam read this twice, in silence, and then tore it to pieces.

"Now, Beau Flintwinch," said Blandois, "the answer to my letter?"

"Mrs Clennam did not write, Mr Blandois, her hands being cramped. She sends her compliments, and says she doesn't on the whole wish to term you unreasonable, and that she agrees. But without prejudicing the appointment that stands for this day week."

Monsieur Blandois descended from his throne, saying, "Good! I go to seek an hotel!" But, there his eyes encountered John Baptist, who was still at his post. "And I demand the service of this contrabandist as my domestic until this day week."

Clennam made him a sign for him to go; but he added aloud, "unless you are afraid of him."

John Baptist shook his head. Mr Flintwinch followed, then Mr Pancks, after receiving with great attention a secret word or two of instructions from Arthur, and whispering back that he would see this affair out, and stand by it to the end.

193

CHAPTER 26

A Plea in the Marshalsea

The sixth day of the appointed week was a moist, hot, misty day.

Light of head with want of sleep and want of food Arthur dozed and woke to see beside the teacup on his table a wonderful handful of the choicest and most lovely flowers.

Then the door of his room seemed to open to a light touch, and, after a moment's pause, a quiet figure seemed to stand there, with a black mantle on it. It seemed to draw the mantle off and drop it on the ground, and then it seemed to be his Little Dorrit in her old, worn dress.

Little Dorrit, a living presence, called him by his name.

"Dear Mr Clennam, don't let me see you weep!"

Looking round, he saw Maggy in her big cap which had been long abandoned, with a basket on her arm as in the bygone days, chuckling rapturously.

Little Dorrit continued, "It was only yesterday evening that I came to London with my brother. I sent round to Mrs Plornish almost as soon as we arrived and heard that you were here."

She took off her old bonnet, hung it in the old place, and noiselessly began, with Maggy's help, to make his room as fresh and neat as it could be made, and to sprinkle it with a pleasant-smelling water. When that was done, the basket, which was filled with grapes and other fruit, was unpacked, and all its contents were quietly put away.

Then they sat side by side in the shadow of the wall and Little Dorrit spoke softly.

"Dear Mr Clennam, I must say something to you before I go. I am not going abroad again. My brother is, but I am not. He only wishes me to be happy, he says. You will understand, I dare say, without my telling you, that my brother has come home to find my dear father's will, and to take possession of his property. He says, if there is a will, he is sure I shall be left rich; and if there is none, that he will make me so. I have no use for money. Will you let me give it you?"

It had grown darker when he raised her in his encircling arm, and softly answered her.

"I am disgraced enough, my Little Dorrit. I must not descend so low as that, and carry you – so dear, so generous, so good – down with me. *God* bless you, *God* reward you! It is past." He took her in his arms, as if she had been his daughter.

"One other word, my Little Dorrit. A hard one to me, but it is a necessary one. The time when you and this prison had anything in common has long gone by. Do you understand?"

"Oh! you will never say to me," she cried, weeping bitterly, and holding up her clasped hands in entreaty, "that I am not to come back any more! You will surely not desert me so!"

"I would say it, if I could; but I have not the courage quite to shut out this dear face, and abandon all hope of its return."

Tenderly wrapping her mantle about her, and taking her on his arm, Arthur led Little Dorrit downstairs.

When it was almost midnight, and the prison had long been quiet, a cautious creak came up the stairs, and a cautious tap of a key was given at his door. It was Young John.

"What is the matter?" asked Arthur.

"Nothing's the matter, sir. I was waiting in the courtyard for Miss Dorrit when she came out. I thought you'd like someone to see that she was safe."

"Thank you, thank you! You took her home, John?"

"I saw her to her hotel. The same that Mr Dorrit was at. Miss Dorrit walked all the way, and talked to me so kind, it quite knocked me over. Why do you think she walked instead of riding?"

"I don't know, John."

"To talk about you. She said to me, 'John, you was always honourable, and if you'll promise me that you will take care of him, and never let him want for help and comfort when I am not there, my mind will be at rest so far.' I promised her. And I'll stand by you," said John Chivery, "for ever!"

CHAPTER 27

Closing In

When the sun was low, three men turned in at the gateway and made for the dilapidated house.

Blandois was the first, Mr Baptist the second and Mr Pancks was the third. They all met together at the steps, and accompanied by Mr Flintwinch and two attendants, they ascended into Mrs Clennam's quiet room where Affery was mending a stocking.

"What do these people want here?" said Mrs Clennam, bending her brows angrily, "Why should I wish them to remain here? Hark! You Pancks! You Casby's clerk! Go. And take that other man with you."

They went out.

"Come!" said Mr Flintwinch at length, "Affery, my woman, take yourself away as well!"

Affery started up. "No, I won't, Jeremiah – no, I won't – no, I won't! I won't go! I'll stay here. I'll hear all I don't know, and say all I know. I will, at last, if I die for it. I will, I will, I will!"

Mrs Clennam spoke firmly. "It is closing in, Flintwinch. Let her alone. Affery, do you turn against me after these many years?"

"I do."

After gazing at her in silence, Mrs Clennam turned to Blandois.

"It would seem that you have obtained possession of a paper – or of papers – which I assuredly have the inclination to recover. The paper might be worth, to me, a sum of money. I cannot say how much, or how little."

"It is your pleasure then, madame, that I shall relate a morsel of your family history in this little family society?" said Blandois.

"I will speak, I will tell it with my own lips, rather than bear the torment of the hearing it from you." Mrs Clennam spoke imperiously. "Repression, punishment, and fear – these were the themes of my childhood. When old Mr Gilbert Clennam proposed his orphan nephew to my father for my husband, my father impressed upon me that this nephew's bringing-up had been, like mine, one of severe restraint. The marriage was arranged. When, within a twelvemonth of our marriage, I found my husband to have sinned against the Lord and outraged me by holding a guilty creature in my place, was I to doubt that it had been appointed to me to make the discovery, and that it was appointed to me to lay the hand of punishment upon that creature of perdition?" Mrs Clennam laid her wrathful hand upon the watch on the table.

"No! 'Do not forget.' It spoke to me like a voice from an angry cloud. Do not forget the deadly sin, do not forget the appointed discovery, do not forget the appointed suffering. When I forced him to give her up to me, when I accused her, and she fell hiding her face at my feet had not I, unworthy and far-removed from them, sin to denounce? When she pleaded to me her youth, and the desecrated ceremony of marriage there had secretly been between them, I was first to be appointed to be the instrument of their punishment. I said to her: 'You have a child; I have none. You love that child. Give him to me. He shall believe himself to be my son, and he shall be believed by every one to be my son. To save you from exposure, his father shall swear never to see or communicate with you more; equally to save him from being stripped by his uncle, and to save your child from being a beggar, you shall swear never to see or communicate with either of them.' If the presence of Arthur was a daily reproach to his father, and if the absence of Arthur was a daily agony to his mother, that was the just dispensation of Jehovah. Was I too, not visited with consequences of the original offence in which I had no complicity? Arthur's father and I lived no further apart, with half the globe between us, than when we were together in this house. He died, and sent this watch back to me, with its 'Do not forget'. I do *not* forget."

Blandois cried with a loud and contemptuous snapping of his fingers.

"Come, madame! Time runs out. You can tell nothing I don't know. Come to the money stolen, or I will! Death of my soul, I have had enough of your other jargon. Come straight to the stolen money!"

"Wretch that you are," she answered, "through what fatal error of Flintwinch's you have become possessed of that codicil, I know no more than how you acquired the rest of your power here – "

"And yet," interrupted Blandois, "it is my odd fortune to have by me, in a convenient place that I know of, that same short little addition to the will of Monsieur Gilbert Clennam, written by a lady and witnessed by the same lady and Flintwinch! Madame, let us go on. Time presses. You or I to finish?"

"I!" she answered, with increased determination, if it were possible. "I,

197

because I will not endure to be shown myself, with your horrible distortion upon me."

"I tell no lies," retorted Blandois. "You know you suppressed the deed and kept the money."

Mrs Clennam was pale. "If Gilbert Clennam, reduced to imbecility, at the point of death, and labouring under the delusion of some imaginary relenting towards a girl, of whom he had heard that his nephew had once had a fancy for, which he had crushed out of him, dictated to me a bequest meant as a recompense to her for supposed unmerited suffering; was there no difference between my spurning that injustice, and coveting mere money?"

Blandois snapped his fingers tauntingly in her face. "One thousand guineas to the little beauty you slowly hunted to death. One thousand guineas to the youngest daughter her patron might have at fifty, or (if he had none) brother's youngest daughter, on her coming of age, 'as the remembrance his disinterestedness may like best, of his protection of a friendless young orphan girl.' Two thousand guineas. That patron was called Mr Frederick Dorrit."

"That Frederick Dorrit was the beginning of it all. If he had not been a player of music, and had not kept, in those days of his youth and prosperity, an idle house where singers and players met, she might have remained in her lowly station. But no! Frederick Dorrit saw that here was a poor girl with a voice for singing music with. Then he is to have her taught. Then Arthur's father became acquainted with her. And so, a graceless orphan, training to be a singing girl by that Frederick Dorrit's agency, worked against me. Lastly, when I suppressed that paper, with the knowledge of Arthur's father, I made no effort to destroy it, but kept it by me, here in this house, for many years. I have seen no new reason, in all the time I have been tried here, to bring it to light. When the paper was at last destroyed – as I thought – in my presence, she had long been dead, and her patron, Frederick Dorrit, had long been deservedly ruined and imbecile."

"Shall I recall something to you, worthy madame?" said Blandois. "The little paper was in this house on the night when our friend the prisoner – jail-comrade of my soul – came home from foreign countries. His true mother had been looked after by the twin brother of my old intriguer Flintwinch."

"I'll tell you!" confirmed Affery, "The person as this man has spoken of, was Jeremiah's own twin brother; and he was here in the dead of the night, on the night when Arthur come home, Jeremiah with his own hands give him this paper, along with I don't know what more, and he took it away in an iron box – Help! Murder! Save me from Jere-mi-ah!"

Mr Flintwinch made a run at her but Blandois caught him in his arms.

"Ha, ha, ha! You're so like your twin, Little Flintwinch. So like him! I knew him in the Cabaret of the Three Billiard Tables, in the little street of the high roofs, by the wharf at Antwerp! I knew when he died. What does it matter how I took possession of the papers in his iron box?"

Flintwinch turned on Mrs Clennam. "It is all your fault. Why didn't you destroy the paper when you first laid hands upon it? I advised you to; but no, it's not your way to take advice. Finally Arthur's ways frightened you a bit, and the paper would be burnt after all. But it was not to be burnt on a Sunday night. We must wait over twelve o'clock, and get into Monday. I took a look at the document before twelve o'clock to refresh my memory as to its appearance – folded up one of the many yellow old papers in the cellars like it – and afterwards, when we had got into Monday morning, and I had, by the light of your lamp, to walk from you, lying on that bed, to this grate, I made a little exchange like a conjuror, and burned accordingly. My brother Ephraim was here that early Monday morning, waiting for the tide; in short, he was going to Antwerp where he made the acquaintance of this gentleman (pointing to Blandois). When Arthur's mother had been under the care of him and his wife, she had been always writing, incessantly, mostly letters of confession to you, and Prayers for forgiveness. From time to time my brother had handed me lots of these sheets and I put them into this same box. I trusted it to my brother to take away and keep, till I should write about it. I did write about it, and never got an answer. I didn't know what to make of it, till this gentleman favoured us with his first visit. Of course, I began to suspect how it was, then."

"This box," intervened Mrs Clennam, addressing Blandois, "can never bring, elsewhere, the price it will bring here. This knowledge can never be of the same profit to you, sold to any other person, as sold to me. But I have not the present means of raising the sum you have demanded. I have not prospered. What will you take now, and what at another time, and how am I to be assured of your silence?"

"My angel," said Blandois slyly, "I have placed copies of the most important of these papers in another's hand. Put off the time till the Marshalsea gate shall be shut for the night, and it will be too late to treat. The prisoner will have read them."

Mrs Clennam put her two hands to her head and uttered a loud Exclamation. She started to her feet, staggered for a moment, then stood firm.

"Say what you mean. Say what you mean, man!"

"Miss Dorrit," answered Blandois, "the little niece of Monsieur Frederick, for her I with my own hands left a packet at the prison, on my way here, with a letter of instructions to keep it without breaking the seal, in case of its being reclaimed before the hour of shutting up tonight – if it should not be reclaimed before the ringing of the prison bell, to give it to Arthur. It encloses a second copy for herself, which he must give to her. What! I don't trust myself among you, now we have got so far, without giving my secret a second life. And as to its not bringing me, elsewhere, the price it will bring here, say then, madame, have you limited and settled the price the little niece will give – for Arthur's sake – to hush it up? Once more I say, time presses. The packet not reclaimed before the ringing of the bell tonight, you cannot buy. I sell, then, to the little girl!"

Mrs Clennam ran to a closet, tore the door open, took down a hood or shawl, and wrapped it over her head. Affery, who had watched her in terror, darted to her in the middle of the room, caught hold of her dress, and went on her knees to her.

"Don't, don't, don't! What are you doing? Where are you going? You're a fearful woman, but I don't bear you no ill-will. Only promise me, that, if it's the poor thing that's kept here secretly, you'll let me take charge of her and be her nurse. Only promise me that, and never be afraid of me."

Mrs Clennam stood still for an instant, at the height of her rapid haste, saying in stern amazement:

"Kept here? She has been dead a score of years or more. Ask Flintwinch – ask *him*. They can both tell you that she died when Arthur went abroad."

"So much the worse," said Affery, with a shiver, "for she haunts the house, then. Who else holds the door sometimes? But don't go out – don't go out!"

Her mistress disengaged her dress from the beseeching hands and said to Blandois, "Wait here till I come back!" and ran out of the room. They saw her, from the window, run wildly through the courtyard and out at the gateway.

CHAPTER 28

Closed

Mrs Clennam stood inside the Marshalsea. The closeness of the place was oppressive and from without there arose a rush of free sounds, like the jarring memory of such things in a headache and heartache. She was at the window, when a soft word or two of surprise made her start, and Little Dorrit stood before her.

"Is it possible, Mrs Clennam, that you are so happily recovered as – "

"This is not recovery; it is not strength; I don't know what it is." With an agitated wave of her hand, she put all that aside.

"You have a packet left with you which you were to give to Arthur, if it was not reclaimed before this place closed tonight."

"Yes."

"I reclaim it."

Little Dorrit took it from her bosom, and gave it into her hand, which remained stretched out after receiving it.

"Have you any idea of its contents?"

Little Dorrit answered, "No."

"Read them."

After a broken exclamation or so of wonder and of terror, she read in silence. When she had finished, she looked round, and her old mistress bowed herself before her.

"You know, now, what I have done. I will restore to you what I have withheld from you. Forgive me. Can you forgive me?"

"I can, and Heaven knows I do! Do not kiss my dress and kneel to me; you are too old to kneel to me; I forgive you freely without that."

"I have more yet to ask, that you will not disclose this to Arthur until I am dead. If you think, when you have had time for consideration, that it can do him any good to know it while I am yet alive, then tell him. But you will not think that; and in such case, will you promise me to spare me until I am dead?"

"I will."

"*God* bless you! With an empty place in his heart that he has never known the meaning of, he has turned away from me and gone his separate road; but even that he has done considerately and with deference. When you have sat at your needle in my room, you have been in fear of me, but you have supposed me to have been doing you a kindness; you are better informed now, and know me to have done you an injury. Even now, I see *you* shrink from me, as if I had been cruel. I have done," said Mrs Clennam, "what it was given to me to do. I have set myself against evil; not against good."

"Oh, Mrs Clennam, Mrs Clennam," said Little Dorrit, "let me implore you to remember later and better days. Be guided only by the healer of the sick, the raiser of the dead."

The first warning bell began to ring.

"Hark!" cried Mrs Clennam starting, "I said I had another petition. It is one that does not admit of delay. The man who brought you this packet and possesses these proofs, is now waiting at my house to be bought off. He asks a large sum. He refuses to make any abatement, because his threat is, that if he fails with me, he will come to you. Will you return with me and show him that you already know it?"

Little Dorrit yielded willingly. Their feet were at the gateway of Mrs Clennam's house, when there was a sudden noise like thunder.

In one swift instant the old house was before them, with the man lying smoking in the window; another thundering sound, and it heaved, surged outward, opened asunder in fifty places, collapsed, and fell. Deafened by the noise, stifled, choked, and blinded by the dust, they hid their faces and stood rooted to the spot. As they looked up, wildly crying for help, the great pile of chimneys rocked, broke, and hailed itself down upon the heap of ruin, as if every tumbling fragment were intent on burying the crushed wretch deeper.

So blackened by the flying particles of rubbish as to be unrecognisable, they ran back from the gateway into the street, crying and shrieking. There, Mrs Clennam dropped upon the stones. For three years she was to live on immobile and in rigid silence, thus living and dying like a statue.

Affery had been looking for them at the prison, and had caught sight of them at a distance on the bridge. She came up to receive her old mistress in her arms, to help to carry her into a neighbouring house, and to be faithful to her.

Parties of diggers were formed. Rumour finally settled that buried within was the foreigner and Mr Flintwinch, but it was night for the second time when they found the foreigner, crushed beneath a great beam.

Still, they had not come upon Flintwinch and it began then to be perceived that Flintwinch had not been there at the time of the fall; but that he had been rather busy elsewhere, converting securities into as much money as could be got for them on the shortest notice. Nor was their belief much shaken by repeated intelligence which came over in course of time, that an old man who wore the tie of his neckcloth under one ear, and who was very well known to be an Englishman, consorted with the Dutchmen on the quaint banks of the canals of the Hague and in the drinking-shops of Amsterdam, under the style and designation of Mynheer von Flyntevynge.

CHAPTER 29

Going!

The Marshalsea walls, during a portion of every day, again embraced Little Dorrit but her part in the life outside the gate urged its pressing claims upon her too, and her patience untiringly responded to them. Here was Fanny, proud, fitful, whimsical, here was her brother, a weak, proud, tipsy, young old man, shaking from head to foot. Here was Mrs Merdle in gauzy mourning – but who came out of her furnace like a wise woman, and did exceedingly well. Here was poor Mr Sparkler, not knowing how to keep the peace between them, and here was Mrs General, got home from foreign parts, demanding a new Testimonial by way of recommendation to some vacant appointment or other. Little Dorrit's sole reliance during this heavy period was on Mr Meagles. He was still abroad but she had written to him. Without disclosing the precise nature of the documents that had fallen into Blandois' hands, Little Dorrit had confided the general outline of that story to Mr Meagles, to whom she had also recounted his fate. Mr Meagles realised the importance of recovering the original papers and wrote that he would not come over to England "without making some attempt to trace them out."

By this time Mr Henry Gowan had made up his mind that though he and Mr Meagles were the best fellows in the world, they were best apart. As a result both Mr and Mrs Meagles were more liberal than before to their daughter, when their communication was only with her and her young child.

With no other attendant than Mother, Mr Meagles went upon his pilgrimage, and when he had "worked round," as he called it, to Paris and had wholly failed in it so far, he was not disheartened.

At Paris, Mr Meagles found a letter from Little Dorrit telling him that Blandois had been known to Miss Wade, then living in such a street at Calais that Mr Meagles quickly found. He was shown into the presence of Miss Wade and immediately came to the point.

"Dear Miss Wade, I believe that you had some knowledge of one Blandois, lately killed in London by a violent accident. Did he, on his way to England last time, leave a box of papers, or a bundle of papers, or some papers or other in some receptacle or other – any papers – with you: begging you to allow him to leave them here for a short time, until he wanted them?"

"Upon my word," she returned, "I seem to be a mark for everybody who knew anything of a man I once in my life hired, and paid, and dismissed, to aim their questions at!"

"Now, don't," remonstrated Mr Meagles, "don't take offence. The documents I refer to were not his own and are sought by the people to whom they really belong. Did he leave them here?"

"No."

"Then unfortunately, Miss Wade, you know nothing about them?"

"I know nothing about them."

"There!" said Mr Meagles rising. "I am sorry for it; that's over; and I hope there is not much harm done. – Tattycoram well, Miss Wade?"

"Harriet well? Oh yes!"

Mr Meagles left. He went next to the London Steam Packet, which sailed in the night; and next to the Marshalsea.

The faithful John was on duty when Father and Mother Meagles presented themselves at the wicket towards nightfall. Miss Dorrit was not there then but she was sure to come back that evening before the bell rang. There was the room the Marshal had lent her, upstairs, in which they could wait for her, if they pleased.

The cramped area of the prison had such an effect on Mrs Meagles that she began to weep. Mr Meagles, who was panting, was facing the door when it opened.

"Eh? Good gracious!" he cried, "this is not Miss Dorrit! Why, Mother, look! Tattycoram!"

No other. And in Tattycoram's arms was an iron box some two feet square. This, Tattycoram put on the ground at her old master's feet then fell on her knees, crying half in exultation and half in despair, half in laughter and half in tears. "Pardon, dear Master; take me back, dear Mistress; here it is!"

"Tatty!" exclaimed Mr Meagles.

"What you wanted!" said Tattycoram. "Here it is! I was put in the next room not to see you. I heard you ask her about it, I heard her say she hadn't got it but I was there when he left it, and I took it at bedtime and brought it away. Here it is!"

"Why, my girl," cried Mr Meagles, more breathless than before, "how did you come over?"

"I came in the boat with you. I was sitting wrapped up at the other end. She never would have given it up after what you had said to her about its being wanted. But, here it is! Dear Master, dear Mistress, take me back again, and give me back the dear old name. I have been so wretched! I have had Miss Wade before me all this time, as if it was my own self grown ripe – turning everything the wrong way, and twisting all good into evil."

Another opening of the door, and Tattycoram subsided, and Little Dorrit came in, and Mr Meagles with pride and joy produced the box. She greeted him with surprise and happiness.

The secret was safe now! She could keep her own part of it from Arthur; he should never know of her loss; in time to come he should know all that was of import to himself; but he should never know what concerned her only.

"Now, my dear," said Mr Meagles, "had I better see Arthur tonight?"

"Not tonight," she replied, "he is very tired."

"Then we three will put up at a City Hotel. Tomorrow morning, Mother and Tattycoram will go down to Twickenham, and I shall go abroad again for Doyce."

They got into the street as the bell began to ring, Mr Meagles carrying the box. He called a coach for Little Dorrit and she got into it. He placed the box beside her when she was seated and in her joy and gratitude she kissed his hand.

CHAPTER 30

Gone

On a healthy autumn day, the Marshalsea prisoner, weak but otherwise restored, sat listening to a voice that read to him and heard in it all that great Nature was doing, heard in it all the soothing songs she sings to man.

Little Dorrit put the book by, and presently arose quietly to shade the window. Maggy sat at her needlework in her old place. The light softened, and Little Dorrit brought her chair closer to his side.

"This will soon be over now, dear Mr Clennam. Not only are Mr Doyce's letters to you so full of friendship and encouragement, but Mr Rugg says his letters to him are so full of help that it will soon be over now."

"Dear girl. Dear heart. Good angel!"

He might have released the little light hand after fervently kissing it again; but that, with a very gentle lingering where it was, it seemed to court being retained. He took it in both of his, and it lay softly on his breast.

"Dear Little Dorrit, it is not my imprisonment only that will soon be over. This sacrifice of you must be ended. We must learn to part again, and to take our different ways so wide asunder. You have not forgotten what we said together, when you came back?"

The hand he held crept up a little nearer to his face, and Little Dorrit spoke.

"You will be sorry to hear what I have to tell you about Fanny. Poor

Fanny has lost everything. She has nothing left but her husband's income. All that Papa gave her when she married was lost as your money was lost. It was in the same hands, and it is all gone. I am very sorry for Fanny; very, very, very sorry for poor Fanny. My poor brother too!"

"Had he property in the same hands?"

"Yes! And it's all gone. – How much do you think my own great fortune is? I have nothing in the world. I am as poor as when I lived here. When Papa came over to England, he confided everything he had to the same hands, and it is all swept away. Oh my dearest and best, are you quite sure you will not share my fortune with me now?"

Locked in his arms, held to his heart, she clasped his hand. "I love you dearly! Oh, if poor Papa may only know how blest at last my heart is, in this room where he suffered for so many years!"

Maggy was now so overjoyed that, after hugging her little mother with all her might, she went downstairs to find somebody or other to whom to impart her gladness. Whom should Maggy meet but Flora and Mr F's Aunt opportunely coming in? And whom else, as a consequence of that meeting, should Little Dorrit find waiting for herself, when, a good two or three hours afterwards, she went out?

"Painfully aware, Miss Dorrit, I am sure," said Flora, "that to propose an adjournment to any place must ever appear intruding even if not a pie-shop."

After eating a hearty meal of kidneys and gravy, spiced with much incomprehensible talk, they parted in the friendliest manner, and with the kindest feeling on both sides.

One morning, as Arthur listened for the light feet, he heard her coming, not alone; she came in with Mr Meagles, sun-browned and jolly.

"Now you see me, at last, my boy," said Mr Meagles, shaking him by the hand stoutly; "and now you shall have any explanation and every explanation. The fact is, I had to start off again to catch Doyce."

"Poor Doyce!" sighed Arthur.

"Don't call him names that he don't deserve," said Mr Meagles. "He's not poor; he's doing well enough. Doyce is a wonderful fellow over there. I assure you he is making out his case like a house a-fire. He has fallen on his legs, has Dan. You won't have occasion to trouble the Circumlocution Office any more. Let me tell you, Dan has done without 'em!"

"What a load you take from my mind!" cried Arthur. "What happiness you give me!"

"Happiness?" retorted Mr Meagles. "Don't talk about happiness till you see Dan. He's medalled and ribboned, and starred and crossed, and I don't-know-what all'd, like a born nobleman. But we mustn't talk about that over here. Britannia in the Manger won't give her children such distinctions herself, and won't allow them to be seen when they are given by other countries. Now, to go back, about catching Doyce. I ran against him among some Arabs. Well! He was coming straight to me, and I was going to him, and so we came back together."

"Doyce in England!" exclaimed Arthur.

"The long and short of it is, Arthur, we have both been in England this fortnight. And if you go on to ask where Doyce is at the present moment, why, my plain answer is – here he is! And now I can breathe again at last!"

Doyce darted in from behind the door, caught Arthur by both hands, and said the rest for himself.

"First, not a word more from you about the past. Every failure teaches a man something, if he will learn and you are too sensible a man not to learn from this failure. Secondly. I was sorry you should have taken it so heavily to heart. We two agreed, that, after what you had undergone, after your distress of mind, it would be a pleasant surprise if we could so far keep quiet as to get things perfectly arranged without your knowledge, and then come and say that all the affairs were smooth, that everything was right, that the business stood in greater want of you than ever it did, and that a new and prosperous career was opened before you and me as partners. My dear Clennam, I thoroughly confide in you; you have it in your power to be quite as useful to me as I have, or have had, it in my power to be useful to you; your old place awaits you, and wants you very much. Am I mistaken in supposing that you would rather not leave here till tomorrow morning? And if this young lady will do me the honour of regarding me for four-and-twenty hours in the light of a father, and will take a ride with me now towards Saint Paul's Churchyard, I dare say I know what we want to get there."

With that they parted for the time being. And the day ended, and the night ended, and the morning came, and Little Dorrit, simply dressed as usual and having no one with her but Maggy, came into the prison with the sunshine. "My dear love," said Arthur. "Why does Maggy light the fire? We shall be gone directly."

"I asked her to do it. I have taken such an odd fancy. I want you to burn something for me."

"What?"

"Only this folded paper. If you will put it in the fire with your own hand, just as it is, my fancy will be gratified."

"Superstitious, darling Little Dorrit? Is it a charm?"

"It is anything you like best, my own," she answered, laughing with glistening eyes and standing on tiptoe to kiss him, "if you will only humour me when the fire burns up."

So they stood before the fire, waiting: Clennam with his arm about her waist, and the fire shining, as fire in that same place had often shone, in Little Dorrit's eyes.

"Does the charm want any words to be said?" asked Arthur, as he held the paper over the flame.

"You can say (if you don't mind) 'I love you!'" answered Little Dorrit. So he said it, and the paper burned away.

They passed very quietly along the yard. Only one face, familiar of old, was in the Lodge. When they had both accosted it, and spoken many kind words, Little Dorrit turned back one last time with her hand stretched out, saying, "Good-bye, good John! I hope you will live very happy, dear!"

Then they went up the steps of the neighbouring Saint George's Church, and went up to the altar, where Daniel Doyce was waiting in his paternal character. And they were married with the sun shining on them through the painted figure of Our Saviour on the window. And they went into the very room where Little Dorrit had slumbered after her party, to sign the Marriage Register. And there, Mr Pancks, (destined to be chief clerk to Doyce and Clennam, and afterwards partner in the house), looked in at the door to see it done, with Flora gallantly supported on one arm and Maggy on the other, and a background of John Chivery and father and other turnkeys who had run round for the moment, deserting the parent Marshalsea for its happy child.

They all gave place when the signing was done, and Little Dorrit and her husband walked out of the church alone. They paused for a moment on the steps of the portico, looking at the fresh perspective of the street in the autumn morning sun's bright rays, and then went down.